BREAK POINT

A BILLY BECKETT NOVEL (BOOK 4)

BY
KELLY HODGE

For Jo Ann, the light of my life

PROLOGUE

The paranoia was growing inside Glen Chapman and growing fast. The bagman had sweated out the last ten miles, convinced the drab brown minivan would at any moment sputter to a stop on the northbound shoulder of Interstate 25. *And then what?*

Chapman had left Midland, Texas, more than six hours earlier, in the dead of night, hopped up on cocaine and Red Bull and determined to keep right on driving until he got to Denver. It only recently occurred to him that he'd need gas somewhere along the way. The needle had dipped below empty, but Chapman could almost coast from here. An exit was finally in sight.

A decorated Army veteran who served three tours in Iraq, he was used to living on the ragged edge. But it had taken a heavy toll. He came home to Colorado a damaged man — disillusioned, angry, suicidal at times — and was just going through the motions as a commercial construction foreman. If not for his ex-wife, Jeri, he surely would have pulled the trigger and ended his life soon after his return.

He wouldn't be here now, somewhere near Maxwell, New Mexico, running on fumes with more than three hundred thousand dollars in cash, seventy-five pounds of pungent, high-grade marijuana, and a loaded pistol in his possession.

Jeri — bless her soul — had sprung for that bucket-list item for his fortieth birthday. One parachute jump was all it took. Before long he had made a hundred jumps. Then five hundred. The constant rush fed Chapman's addictive personality, and he went from feeling vulnerable to invincible.

Two years later his wife was gone, but he had an airplane and a drop zone for his own skydiving business. He had a future.

Chapman took the exit and wheeled into the first gas station on the right. There was a sigh of relief. He would fill the tank and be back in Denver soon after lunch.

He'd still have to explain why he showed up late in a rental van with Texas tags, considering he had supposedly left town in a Cessna 182. But his associates would understand. Plans in their line of work tended to be fluid.

Before he could shift into park at the pumps, Chapman felt the contact. An older-model gray sedan had slightly clipped the rear bumper of his van. Instead of stopping, the driver continued to the front of the convenience market.

The rage came to the surface quickly, as it often did, and Chapman couldn't hold back. He approached the vehicle, pounded his fist on the windshield, and threatened to pull the driver out. His weathered face was flushed, and the veins bulged from his neck to his forearms, which were covered in sleeves of bold battle tattoos. He would not be disrespected this way. He was primed for a fight.

Chapman hadn't noticed the Colfax County Sheriff's Department cruiser parked around the corner of the building. Within a minute, a deputy who had been in the store was ordering the other driver out of his car. The man opened his door and staggered to his feet, apparently drunk or high on something. When he began to turn belligerent, he had the officer's full attention.

Chapman slinked past the bystanders that were gawking. He could feel his heart racing as he jumped back in the van and started the engine. Four hours from home.

Merging into traffic, still hot and a bit lightheaded, he realized his folly. The drugs were playing games with his mind again.

What was it his counselor had written? *Patient is subject to intense feelings of euphoria followed by the inevitable crash.* She knew him too well.

Slowing to a stop off the left lane of the interstate, Chapman cursed himself and pounded the steering wheel. He pondered going back to a different gas station. Or should he roll the dice, press on another eight or ten miles toward the next exit on this godforsaken stretch of road? He had always been a gambler.

The air in the van was deliciously fragrant, a dead giveaway. He raised the snuff bullet to his nostril and gave it another hard pull. The sweat was beading on his brow.

One way or the other, he had to move.

If it were any consolation, Chapman had a way of extricating himself from dire circumstances. At least he wasn't hunkered down under enemy fire in Fallujah or running low on fuel as he circled in the clouds. This was a relatively minor problem — with major implications if he suddenly found himself stranded on the side of the highway.

Chapman took a long look around the desolate landscape. He tugged at his thinning auburn hair and rubbed the stubble on his cheeks before putting the van back in gear. *Time to move.*

The abrupt U-turn through the median caused a swirl of dust that trailed him as he reached the pavement heading south.

Perhaps the trooper was already looking for the vehicle. Or maybe it was just a stroke of bad luck that was long overdue. The siren was wailing before Chapman even got back up to speed.

The bagman pulled over again, and the cluster of flashing lights soon loomed large in his mirrors. He could see the officer talking on the radio before slapping on the broad-brimmed hat and stepping from his cruiser.

Chapman opened the glove box and stared intently at the Glock inside. The inevitable crash was again at hand.

PART I

CHAPTER 1

The glare of the morning sun was becoming uncomfortable along Florida's Gulf Coast. The budding star had been going through his practice paces for almost two hours at a tennis academy near Bradenton, where young players were groomed for greatness. The constant soundtrack — groans and grunts, balls struck with purpose — echoed throughout the place.

On center court, the coach seemed agitated. He was standing at the net and hitting one crisp volley after another at the sweat-drenched player on the baseline, barking out instructions as the returns flew past him in rapid-fire succession. Many of the shots were missing their mark. The intensity picked up.

Finally, the tall left-hander with the wispy blond curls rifled a backhand into the net and erupted. He smashed his racquet head on the hardcourt, and then again for good measure, cratering the bright yellow frame with a bone-snapping resound. He tossed it aside with a string of expletives.

"That's enough," his coach said.

The youngster stormed off the court and collected his gear without another word.

Billy Beckett had been watching from a courtside bleacher. He removed his sunglasses, wiped his forehead with the back of his hand, and glanced over at the man sitting next to him. They both arched their eyebrows knowingly. *Shouldn't we be past this? Is Simon Shay ready to take the next step?*

There was a fire burning inside the kid, obviously, but also a callowness that had kept him from harnessing all that ability and staying focused on the big picture. *Did he really want to be a star?* It had been a recurring conflict in Simon's short but tempestuous professional career — talent versus temperament — and a frequent topic of conversation with his agent.

Almost a year after they first met, Billy still wondered how to best manage the two. After all, Simon had just turned nineteen and was very much a work in progress — on and off the court.

Zander Fleming twisted the cap off his bottled water and took a big swallow. He looked impatient. Zander had facilitated this experiment, steered the player into Billy's purview, confident that the agent's reputation as a mentor to other high-strung athletes would pay dividends. Now he was a little less sure than when the day began.

"Seems like the fuse is getting shorter," he said.

Billy nodded. Tan and toned in a white Polo shirt and khakis, he readjusted his glasses and ran his fingers through his dark hair.

"If he blows a gasket in practice, how's he going to hold together for two weeks at a major?" he said.

"Unless something changes, he won't be there for two *days*. He just needs to grow up. Soon."

Billy chuckled at the thought. *Just grow up.* He had heard that about clients more times than he could count. He'd told them himself.

"You can't rush it with some kids. It takes time. Simon is good — very good. But he's still a long way from slugging it out with Nadal in Paris."

A text message pinged on Zander's phone. The pilots were waiting. "We're clear to go," he said. "I think we've seen about enough here."

The plane sat at a nearby airstrip, ready to take the men on to Knoxville, Tennessee. They were old friends and had spent the last few days relaxing at Zander's home in the Florida Keys — fishing, playing on the water, catching up. Billy needed to get back to the real world and schedule meetings with several clients who required his immediate attention. Soon, he would be back on the road.

For Zander, there was still some leisure time left. A car was waiting at the Knoxville airport for him to drive to Jonesborough, a small town about a hundred miles to the east, to visit his parents. His shipping business was booming, but he still went home religiously. He was grounded in the rolling countryside of Northeast Tennessee.

The men had decided this morning to stop in Bradenton first and see for themselves how Simon was doing. He was a special project for Zander, who had agreed to loosely sponsor the player, give him every opportunity to succeed as a pro, if he worked hard and stayed in line. But Simon was a handful.

He played masterfully at a Challenger event in Orlando two weeks ago — his most impressive showing face, he would gladly stay out there and battle all day if that's what it took.

Simon had yet to develop that mindset. He was still the gifted kid capable of winning spectacularly when he was on, which was most of the time, or losing in similar fashion when he wasn't.

Carter recently arranged for the two to speak by phone, giving Hewitt a chance to offer some sage words of encouragement from a distance. The coach wasn't sure the generations connected — Simon was born about the time Hewitt was a force on the tennis scene — but it was worth a try.

"They don't make racquets like they used to, huh?" Billy said, holding up the offending equipment. "There goes another two hundred fifty bucks. What are racquet sponsorships for, anyway?"

That prompted a sheepish smile from Simon. "I apologize for that. Just a little outside the lines today."

"What about last week?" Zander asked. "That was *way* outside the lines."

"I apologized for that, too. I sent the lady flowers."

Billy shook his head. He appreciated free spirits – he considered himself one – but he was not yet sure about Simon. That question always got in the way: *How much did he want it?*

"We need to be firming up plans for the new year, not smashing racquets," Billy said. "Australia is already on the horizon. Is Team Shay going to be ready?"

"I'm ready," Simon offered quickly.

Billy turned to the coach. "What about you, Darren?" Carter's face was blank, noncommittal. He seemed less sure.

"We'll keep working at it," he said. "We can get better. We've still got time."

The Australian Open in mid-January was a milestone event; it would mark Simon's first appearance in a major tournament. Carter wanted his new man to make a good impression in Melbourne, maybe win a couple of matches, earn some valuable Grand Slam points, and set the tone for the long grind ahead. It would also signal that the veteran coach was back on the scene; that he still had a rightful place in this ultra-competitive environment. Perhaps that explained the growing tension on the court this morning.

Carter stood stoically and listened as Simon was peppered with a mix of praise and pragmatism. Zander punctuated the conversation with a little added incentive, like he often did with his shipping managers. He told the player that he'd fly him down to Key West for a few days of fun if he kept working hard.

"We'll even take the big boat out for a spin," he said. "Or you can stay here and keep pissing off Darren. Looks like he's about ready to whip your ass."

"The fun's getting harder to find around here."

"Second that," Carter said.

Simon admittedly wasn't happy about his living situation in Florida. He felt confined and missed Colorado, his father, and his friends. Even though he had cracked the top one hundred in the world rankings — currently one of only eight Americans included — the frustration had been building.

He mentioned again that he could be on the pro snowboarding tour, doing what he loved most in the mountains somewhere, maybe trekking around Europe. That was once a distinct possibility, but his father pushed for a move to Florida, home base for many of the world's best tennis players. Once considered a prodigy, Simon would train at the Branson Academy, see if he had the goods to make a living with a racquet in his hand like Michael Shay had dreamed of doing. He could always go back to playing in the snow later.

Carter finally clenched his jaw; he wasn't one to humor young players for long. And he didn't give a damn about snowboarding.

"Simon, don't be a tosser," he said. "You have the game. Hell, I keep hearing that you could be the biggest thing in tennis one day. People are paying attention to everything you do, for better or worse."

He pointed to a group of smiling young ladies gathered near the clubhouse gate who were keeping a close eye on the player and his entourage.

"But you have to have the head and the heart — they work together." Carter pounded his chest and raised his voice. "You have to want it, mate. You have to work for it. Every day. No shortcuts."

"Amen," Billy said. He praised Carter's efforts and credited Zander for his involvement in Simon's career, and then came eye to eye with the player. "It's all out there for you, and you couldn't have a better team behind you."

The agent had a serious look on his face. "In that spirit, Zander and I have been kicking around some ideas with your father. You've got a little break in the schedule, before the new season gets cranking, and we think a change of scenery might sharpen your focus. Call it a quick recharge."

"Christmas in Colorado?" Simon asked.

"No."

Simon let out a deep sigh. "Where?"

"Tennessee," Billy said. "I want you to come and stay with me."

CHAPTER 3

The big rig truck was loaded and scheduled to leave the loading dock before midnight. The driver locked the trailer and stopped to stretch his paunchy frame a few times to prepare for the long haul.

As he eased down the steps toward the cab, a short man walked up and handed him a cup of coffee. "Mack?" he said, extending his hand in the darkness. "I'm J.T. They tell me we're going to share this ride."

J.T. had a large backpack slung over his shoulder and looked out of place. Mack Luttrell had never seen him before. "You're what? A team driver?" he said. "They didn't say anything to me."

"I was an owner operator for years, but it about broke me. Trying to catch on now as a company driver. I just need the miles and look forward to making the run to Michigan. De-troit, Michigan. Haven't been there in a while." He laughed when Mack turned his back and kept walking. "I can see you're not happy. Don't worry, it won't cost you anything."

J.T. put down his pack and flashed some papers, but Mack waved him off. The days on the road were long and monotonous and having company occasionally wasn't a bad thing. Mack just didn't want to make a habit of it.

"Whatever," he said. "Let's go."

The black Freightliner roared to life and was soon rumbling east along I-70. Detroit was more than thirteen hundred miles away, which translated into a nineteen-hour trip including stops.

Mack had given the manifest only a cursory look before he left. The veteran hauler generally didn't care what the dockworkers rolled onto his trailer. His priorities were consistent: move the cargo, stay on schedule, and keep cashing paychecks.

Once an independent driver in serious debt himself, he now saw the steady work in a company rig as a godsend. But rarely had he been asked to share the load with another driver, much less a complete stranger who was probably twenty years younger. In close quarters, chemistry was important.

Mack was used to switching his brain to autopilot once he got on the open road; he turned on the radio and just drove. But he could already see this trip was going to be different. J.T. was a chatty guy with a lot to say about anything and everything. Worse, he expected a response, so the conversation could be endless. That was going to grate on Mack's nerves.

"Weather in the Midwest looks ugly this week," J.T. said. "I'd rather be down in South Beach, breathing that sea air. You know what I mean, brother?"

"What does Florida have to do with anything? You from there?"

CHAPTER 4

The Freightliner rolled into a busy travel center outside Kansas City, and Mack parked in a large lot beyond the pumps. He often stopped there when taking an easterly route out of Denver.

A new day was dawning in the Midwest. It was going to be the last nice one before the rains swept through. The sun was working its way into a cloudless sky. Mack flexed his arms and craned his neck to look behind him. He'd almost forgotten he wasn't alone.

"Kansas City," Mack announced. "I'm going inside to get a bite. The food here is pretty good. You hungry?"

J.T. sat up and shook his head. He'd spent much of the morning on his phone, texting with someone and tapping away at the screen. "Nah, I'm good. I'll just stay and catch up on the latest."

"You do that. Maybe they caught those guys down in Miami," Mack said with a laugh. "We'll get fuel on the way out. Got a big chunk of Missouri to cover before we turn north. You can drive for a while if you want."

"Just leave the key, and I'll top off while you're inside. We'll tag-team this sucker all the way to the Motor City."

Mack wasn't used to being idle for long. Truckers like him tended to think they were wasting time when their hands weren't on the wheel. At the moment, just the thought of being a passenger felt strange.

He grabbed his jacket and gingerly climbed down from the cab. He was dressed in his standard gear — faded red ball cap, green flannel shirt, jeans, and work boots. A scruffy, mostly gray beard framed his round face. The miles were starting to show.

Mack resisted the urge to smoke a cigarette as he stopped to talk to another driver in the rest area. He was trying to quit again but still kept a pack in his jacket pocket, just in case. After a few minutes he and the other driver, a younger man named Cliff, shuffled toward the diner together.

"You're heading north to Detroit this morning?" Cliff said as they sat down to order breakfast.

"Yeah, and it's already been kind of a strange start. I've got backup that I wasn't expecting along for the ride, and he's a talker."

"Well, sometimes it's good to hear another voice."

"And sometimes it ain't. I'm not used to it. Makes me feel like my cab has shrunk if you know what I mean."

Cliff nodded. "Could be worse. Could be your wife along for the ride. Or your girlfriend."

"How about both?"

Mack tossed his menu down just as the waitress arrived at the table with a pot of coffee. She was maybe sixty and wearing a faded blue uniform with a name badge that was barely legible anymore. She poured them both a cup while taking their orders without writing anything down.

"Pearl, you're old school," Mack said.

The waitress reacted with a sly smile. "I just lost my pen. We'll see how good my memory is today. It goes up and down."

"Mine, too," Cliff said. "I can barely remember where I'm driving to anymore. It's just all a blur."

"I thought those trucks drove themselves."

"That's the direction we're going with everything," Mack said. "Just gonna be robots running the world. I saw a show the other night where they were testing automated trucks. UPS has some of them out on the highway now, down in Arizona."

"That's all we need — forty-ton trucks rolling down the interstate with nobody's hand on the wheel."

"The world today," Pearl said. "Pretty soon we won't need waitresses either."

Mack wolfed down his Hungry Man breakfast — three eggs, scrambled, country ham, hash browns, biscuits and gravy, grits —and hit the restroom. He was anxious to get back on the road.

When he turned the corner, he stopped dead. His eyes grew large. *Where was his black Freightliner? Where was J.T. McClanahan?* After circling the property, panic started to set in. The truck was gone, along with all his belongings except for his cell phone and the clothes on his back.

Missouri state police arrived within minutes. They had initiated a search along Interstate 70, an officer said, and expected to quickly locate the missing truck. "He got a head start, but it's hard to hide these things. Especially in this part of the country."

Mack was already kicking himself and worrying about his job. There was no good excuse for a driver losing his rig. He began to wonder about J.T., whether he was legitimate. *If not, who was he?* As he waited beside the trooper's unmarked car, Mack kept thinking he should have been smarter.

The first notice came across from Missouri Highway Patrol about an hour later. "Ten fifty-two at Highway 291 and White Oak."

"What does that mean?" Mack asked.

"They're calling for an ambulance out on a state route. Wait over there."

The trooper slid inside his cruiser, shut the door, and got on the radio. Police had found the truck parked on the shoulder of a Missouri state route. The driver was reportedly slumped over the wheel.

After a few minutes, the trooper stepped back outside with the news. "Looks like whoever took your truck is dead."

CHAPTER 5

Billy and Zander boarded the Gulfstream G280 for Knoxville. The glistening white jet with gold trim was a recent acquisition for AAF Transport, further evidence that Zander's business was quite literally taking off. His travel had become so frequent and extensive that he decided it was worth the twenty-five-million-dollar investment.

The men were still going on about Simon Shay and his tennis prospects as they took their seats. Zander remained exasperated. "You sure you want to see this through?" he said. "I know we're a year into it, and it's been a mixed bag. There are no guarantees with this kid. I'd hate to see it all blow up in our faces."

Billy took a second and smiled. "Not many of my clients come with guarantees; it's mostly potential. This could be fun. Or a huge pain in the ass. Both, probably. It just takes a little while to play out."

"Don't humor him, Billy. He's a teenager, but it's still a business deal. His dad knows that. We all know that."

"I know all about teenagers and their parents. How much influence do you think Michael has in this situation?"

"A lot. This is his dream, getting his son onto the ATP Tour and into these big tournaments. No, the dream is *winning* big tournaments. He's constantly in Simon's ear."

"I haven't spoken with him lately. I never know exactly what he's thinking anyway."

"What do you mean?"

"We've just never really clicked, I guess. It's unusual because I make it a point to hit things off with the parents. They tend to love me."

"Michael is hard to read, just one of those adventurous western types," Zander said. "Always doing something crazy — skydiving, skiing the backcountry, running the rapids. I've ridden a lot of miles with him on mountain bikes."

"And what was the extent of his tennis career?"

"I think he was good enough to turn pro. At least that's what he said. Things just didn't work out. Now that he's got a son who's capable of moving up the world rankings quick, he's fully involved."

"Seems at times that Michael is more into the tennis than Simon is," Billy said. "He wouldn't be the first father living out his fantasies through his kid. I hate to judge him too harshly. I know he lost his wife a while back."

"Michael has his own idea about things, but he's been a team player for AAF. I appreciate that and have given him a longer leash than some. And he seems to be a good dad; he wants what's best for his son. I've known them both for a while now, since Ellen got sick."

Billy shrugged. "I guess I'll know them better soon, and hopefully that's not a bad thing. I really haven't been able to fully invest until now."

"Always have those plates spinning in the air, don't you?"

"Billy Beckett, plate spinner. I like that."

"I appreciate what you've done so far for Simon. I'm thinking the next few weeks could be a turning point for him. I know you've got a plan."

"It's fairly simple. We'll bring in Darren to work with him at one of the local clubs. We're talking about a short-term arrangement, and Simon can clear his head and get ready for the season. He'll be on his own most of the time, but I'll be there if he needs me. And we'll talk often and build on our relationship. I think it'll be helpful long term."

"You'll work it out?" Zander asked.

"Of course. I'm pretty good at handling firecrackers, as you know. Based on what I've seen, Simon is fearless and a helluva talent."

"Easy to be fearless when you're nineteen."

"I really think he can beat anybody outside the top ten when he's on — right now." Zander seemed pleasantly surprised to hear that. "And he's piling up points, which is key at this stage of his career. He's got that charisma, too. To be perfectly honest, he could be one of the most interesting players in the game this coming year."

"Not a bad thing for his agent, right?" Zander smiled and stretched his legs into the aisle. "You know I'm no tennis expert — not long ago I didn't know a volley from a Volvo — but I do like a challenge. I see a lot of untapped potential in this kid if he gets his head right. I believe you're just the man to make it all come together."

"We'll see."

"I'll leave the worrying to you, if that's all right."

"Believe me, I've got plenty to worry about *without* Simon. It's all waiting for me in Knoxville." He shook his head. "Whatever happened to simple times?"

Zander laughed. "Those are long gone."

"I remember you always saying how much you wanted to leave school and just start making money. Careful what you wish for, rich boy. You're aging fast. So am I."

The men were pushing forty and dealing with problems they had never imagined as college buddies. Business demands, parents, shifting priorities all around. At least there were no wives to consider. Neither man was married, though Zander tried it once and couldn't make it work.

"You haven't outgrown those Tennessee roots?" Billy asked.

"No way. When everything gets crazy, I find myself wanting to breathe that mountain air for a couple of days. Clears the head. Don't you feel the same way about the Smokies?"

"I guess I do when I stop to think about it. My father being there in Sevierville is a good thing. Even though I'm always on the road, it's nice to come home."

"Let's get on home then," Zander said. "People are waiting."

CHAPTER 6

Northeast Tennessee wasn't known as a hotbed for entrepreneurs, and Jonesborough was even less likely to produce a business titan like Zander.

The state's oldest town had just over five thousand residents at last count. Springing up where the watersheds of the Watauga and Nolichucky rivers met, it was founded seventeen years before Tennessee's statehood was declared. The locals took pride in the notion that the place hadn't changed all that much since then. They liked to call it "God's country," and the countless churches that dotted the landscape were a testament to the truth of the phrase.

An ambitious tone was set from the start for Ben and Alice Fleming's only son. They named him Alexander Augustus, and then called him Zander with a Z. He always stood out in little, unpretentious Jonesborough.

The entrepreneurial spirit came naturally. Zander's family used to operate a small hotel on the main drag that ran through town near the International Storytelling Center. They owned a restaurant nearby, too. A few years later, they sold the hotel and opened a bed-and-breakfast down the road from the oldest microbrewery in the area.

As always, going back to Jonesborough conjured up all sorts of imagery for Zander — home-cooked meals, maybe a hike in the Cherokee National Forest, or a bike ride on the scenic country roads. He could walk down to Depot Street Brewing, chat with old friends, and sample the Loose Caboose lager or Grand Phunk Railroad pale ale. Then he'd transform himself back into the enterprising shipping executive and be off again.

He was scheduled to make the rounds at AAF facilities in the coming days. The last stop would be a distribution center outside Denver, in Aurora, where he'd meet with Michael Shay, who was leading his management team there.

Busier was better for Zander. It had been his nature from the start to test the limits of his imagination, and those thoughts always trended toward business.

He began to lay the groundwork for a trucking company while still pursuing a business degree in Knoxville. The idea of constant movement — shipping cargo all over the country, and maybe the world — intrigued him. It was an extension of his personality.

Late in his senior year at the University of Tennessee, with graduation in sight, Zander lined up a few investors and suddenly dropped out of school to start what would become AAF Transport. His parents were stunned. They were pragmatic people who had saved for years to ensure their son would get a proper education. But Zander was a risk taker; he saw a business opportunity and didn't hesitate to go for it. That degree would have to wait.

All these years later, it was still waiting.

"Your folks still badgering you about that degree?" Billy asked.

"Of course. One of these days, maybe."

"I know they're really proud of you, diploma or not. I like your parents."

"Yeah. Me, too. They keep me focused."

"Focused? You?"

Zander let the sarcasm go. "What about *your* father? He's getting better?"

Franklin Beckett, the Sevierville police chief, had been battling cancer for the last year. His prognosis was still bleak, but he was holding his own. He was a former Marine and longtime cop. He was tough.

"He's actually made a lot of progress," Billy said, "but it's a day-to-day thing. He's been feeling good lately. I'm trying to get him to retire from the department and start working for me. It's hard to break away. You know, once a cop, always a cop."

"He's a smart dude. You'd be lucky to have him. He'd keep you out of trouble."

"Maybe," Billy said. "I just want to keep him busy. To be honest, Zander, I'm afraid he's going to slip away from me. The more I can keep both of our minds occupied, the better."

Zander smiled and nodded, the way old friends do. "You still think a lot about your mother?"

"Every day. It's been quite a few years now, but it never goes away, especially under those circumstances."

"It was an accident," Zander said. "You were a teenager."

"Doesn't matter. She's gone, it's my fault, and those things never change. What I did impacted everything — the course that my father and brother's lives took, too. John might still be here if it wasn't for that. Sometimes I wish it had been me instead."

Zander swallowed hard. The emotion was surprisingly raw after all this time. He hadn't meant to stir it up and wasn't sure what to say next.

"The thing I really hate," Billy said, "is I've almost forgotten what she looked like in person. I said I'd never let that happen, but the years go by. It's hard to look back at the pictures now because I know the pain I caused."

"I'm sorry, brother. I didn't mean to go there."

Billy smiled. "It's okay. Just be thankful that you've had two healthy, happy parents for so long. It's a blessing."

CHAPTER 7

Billy's cell phone rang in the seat pocket beside him. Claire Bosken, his business partner, was checking in. She wondered when he'd arrive in Knoxville and wanted to share some good news about a new client, an indie rock band she had brought into the Premier Sports and Entertainment fold.

Claire was another University of Tennessee alum, a vibrant and sexy redhead, and Zander always had a thing for her. He wondered how she was doing. Billy mentioned that Claire was still getting over her divorce and was in full business mode.

"She's spending a lot of time in Nashville," Billy said. "You know, that's home. She has a lot of connections there."

"Is she seeing anyone?" Zander asked.

"Not officially."

Billy smiled and told him about Ty Nelson, the young country music star who was the first artist to sign with Premier. His career had taken off, in large part because of Claire's management decisions.

"I don't know where things are headed," Billy said, "but they're old family friends who have grown closer."

"And she's his agent? Lucky guy."

Zander recalled his last conversation with Claire, a few months back. He wanted some feedback on a legal matter and was picking her brain, just like the old days. He enjoyed hearing her voice.

"She didn't mention talking to you," Billy said.

Zander smiled. "I asked her to keep it quiet."

"Really? Why?"

The co-pilot announced over the speakers that they were almost ready for departure. Before Billy could pick up the conversation, Zander glanced at his phone and immediately slid out of his seat and walked toward the cockpit.

"Let's wait for just a minute," he told the pilots. "I have a call I need to make. I'd rather do it right now."

Zander pulled the curtain behind him. He had just received a text from Michael Shay in Colorado. *Trouble. Call when you can.*

Zander pulled up Michael's contact and initiated the call.

"I got your text," Zander said. "What trouble?"

"Had a driver killed this morning in Kansas City."

"In an accident?"

"No, he was with one of our regular drivers and had left Aurora about midnight. They had stopped at a travel center."

"And?"

"Well, you're not going to believe this. The regular driver went inside to eat and came back, and the truck and this other guy were gone."

"Gone where?"

"They found the rig on a back road a few miles away. The driver was dead. Shot in the head."

The news briefly took Zander's breath. He needed a few seconds to compose himself.

"Suicide?"

"I don't think so. The state police just contacted me, so the information is still sketchy. But it looks like a murder. An investigation is under way there, obviously."

"I'm getting ready to leave Florida with Billy Beckett. I'll call you back as soon as we land in Knoxville. I'd planned to drive up to see my parents, but I can come straight on to Colorado if I need to."

"Let me stay on it, and I'll let you know. I don't see why I can't handle it from here. I'm just waiting for more information."

"Okay, I'll call you back."

Zander ended the call and rubbed the phone against his cheek. He was shaken. AAF had never been involved with anything like this before.

He opened the cockpit door and told the pilots they were ready to go. The curtain parted and he took his seat again across from Billy, who had already clicked his lap belt and was checking his email before takeoff.

"Where were we?" Zander asked.

"We were talking about Claire. You said you had spoken with her recently and asked her not to mention it. Why?"

"I don't even recall right now. Does it matter? Can't Claire and I have a private conversation?"

Billy looked curiously at his friend. "Sure."

"Good. Let's get out of here."

CHAPTER 8

The plane landed in Knoxville and taxied toward the private hangar. The cars were parked in a fenced lot behind it.

"I really appreciate the hospitality," Billy said, stretching in his seat. "Your life is amazing. Still can't believe how the small-town boy hit it so big. One day you're riding around campus with that ponytail and ratty Grateful Dead t-shirt, and the next day you're flying around in your own jet. Still look like a hippie though."

Zander was subdued but still managed to smile. He hadn't shared the information about the driver's death.

"What's a hippie look like?" he said, gathering his long, sandy hair into a ponytail. He was wearing a pair of colorful cargo shorts and sandals with a short-sleeve shirt, defying the December chill. He never seemed to be affected by weather.

"It's a compliment. Hippies were unique and idealistic and creative. I guess a few of them ended up in corporate America, like you."

"Didn't happen overnight," Zander said. "But yeah, it's been a crazy ride all around."

"Getting harder to stay humble, right?"

"That's why I go home so often. My mom keeps it real. Her cooking isn't bad either."

Zander gazed out the window at the familiar landscape. The area had received an abundance of rain over the last few months; it was lush and green. He nodded approvingly.

"Nothing like Tennessee," he said. "Ain't no place I'd rather be, as the old song goes. By the way, I'm thinking about building a home up here somewhere, maybe out on the river near you."

The news surprised Billy. "You are? When?"

"Not sure. Just have to figure out a few things first. We're branching out more, and it looks like we may put a warehouse facility in west Knoxville. It's a good business climate and fits into what we're doing with the fleet."

Billy was used to being caught off guard by his friend. As well as they knew each other, Zander was still a man of mystery in many regards. His offbeat personality made him hard to read, and that's the way he liked it.

"You sure you want to live in Knoxville? Once upon a time, you couldn't wait to get out of here."

"I didn't say I was going to live there. Just thinking about building a house. Would be closer to my parents, but not too close."

"And *we'd* be closer. Not sure if that's a good thing or not."

"Seems like a lot of trouble follows you, Billy Beckett. And the women, of course."

"I'm a mixed bag, right?"

"Something like that."

In the last decade, the men had tried to get together a couple of times a year in Knoxville and rekindle their friendship. Usually, it was during football season. Billy would invite a few regulars to tailgate on his houseboat outside Neyland Stadium, on the Tennessee River. The Vol Navy was a force to be reckoned with on game days, even if the team wasn't.

Billy still dished out grief about the last time Zander showed up, riding a mountain bike that had traveled with him on his new jet. He drank a beer and then pedaled on to the school library before kickoff because he wanted to look up something none of his friends had ever heard of.

"You come all the way up here just so you can go to the library?" Billy asked. "Don't they have libraries in the Keys? Probably not."

Zander was not a football fan, or even a sports fan, for that matter. He was more interested in the networking opportunities the events offered, the chance to talk to a variety of people and pick their brains. They were usually more receptive after they'd had a few beers and were in tailgate mode.

There never was any question about his ability to solve problems. It didn't matter how complex the obstacle; Zander could see a way through. He and Billy were both like that.

When it came to sports, each had strong opinions.

Billy, whose life had always revolved around the games and those who played them, enjoyed mocking his friend whenever possible.

"When you buy that pro franchise, or at least a piece of one, you can hire me as your general manager," he said. "I know that's high on your priority list."

"Can't think of a worse fit for me. You do realize how pervasive the sports world is? Overblown and full of pain."

"How so?"

"There's just too much money and too many huge egos."

"Unlike the business world, right?"

"Well, just look at all the problems you've had with these athletes. *And you're trying to help.* You've made a good living, brother, but in all seriousness, you should be dead."

Billy laughed. "What about Simon Shay? Being an agent can be a noble cause. These kids need guidance and direction, especially the ones that come from nowhere."

"What about Russell Mann?" Zander asked. "He came from nowhere. Did he need guidance? Hell, he just about killed you himself on his way out. And you think *I'm* leading an exciting life?"

CHAPTER 9

Glen Chapman pulled the minivan around to the back of the growhouse, where some of the best marijuana in Colorado was being cultivated. Sour Diesel. Green Crack. Strawberry Cough. Pineapple Kush. The strains had a cult-like following in the marketplace.

Denver alone had more than six hundred grow facilities, so it was possible for an illegal operation to hide in plain sight. Good Budz had proven that. It had been posing as a legitimate business for the last two years.

The huge footprint and electricity bills, the flurry of activity involving suppliers and exporting of harvests — none of it raised red flags. Or if it did, city inspectors didn't notice. They passed through regularly, but the paperwork seemed to be in order. They never grew suspicious enough to investigate further. Not yet.

Sierra Reed, a muscular woman with long, dark hair, met Chapman at the gate. She smiled and activated the mechanism to let him in. The reinforced steel door slid to the side and stopped with a loud clang.

"People were starting to worry about you, Glen," Reed said. "Everything okay?"

He nodded. "Where is Khai?"

"Should be here soon."

"Good. I need to talk to him."

"I've got some things to discuss with him myself. It's crazy around here and getting crazier." Reed cocked her head and studied Chapman carefully. "You don't look so good, Glen."

"Just got off the road," he said. "Long trip. Longer than expected."

Reed was Khai Le's younger sister. She used to own a local gym before going to work for her brother. Her official title at the growhouse was production manager; co-workers affectionately referred to her as "The General." She coordinated operations in six thousand square feet of growing space, with forty-five-thousand-watt lights shining down on a thriving sea of green.

The place stood out for its sophistication and micromanagement in speeding up harvests. Reed and her budtenders were getting three pounds per plant per harvest — far more than other growhouses. Bigger harvests, more harvests, more money. It was a winning combination.

Good Budz, in fact, had generated more weed, and cash, than it knew what to do with. Despite the plant's growing popularity nationally — nineteen states and the District of Columbia had legalized recreational consumption — the federal government still outlawed it. That meant that banks wouldn't do business with dispensaries, so cash was piling up everywhere in Colorado. Growers needed armed security full-time.

Things had gotten to the point at Good Budz that Khai was filling thick rubber duffel bags with money and hiding them in the Rockies wilderness for safekeeping.

They had GPS tracking devices attached and would be retrieved later, after he found a way to launder the cash.

Chapman didn't get drawn into the operation immediately, but he and Khai were childhood friends. He couldn't resist for long. His fledgling skydiving business was still a shaky proposition, and, with the soft underbelly of Colorado's early cannabis industry, there were opportunities. Huge opportunities. Even with legal weed coming online, the black market still flourished, if you had the stomach to get involved.

Chapman had a strong stomach, and he had become more ambitious. He wanted to make enough money to buy a couple of bigger planes, expand his business, maybe walk away debt free at some point. He began as a driver for Khai's operation, and one thing led to another. He was on his way.

"Where's your car?" Reed asked.

"It's in the shop. Had to get a rental."

"Have you done anything more about the trucks? Khai asked me when we talked this morning."

"No."

"I guess he'll be in touch."

Chapman nodded. He was in a bit of a mental fog, but that wasn't unusual. The marijuana trade had that effect on a lot of people. It was one surreal experience after another.

There had been sketchy offers from potential smugglers from the moment he began the process of securing a pilot's license. Everyone, it seemed, had designs of delivering large shipments by air. But the thought had scared Chapman. Hell, at the time he only had a student pilot certificate and barely knew how to fly.

The first run he made to a small airfield in Wyoming, he almost ran out of gas over Cheyenne. His single-engine plane was coughing as it reached the pumps. Chapman had landed with multiple duffels stuffed to the gills with sticky Rocky Mountain weed that occupied the other three seats in the plane. Even a cursory glance inside would have tipped off authorities that something was amiss, but the municipal airport was lightly patrolled. He was in and out without notice.

A second close call in the early days came when he unknowingly flew through a military operating area (MOA) in South Dakota. When Chapman landed, a cop that had been alerted rolled through the parking lot and stopped less than a hundred feet away. Chapman, who had the gift of gab, got out and casually chatted with the officer for a few minutes, and that was it. He moved on.

By then Chapman had discovered that drug smuggling and skydiving were similar. There was an adrenaline rush associated with doing something totally crazy and getting away with it, your life intact. And you had a chance to keep chasing the same thrill, to ratchet it up until you cashed in or crashed.

Chapman had reaped the rewards and was still alive and well. For the moment.

"You know we can do more with the trucks, if it's done right," he said. "I've got some ideas."

Reed turned away. "We may already have problems."

"What do you mean?"

"That's not in my ballpark. You'll have to talk to my brother. Good luck with that."

CHAPTER 10

Khai Le had piercing brown eyes. That was the first thing most people noticed about him. A slender man with a wistful smile and affinity for gold jewelry, he was typically calm and personable, but the eyes were unsettling.

Chapman wasn't completely sure what he was going to say, or what Khai would do once he heard the story. If the bagman returned from a big delivery empty-handed, there were no good explanations. Chapman had to hope their long, profitable relationship meant something now.

Khai walked into the office with his imposing bodyguard close behind him. Big Butch was six-foot-seven and well over three hundred pounds; he filled the doorframe as he entered. Butch didn't look like a cop but had served for years as an investigator in the Denver suburbs. He was still well connected with area police departments and had become more of a valuable resource at the growhouse in recent months.

There was a decidedly grim look on the boss's face today.

"We lost track of you, Glen," Khai said. "I thought you were going to fly back last night. What happened?"

"You're not going to like it." That's all it took to get the juices flowing again.

"Tell me," Khai said. "Go slow and be clear."

Chapman's life had been in danger many times through the years, but this one was different. It was a Hail Mary that would test the bounds of trust, faith and friendship. The fallout was potentially devastating for everyone involved.

Good Budz had begun as a group of longtime acquaintances who joined forces to take advantage of Colorado marijuana laws, looking for a lucrative niche. The Trust, they called themselves. It was a game at first, and Khai was the undisputed leader, the organizer. He made up the rules of the road as he went.

His family had emigrated from Vietnam when he and his sister were very young. Their parents had been tea farmers before the war intervened and sent thousands in the population scrambling to safety. They eventually came to the United States to piece together a new life, and tending crops was in the bloodline. Marijuana was a natural fit.

Khai was always ahead of the curve when it came to cultivating plants and trying new things, and he was quick to tap into the possibilities after Colorado became the first state in the union to legalize weed in 2012. He had already secured a license as a "caregiver" for medical marijuana patients, which shielded Good Budz from overzealous inspections. Restrictions on quantity limited his potential as a grower, but they didn't curb his ambitions.

All the while as a caregiver, Khai was expanding operations behind the scenes, with designs on one day being a major player in the state's recreational market. He brought others he knew that were useful into the fold. One was a chef interested in starting a line of edibles, another owned an LED lighting company, yet another was a security expert. They were all looking for ways to grow the business.

Khai handled the finances and built the organization to where sixty employees were on the payroll. Good Budz brought in more than twenty million dollars during a four-year run and was poised to transition as a commercial supplier for legal dispensaries. One dispensary even reached out to investors and potential partners in 2014, and a deal was close. It never happened.

Without government intervention, Good Budz continued to flourish in the black market. But the game was getting more complicated, more lucrative — and more dangerous.

Chapman stared down at the floor and began to wring his hands. His position was hard to reconcile. There had been a sense of honor serving in the military, but running drugs was different. It was mostly exponential greed, finding ways to keep the money machine running, no matter what. To hell with collateral damage.

The pressure had worn on Chapman more than he realized.

Maybe he should have done the right thing, taken one last plunge without a chute. Quick and easy. He wouldn't have to explain anything. He wouldn't have to live with the consequences.

Khai sent Big Butch out of the room. He closed the door and motioned for Chapman to sit on the couch, and then rolled a chair from behind his desk directly in front of his old friend. The weapon strapped on the boss was plain to see.

"Go ahead," Khai said. "Let's hear it."

"I don't have the money. I did have it, but I don't now."

Khai took a long, deep breath and exhaled slowly. "Glen, that was more than three hundred grand. *Three hundred grand!*"

"Three hundred and seven, to be exact. There was still some product left."

"Where is it?"

"We got double-crossed."

"*We?*"

"I flew down to Midland with a friend. He owns another skydiving outfit and has a Twin Otter and …"

"Wait," Khai said, standing with an incredulous look on his face. "You brought in somebody else? I thought you left in your Cessna by yourself. Same as always."

"He has a bigger plane, and I thought we might try it once. We've talked about finding ways to move more product. I trusted this guy."

Khai clenched his jaw and leaned in close to Chapman. "You brought in somebody else without talking to me? You *trusted* him?" He tried to collect himself. "That alone is a huge problem, Glen."

CHAPTER 11

It wasn't the first time that money — and lots of it — had gotten away from the business. In the freewheeling early days, Good Budz was susceptible to other criminals, gangs who were always aware and keeping watch on the growers. They were a clear and present danger, more so than the cops.

At least two break-ins had resulted in large thefts of product. In one, the whole warehouse was cleared out — about six hundred thousand dollars' worth of plants. In another, a fifty-five-gallon soy sauce drum was loaded with weed and rolled away into the night.

Khai was convinced they were both inside jobs, and he began to harbor deep suspicions about those working for him. The cracks in the organization had begun. At times it was hard to distinguish sloppiness from outright treachery. Either way, Khai was trying hard to clean up the company's act.

In all that time, there had never been a problem with Glen Chapman.

Khai sat back down and folded his arms. "Go on."

"When we got to Texas, the customer told me he hadn't been able to raise enough cash for the whole shipment. First thing out of his mouth. He threw down what he had in a couple of suitcases, and I counted it out. I didn't like what was happening, but what could I do? So, I kept seventy-five pounds of the weed and took the money."

"Seventy-five pounds is a helluva lot left over. That wasn't our agreement. It should never have gone down like that."

"I know, but again, what was I going to do? I wasn't going to leave the product there or take a damn IOU." He swallowed hard. "The real problem was what came next. My friend, the pilot, got scared and decided he wasn't smuggling anything back in his plane. He started freaking out and convinced himself the authorities would be waiting for us. I couldn't settle him down."

"That's why you don't bring in new people like that. It was foolish."

"I understand that now. So, he flies home and leaves me with a shitload of cash and this big duffel of weed. I'm on my own and suddenly feeling exposed. I don't really know these guys — and I'm six hundred miles away from here."

Khai was shaking his head over and over at this point. "So now we've got a local pilot running loose who knows about what we're doing. All because of you."

"He only knows about me. He thinks I'm the mastermind of the operation. Like I said, I know him from my business. I believe he was testing the waters to see if there were opportunities down the road, and he just couldn't handle it. He doesn't care about you or anybody else here. He was worried about himself."

"How long before he starts talking?" Khai stood threateningly over Chapman. "And we haven't even gotten to the heart of the problem. *Where the hell is my money and the rest of the product?*"

"I'm getting to that. When I saw what was playing out at the airfield, I knew I needed to get out of there quick, just get away. So, I decided to rent a car and drive back."

"And …"

"I'm not even ten miles down the road," Chapman said, "when I get a call from some other guy who claimed to be partners with our customer. He said the rest of the cash had just come through and wanted me to meet him. So, I pulled off at the next exit and went down the road to this old warehouse and waited at the loading dock in the back. After a few minutes, a pickup truck pulled in behind me, blocked me in. I knew right then it was a setup. As soon as I got out, he pulled a gun on me."

"Let me guess. He took the money and the weed — and then let you drive away scot-free." Chapman nodded. He knew the story sounded unbelievable. "Why would he do that? Why didn't he just kill you?"

"I can't answer that, Khai. He could've."

"Are you lying to me, Glen? This bullshit is over the top. I can't believe you'd be foolish enough to lie to my face this way, when so much is on the line. Let me be clear: We're friends, but that only goes so far. People are killed every day for a whole lot less."

"I know what it looks like, but you have to believe me, brother. I've been on board from the start. We've made a lot of money, all of us, and I'm not greedy. I was just trying to do my job, help the Trust. We're always walking the line between boom or bust in this business."

"We've never gone bust like this. If you'd flown down there in your own plane, just done what you were supposed to, none of this would have happened. This is all on you."

Khai rubbed his face and began to shake his head. "Wait here," he said. He walked out of the room, slamming the door behind him.

Chapman felt flushed again. He knew Khai was vindictive but had rarely resorted to violence in the past. Of course, he never had so much money disappear at once. And the pressure to produce had been growing year by year. This, Chapman feared, may be the day to send a violent message.

The door finally opened again. Khai stepped inside and stopped. For some reason, he was smiling. At least, it seemed like a smile.

"Glen, I'm giving you a chance to change your story. Are you sure this is how it went down?"

Chapman didn't waver. "Swear to God."

"I just called our friend in Texas," Khai said. "He backed up what you're saying, to a point. As far as he knew, everything was fine when you left. He said they fell short on the cash, and that he regretted that. Circumstances beyond his control."

"That's right."

"But he didn't know anything about anybody else. If they claimed to know what had gone down, this guy doesn't understand how. Or who it would be. Again, are you sticking to what you said?"

"I'm just telling you what happened. Everything was fine, and then it wasn't. Before I know it, some guy with a mask is putting a gun in my face."

"And just like that, three hundred thousand dollars is gone. That's what you're telling me?"

"I'm afraid so."

"This is a huge blow to the organization, obviously, and to me personally. I'm going to have to give this some thought before I do something we may both regret. I don't want you to do anything before I decide. By the way, I knew your plane never left the airfield. I had someone check. I knew something was up."

"I explained that."

"You just go home and wait to hear from me. If I find out you're lying, that'll be the end, Glen. You're forcing my hand with this one."

Chapman stood and tried to put on his best face. Like skydiving, he felt relieved to be able to walk away again, but he knew time was running out. One day the chute wouldn't open.

"I'll make it up if you give me a chance," he said. "It may take a little while, but I can do it. You know I can. Let me talk to Michael Shay."

CHAPTER 12

Billy and Zander walked off the jet and headed to their cars together. Claire was waiting in the parking lot and stepped out of her red BMW with a smile as they approached.

Zander was pleasantly surprised when he saw her. For a moment, the distressing news from Colorado was forgotten.

"Good to see you, Claire," he said, offering a hug. "Billy didn't say you were coming out."

"He didn't know. I just thought I'd see how you're doing."

"I'm fine. A few days with my friend here helped." Zander opened the door of a heavy-duty black Ford pickup and threw his travel bag in the back seat.

"Can't get away from those trucks, huh?" Billy asked. "This one's a little different than that beat-up Ram you had in college."

"I always tell the dealer to leave me something interesting to drive, just for the hell of it. Not sure where they came up with this. They must think I'm going to work on a ranch."

Billy looked at the window sticker and raised his eyebrows. "Not your typical work vehicle."

"Last time it was one of the new Vettes. You've seen those mid-engine beasts. Look like Ferraris."

"Got a client or two who've bought one."

"This one was an exotic color — Sebring orange, they called it — and it ran like a rocket ship. Next time they'll leave me something else. Maybe a Harley."

"Man on the move," Claire said.

Zander was reminded of the classic Corvette Sting Ray that Billy's father used to own. He'd made a standing offer to buy the car years ago if Billy ever got tired of it just sitting in his garage. He never failed to mention it.

"Still looking good and going nowhere fast," Billy said. "My father would kill me if I let it go."

He pointed to the leased Lexus sedan he had been driving daily. "I must be getting old," he said.

"At least you still have the Escalade, too. And the houseboat. Can't have too many toys, they say."

"You should know."

Zander turned his attention back to business. "I have to go," he said. "Got a problem that just came up. We'll talk soon."

"Thanks again," Billy said. He and Claire waved as Zander pulled out of the lot and headed east toward I-40.

"What a guy," Billy said. "I'm exhausted from spending a few days with him; he's a whirlwind. It's like we were back in college again."

"I just hope he's not overdoing it," Claire said.

"You know something I don't?"

"No, but I know playtime is over — for you, at least. There's a pile of stuff waiting at the office."

"Why did you drive out here anyway? I told you I was coming in after I go by to see my father."

Claire said again that she was nearby and just wanted to stop and say hello to Zander. She shrugged when Billy mentioned that Zander still had feelings for her.

"He's crazy," she said.

"I liked what you were saying about this new music act. So, the deal is done?"

"They're a unique group, and they're building a nice following and have a lot of room to grow. They could use our connections. That's what it usually comes down to."

"Sweet."

Claire had lobbied hard for Premier to get into the entertainment business, and she was making the most of it. She was getting a better feel for the music landscape in Nashville and considering whether to rent a small apartment there.

"I'm hearing good stuff from a lot of people," she said, "but things are changing fast. We just need to maintain a presence."

Billy laughed. "You definitely have a presence."

Claire grew up in Belle Meade, a Nashville suburb, and felt comfortable in Music City, even though it seemed to be bursting at the seams. The big agencies representing high-profile performers still controlled most of the action, but there was always a place for newcomers with Claire's skills.

"What's the latest with Ty?" Billy asked.

"A couple of the guys in the band have been sick — nothing serious — but the tour is going great. Everybody is excited."

"What about *you* and Ty?"

Claire pursed her lips and shrugged again. She had an attractive way of being evasive.

"We're good, I guess. I'm still getting used to being single. I'm going down to Austin in a few days to see the Austin City Limits taping."

"Wish I could go along, but I'm covered up."

"I think you've probably burned all your vacation days already. Somebody needs to be working. Besides me."

"Okay, boss. I'm heading to Dad's. Keep up the good work."

CHAPTER 13

Billy drove out to Sevierville, about thirty miles south-
east of Knoxville. As he stood in the driveway, looking around his childhood home, Franklin Beckett
pulled in after a quick trip to the office.

His dog, Lucy, had her head hanging out the passenger window of his red truck. The miniature golden-
doodle looked excited to see Billy and was ready to bolt
toward him as the door opened, but Franklin snapped a
leash on her and laughed. "Let's keep you close," he said.
They bounced out of the truck together.

Franklin seemed to be energetic and doing well, despite
the grim medical prognosis. Most mesothelioma patients
weren't expected to live more than two years beyond their
initial diagnosis, though some had survived the cancer
several more years with treatment. Franklin had gotten to
know a few people who had battled it for over a decade.

He had taken a leave of absence from the police
department and, much as he hated it, was planning to
soon make his retirement official. The daily grind was
more than he could manage in good conscience.

Billy had offered him a role at Premier; he could use
Franklin's expertise on several fronts. And he just liked

having his father around. After all the other heartache, he couldn't imagine losing him, too.

Franklin patted Billy on the back, walked to the mailbox, and pulled out a stack of stuff. He smiled when he noticed the letter on top. The stationery was distinctive, an attention grabber like its sender. It was from Dolly Parton, Sevierville's iconic native daughter, who was beloved around the Great Smoky Mountains and generally regarded as a national treasure. The buxom songwriter, singer, businesswoman, actress and philanthropist, well into her seventies now and busier than ever, was in fact the most popular person in the country, according to one recent poll. A living legend that hadn't been poisoned by politics or scandal.

Franklin had known Dolly and many of her relatives for decades. There had been any number of issues arise regarding Dollywood, her bustling theme park in Pigeon Forge that was in a constant state of growth and impacted the entire Sevier County area. Franklin was also a member of a task force that helped direct her philanthropy in the aftermath of the 2016 wildfires in the Smokies that ravaged Gatlinburg and nearby communities. Dolly gave displaced families a thousand dollars a month for six months while they tried to get back on their feet. It added up to almost nine million dollars.

The men walked into the house through the carport door. Franklin dropped the other mail on the kitchen table, sliced open the light pink envelope, and began to read her handwriting. His face lit up again.

He passed the letter to Billy, who was immediately impressed. Dolly was checking on the ailing police chief and expressing more support in her own unique way.

"She's been very helpful," Franklin said.

"How so?"

Franklin said she had connected him with cancer specialists and even offered to assist with any expenses he couldn't handle. She made sure her Sevierville representatives stayed in touch.

"Is there a better human on the planet?" Billy asked.

Franklin beamed. "Not that I know of."

"How often does she get back home these days?"

"Not as much. Still lives there outside Nashville, in Brentwood. It's always a special treat to hear from her."

"I remember you and Mother taking us backstage at a couple of her shows. We were young, and I guess that was our first brush with greatness outside of sports. Dolly is larger than life, even if she doesn't act like it."

Franklin smiled and nodded. So many good memories rolled into one.

"I know you just got back from Florida," he said. "How is Zander?"

"Good ol' country hippie, as always. Just richer."

"I always liked him; he's earned his success. What about your tennis player?"

Billy summed it up: freakishly talented, unpredictable, good-hearted for the most part. Still a wild card at this early stage of his career. The agent was hoping for a breakout year if everything fell into place.

"It's never going to be easy with some kids," Franklin said. "I guess you knew that from day one with Simon."

"Yep, and there haven't been many dull moments since. I appreciate different strokes from different folks, to use a tennis analogy, just as long as we're going in the same direction. Simon is coming to Knoxville soon; he'll be staying at the house. We'll get a chance to know each other better."

"You're the guiding force he needs right now."

"Yeah, people keep telling me that."

Franklin walked to the refrigerator and pulled out a pitcher of ice tea and some lemon slices. They sat at the kitchen table and talked for a while. Billy appreciated those moments now more than ever.

"Since we're catching up, I got a text from Rachel a couple of days ago," Franklin said. He fumbled with his phone for a moment before turning the screen toward Billy. It showed a little girl smiling in a green dress.

Billy grimaced. "So that's Dani? She's growing fast."

Danielle was his niece, and Franklin's only grandchild. Billy was still hurting from the revelation that his former girlfriend, Rachel King, had a fling, and a child, with his deceased brother. That was a huge betrayal on both sides, one that had haunted Billy ever since. It stuck in his gut.

Still, he had tried to patch things up with her, to the extent possible, for his father's sake. She brought Dani to Tennessee to visit with Franklin a while back, after she learned he had cancer. The child was an extension of the son he tragically lost to suicide, and he was admittedly smitten.

It remained a delicate subject, but Billy could tell his father wasn't going to shut the door on the little girl, or her mother. Not with his illness clouding the future. And that was how it should be.

"She looks like John, doesn't she?" Franklin asked.

Billy expanded the picture, stared at the face and nodded. "She's beautiful, like her mother." He handed the phone back and started moving toward the door.

"I really should get back to the office," he said. "I'm glad to see you're feeling well. We need to sit down and talk business here real soon. I've been stockpiling some things I want you to look at. It's not police work, but I think you'll find it interesting."

"I'm excited about it." Franklin opened the door and squeezed his son's shoulder as he passed.

CHAPTER 14

The two agents stood in the hall outside the small conference room at the Drug Enforcement Administration's district office in Albuquerque. They were waiting for a briefing from Special Agent in Charge Carlos Diaz, who had been juggling a variety of concerns all morning.

Trafficking in most sectors in New Mexico had been on the rise for months, and the caseload reflected it. The agents in the hallway weren't sure where this one fell on the priority list.

Diaz turned the corner with a Styrofoam cup of coffee in one hand and a manila folder in the other. "Sorry for the wait," he said. "Come in." He waited to shut the door behind them and then dropped the case file on the desk before taking his seat.

"I've just spoken again with Special Agent McGuire in Denver," Diaz said. "He's heading up a drug task force there and tells me that the suspect, Mr. Chapman, is still cooperating in this case, to a point."

Leslie Miller, a sturdy woman in her mid-thirties with sandy blond hair, looked puzzled. *"To a point?"* she said. "Didn't look like he had much room to maneuver here. Cut and dried."

Diaz smiled. "You know nothing in this business is ever cut and dried. There's always wiggle room if you play the game right. Mr. Chapman is playing the game."

"Sounds like he's playing the long game."

Diaz flipped open the folder and slipped on his reading glasses. He was a veteran lawman with gray-flecked hair and a rumpled appearance. He'd dealt with countless drug runners through the years. The younger agents considered him a mentor.

"To refresh your memory," he said, "the suspect was stopped in the I-25 corridor. There's been a lot of action along the Colorado border lately, and this guy was supposedly heading home from Texas."

Eric Quintana, the third agent, chuckled. "Equipped for a party."

"Helluva party. Three hundred seven grand in cash. Seventy-five pounds of weed. Loaded handgun in the glove box. Had a small amount of cocaine on his person."

"Sounds like a drug runner to me," Quintana said.

"The arresting officer, Montgomery, wrote that Mr. Chapman was about to run out of gas and cut through the median to get back to the last exit. He noticed a strong odor of marijuana when he approached the vehicle, and a search turned up all of these goodies inside."

"Stupid," Miller said with a shake of her head.

"He wasn't going to make it back to the gas station anyway. The van wouldn't even start when the tow truck driver came. Anyway, Mr. Chapman was apparently eager to speak with the DEA. McGuire said that was the first thing out of his mouth when the officer came to him. We saw him a short time later, if you recall, and facilitated his return to Colorado."

"Where is he now?" Miller asked.

"That's a good question. Everything in this case is running through the Denver office, so I don't know. McGuire told me that they have an eye on him. Colorado is used to handling all kinds of interstate trafficking; they're the hub for a lot of this. Of course, we in New Mexico have plenty of our own problems to deal with, particularly the rise of meth and heroin. I just wanted to brief you and get this case off our books. It's Denver's problem now."

"Why isn't he in custody?" Quintana said.

"McGuire thinks he's part of an organization that's trying to extend its reach. They've put together a task force up there with state and local officials, and this case falls under its domain. They're interested to see where the investigation may lead, so Mr. Chapman is still running free as long as he continues to cooperate. He has his pilot's license and claims to be a bagman for this group."

"And he didn't come back with three hundred large?" Miller said. "That's a very forgiving group. He sounds like a flight risk."

"Maybe. I'm surprised he's still alive."

"He may not be for long. But again, that's not our problem."

"What do we know about this group?" Quintana said. "Is it going to be a problem for us down the road?"

"They've apparently been out there for a while, but they were small fish in the sea. A bunch of guys who knew each other and were just looking to find a hole in the system in Colorado to make money. Started out as caregivers. Have you heard that story before?"

"And just got carried away when cash started raining down from the heavens? Yeah, I've heard that one."

"We'll get an update from McGuire at some point and may be able to track any future activity in this direction. I'm guessing we won't see Mr. Chapman again, but who knows? They may be a problem later. Or they may get shut down soon and thrown in prison."

"The amount of money that Chapman was carrying suggests they're getting bigger," Quintana said. "And the fact that he was coming from Texas … well, we *are* part of the El Paso division. It's something to remember."

Diaz removed his readers and closed the file on the table. "Yes, it is."

CHAPTER 15

Glen Chapman had always split his allegiances. His skydiving buddies were on one side of the line. The growers and smugglers were on the other.

From the beginning, the marijuana syndicate was the means to an end, a way to exploit the system and make money. Potentially obscene amounts of money. But those personal relationships with childhood friends had diminished in the face of rampant greed to the point that they became a throwaway in Chapman's mind, something to be discarded down the road when the time was right. They weren't really *friends* anymore. Once his pockets were full, he knew he could turn his back and simply walk away.

Skydiving was different. The camaraderie that grew from squeezing into small planes, looking out over the fruited plain, and then taking the plunge together — that was special. Those were his *real* friends.

The line had gotten blurred with Michael Shay.

The door to the stylish condo in Aurora opened, and Chapman stood on the porch with an uneasy smile.

"Sorry to bother you, but like I said on the phone, I was hoping we could talk."

Michael glanced suspiciously around the parking area. Nothing seemed unusual. "Okay. Come in."

Chapman stopped just inside the doorway of the end unit. The condo was sparsely furnished, like a bachelor pad. Michael had paid cash for it and was using it more as a place to crash when he wasn't at work.

The family home in Eagle, where he and Ellen had raised their son, had become an Airbnb property, mostly for renters who liked the proximity to the ski resorts. Michael didn't have time to get to the mountains much anymore.

"I'm in a bit of jam and need your help," Chapman said.

"I don't like the sound of that. Sit down and tell me what's up. Want something to drink?"

"No, thanks."

Chapman took a seat on the couch and squinted as bright sunshine streamed through the transom window. "You know we've been turning a nice profit for a while now, and I know you feel good about how our arrangement has produced."

"Of course. It has improved my outlook on life, so to speak." He gestured toward their surroundings. "I'm able to do things I've never been able to do before."

"Good. Well, it may be time to ramp up. I think we can do more. We *need* to do more."

"You know we've discussed this before," Michael said. "I'm not comfortable with that right now. We have to go slow."

Chapman took a deep breath; he seemed rattled. "Things have changed."

"They've changed on my end, too. Don't forget how close we came to disaster with the truck in Kansas City. When people start getting killed, everything changes."

"So, they haven't arrested anybody?"

"No, and no motive yet as far as we know. They're going through the shipment to see what might stand out. You don't know anything about that?"

"No," Chapman said. "What I do know is that we need for that shipment to move on. The customer is waiting."

"They'll get it as soon as possible. Hopefully it's still intact, the way it was loaded."

"If it is, then this must be a random thing, maybe something personal with the driver. If not …"

Michael shook his head. He always appeared cool under duress, whether he was firming up new business plans, preparing to make a jump, or dealing with smugglers. But he needed to know that the benefits outweighed potential consequences.

"I'm trying to understand this situation," Michael said. "We'll move forward when it's appropriate and not before."

He had been given wide latitude to make decisions at AAF Transport, almost from the beginning. The stream of cargo coming through Aurora was building, moving faster by the day. It had become a key cog in the company's plans to expand routes into more western markets.

Michael had hit it off with Zander Fleming from their first meeting. He was a handsome outdoorsman with a background in transportation and a certain swagger that played well in that part of the country.

Michael's personal story was just as compelling. He had battled through the tragic loss of his wife and was a single father who was working hard to make ends meet. His son Simon's rising profile in the tennis world made the story even more interesting.

Zander was inspired by it all. So was Chapman.

"You said you're in a bit of a jam," Michael said. "What are you proposing?"

"It's fairly simple. We're stockpiling more product in Denver than we're able to distribute. Moving it by air is problematic, and it's on me to come up with solutions."

"Well, you're the boss. Is it possible that some of your people are involved — an inside thing? I know you've had problems with that before."

"Only a handful of people know. I trust all of them. The problem is with criminals, not my associates."

"Funny choice of words. They can be one and the same."

Michael smiled and shook his head. "I said I've been comfortable with our arrangement. Assuming what was stuffed into that wing hasn't disappeared, I'm still comfortable with it. But you want to push harder?"

"You know me, Michael. Always higher, bigger, faster. And richer."

"Tell me exactly what you want."

The men had become skydiving buddies during the early days, when Chapman was determined to build his business, regardless of the cost. Simon Shay had recently left for Florida, and his father was alone for the first time. Michael fought depression for a while before seeking a new outlet to occupy his mind. What could be more invigorating than jumping out of airplanes?

When Glen started his skydiving company, Blue Yonder, the men's relationship got tighter. The sky was the limit in so many ways.

By then, Chapman had already been sucked into Khai Le's burgeoning marijuana schemes. He began by driving shipments from Good Budz growhouses to a handful of outlets in the Denver area, between Fort Collins and Colorado Springs. Drop product, bring back cash. It was hazardous work, but nothing Chapman couldn't handle.

Once he earned his pilot's license, and the group became more brazen. The Trust could extend its reach to neighboring states where marijuana was still illegal but in greater demand than ever. Even down to Texas. That's what drove the black market in Colorado.

The potential bonanza ultimately outweighed the legal jeopardy and limitations on how much weed could be smuggled aboard a small plane.

That's where Michael Shay came in.

"I want to get another shipment ready to go within a week," Chapman said. "Let me see what I can do, and I'll be back in touch."

"I'll wait to hear."

"By the way, how's your son doing down in Florida? I know he's a helluva tennis player. That was *your* sport, right? Chip off the old block."

"He's getting ready for the Australian Open. First major."

"Big time."

"Yeah, and it doesn't look like he'll be home for Christmas this year. He's going to spend the holidays in Tennessee with his agent. I miss him, but it may be better if he's not around right now."

Chapman stood and headed toward the door. "Good luck to him. And to us all. I'll be in touch."

CHAPTER 16

Zander was back in Knoxville early. The news about the murder had been gnawing at him, more because of what he didn't know than what he did. His parents encouraged him to go to Colorado and see for himself.

First, he was going to check out a tract of land for possible construction of a new distribution center. It was a long shot but worth the stop. He'd then make the short drive south to Blount County, where the airport was located.

The pilots were getting ready for an early-afternoon departure when Zander called Billy. "Want to grab some lunch?" he said.

"Are you back in Knoxville?"

"Yeah, I need to get out of here, but I want to look at that land I was telling you about. Can we eat somewhere on the west side of town?"

"How about Harvest, out on Kingston Pike? Helluva brunch."

"I remember the sign — land, sea and vine. Seems to cover it. If you're free, I'll meet you there in an hour."

Billy was already seated with a glass of ice tea when Zander walked into the restaurant. "I'll have one of these," he said to the waiter, pointing to Billy's drink, as he pulled up a chair.

"Sweet tea with lemon. You know we don't get that down in the Keys, or out West, or up North — except at McDonald's. Why is that?"

"Never understood unsweetened tea anywhere. Better get your sugar rush here while you can. What did you think of the tract?"

Zander shook his head. "Don't think it'll work. Nice area but the access isn't right for our purposes. I've got people looking."

The waiter returned to take their orders. Billy went with the Bubba Benedict — Benton's bacon, biscuit, over-easy egg, sausage gravy, and roasted Yukon gold potatoes.

"That's a killer," Zander said, before ordering the Harvest salad with raspberry vinaigrette.

"Did you have a good visit with your folks?"

"Short and sweet. They're doing well."

"Why so short?"

"I just had something come up in Colorado that needs my attention."

Billy didn't pry, but Zander wanted to get it off his chest. "We had a guy on one of our trucks who was shot and killed," he said. "First time that's ever happened."

"The driver?"

"There were two drivers making a haul from Aurora to Detroit. They stopped in Kansas City, and things apparently went bad in a hurry. One of them was shot. Still a lot of questions — and no suspects."

Billy furrowed his brow. "So, you're going on out to Denver? What can you do?"

Zander shrugged and squeezed the lemon into his tea. He took a long drink and nodded his approval.

"Not much I can do," he said, "but I was going anyway. It's just been weighing on my mind."

"Sorry to hear."

"Just something else to worry about. Right now, I want to know the latest on Simon. Is he coming?"

"He flies in tomorrow. Anything I should know before he gets here?"

"I can't think of anything you don't already know. Hopefully he'll be a gracious guest while he's here and a better player when he leaves."

"That's the idea," Billy said. "Have you already made plans for Australia?"

"I haven't had a lot of time to think about it. Guess I'll be flying commercial for that one. Haven't been on many international flights lately. Wish you were going with me."

"I'd like to, but I just can't make it happen this year. The football stuff is really starting to pile up. It's amazing the way these teams change their rosters now from year to year. You always have to be ready to move."

"I thought you liked that part of the business."

"Sure, as long as the salary cap keeps going up and you can find somewhere to plug in your clients. There's just no such thing as job security in the NFL. It's brutal." The waitress set down a fresh glass of tea. "So, what about Simon's father? He's definitely not going?"

Zander shook his head. "Under the circumstances, Michael and I shouldn't both be gone at the start of the year. And depending on what happens the next few weeks, I might have to cancel, too. I'd hate to, but I want to get this legal matter behind us."

"I'm sure Darren can handle everything, but you know Simon. You can always expect the unexpected."

CHAPTER 17

The snowboarders were happily carving their way through deep powder, on a steep and difficult grade just outside the boundaries of the Vail Mountain ski resort.

Recent storms had dumped more than two feet of snow in the area, creating a winter wonderland in early December. The Colorado sky had cleared to a majestic blue, and the mountain sparkled under the intense sunshine. The freedom and sheer joy of the moment was apparent on the boarders' faces. The unspoiled playground was all theirs.

Suddenly there was an ominous warning above them. Whoomph! A slab of the snowpack broke loose and began to funnel down the face of the mountain, slowly at first but building with remarkable speed, burying everything in its path.

Terrified, the boarders scrambled to find refuge. Simon came to rest amid a tangle of evergreen branches, dazed but unharmed. Miraculously, he managed to free himself after a few minutes.

Jenny Riddick, Simon's childhood friend, was nowhere to be seen. But she couldn't be far away.

Relying on his training for just such an emergency, Simon checked for a signal from her avalanche beacon. They were both wearing one.

He was locked on now and repeatedly yelled Jenny's name while methodically wading back and forth through the deep snow. The signal brought him closer. He began to probe. She was right there, buried perhaps two feet under.

Simon assembled the small shovel from his backpack and dug, quickly but carefully, continuing to yell her name. Jenny! Jenny! I'm coming! He heard the muffled response and knew Jenny was struggling for air, but she must have cleared a small chamber around her face. If he didn't get to her soon, she would die of carbon dioxide poisoning.

There were typically about thirty avalanche victims in the United States every year — and Simon would bear the blame for this one. He was the wildly adventurous friend, the one who always flouted rules and tested limits. He had suggested to Jenny that morning that they leave the back bowls of Vail Highlands and cross the boundary, outside the area where the resort routinely blasted to mitigate the avalanche danger, to play in the fresh powder.

Since they were kids, he had looked after Jenny on their many forays into the mountains. He'd been like the big brother she never had, and she trusted him implicitly. Now it was up to Simon to save her.

Another five minutes had passed, and Jenny's chances were getting slimmer. There was no one else to help. Simon was breathing heavily in the thin air. Time was running out.

***

Simon and Jenny were sitting around a crackling fireplace in the den and watching the GoPro footage on the big television screen for the third time. Cameras mounted on their helmets recorded the action — the exhilaration and the terror. They were laughing now, drinking hot tea and casually discussing the second avalanche of the young season to affect adventurers in the Vail area. Two skiers had died in the first one.

No big deal, they seemed to suggest. There was always an element of danger in the Rockies. This time they were lucky. Very lucky. Finally came the moment the white field cleared, and the gloved hand began to clear away the snow from Jenny's face. She was safe.

The quality of the picture was remarkable. Simon was looking down at her with those icy blue eyes, and his expression changed, from panic to relief. His electric smile lit up the frame.

"There you are," he said.

Sprawled out and frozen in place with her red snowboard, Jenny took a deep breath and managed to laugh. "I thought you said this would be fun," she said.

***

Billy stretched out in his Escalade outside baggage claim at the Knoxville airport, recalling the day they first met. He had flown to Denver and then driven out to Eagle, just to talk to the kid Zander had been raving about.

"It may take some time to get used to him," his friend had warned. "He's different, and so is his dad, so it may take a few minutes to warm up."

Billy remembered his response: "I don't mind different, and I warm up pretty fast. Just a normal sit-down would be a great start." Instead, he ended up reliving the near-death experience on the screen. It shaped the agent's opinion of his new client.

Simon's plane had just landed in Knoxville, and Billy seemed unusually anxious as he waited. He had been covered up as the holidays approached and hadn't had time to think about the visit or his reasoning for suggesting it. The one thought that kept rolling around in his head: *Maybe this wasn't such a great idea after all.*

After a few minutes, Simon rolled his luggage out the sliding doors and to the curb where Billy was parked. His bag of racquets was slung over his shoulder, and his hair was wild and woolly. He looked every bit the tennis renegade.

Billy popped the rear gate and got out to greet his guest. "Glad you're here," he said. "How is everything?"

"Not sure, dude. I've never been in Tennessee, so we'll see."

Billy could tell the youngster was less than thrilled to be there, and he wasn't in the mood to hear any whining.

"You wanted a break from Florida, and this qualifies," he said. "Just to be clear, it's not a break from tennis. It isn't a vacation."

"Don't worry, I'm definitely not looking at it that way. I wouldn't come here to vacation."

Billy chucked the bag in the back and slammed the gate shut. "Get your head right and you might be surprised."

They headed toward Billy's home on the Tennessee River. The mood was subdued until Simon broke the silence with an admission that caught his agent off guard.

"I'm not sure how welcome I am at the academy right now," he said.

"Why do you say that?"

"I had a little incident involving Jack Branson."

"The founder? What happened?"

Simon stared out the windshield. "It had something to do with his wife. He's pretty upset with me."

"Don't tell me you insulted his wife. What's her name? Ashley?"

"No, it wasn't like that. She and I, uh, got a little close at a reception the other night. He didn't like it and made a few threats. I apologized." Simon was gauging his agent's reaction. "Don't worry, he'll probably cool down while I'm gone. Don't know about his wife."

Billy took a big breath and exhaled slowly as he turned onto the winding road toward Rocky Top Estates. There were expansive river views everywhere.

"Seems like you do a lot of apologizing. Is that a tennis thing? You're a little young for that kind of drama anyway."

"She didn't think so," Simon said. "It wasn't my idea. I'm just trying to play tennis and stay out of trouble."

"Then stay away from the tennis babes, and especially the married ones. They're radioactive. Haven't we discussed this before?"

Simon smiled. "There's a bunch of them in Florida. And this one ... she's probably twenty years younger than her husband. All I did was compliment her on how nice she looked, and one thing led to another."

"And?"

"I think I was able to smooth it over. Maybe."

"You're a charming young man, Simon, and I know you're popular with the ladies. But here's the voice of experience: Sometimes it's better to observe than comment. Just keep your mouth shut and stay in your lane. That'll hold you in the good graces of people who can help further your career."

Simon chuckled. "Such a wise old man."

CHAPTER 18

The gray contemporary on the hill suddenly came into view, and Billy slowed at the driveway to let his guest take it all in. He was proud of his home.

The garage door was open by the time they reached the house. The covered car drew Simon's interest immediately. "That looks like an old Corvette," he said.

"Not old — *classic*. Nineteen sixty-three. Used to be my father's."

"Nice. Can we take her for a ride?"

"Maybe we'll get to that eventually. Grab your bags, and I'll show you around."

They walked to one of the downstairs bedrooms that looked out over the river, and then on to the wraparound deck. It was a quiet, overcast day.

"So that's your dock?" Simon asked, pointing down to where Billy's white houseboat was secured below. "I think I've read about that, what happened."

"You can't believe everything you read. C'mon, let's take a little walk."

They ventured down the path to the river and onto the dock. There were few signs of activity on the tranquil bluish-green water.

Simon jumped on the deck of *Agent Orange* and smiled. "Not quite like Zander's yacht, but not a bad party boat," he said. "Maybe this *could* be a vacation."

"Could be, but not this time. We're going to hash out what the next few months look like for your career. Then it depends on how successful you've been, how much progress you've made. It could be a helluva year."

"I hope so."

"You won't be here long, so just work on your game and your focus and try to become a better player. I tell all my clients —"

"I know. Embrace the process. Carry yourself like a pro at all times."

"Very good," Billy said. "It's simple, right?"

"Not really. When can I drive the Vette?"

"I'll let you know."

Simon gazed around at his surroundings and nodded his head approvingly. "Looks like you're doing pretty well here, Billy. I know a lot of agents do well, but you're different. At least that's what people say."

"Is that right? What else do they say?"

"Just that you're not afraid to get your hands dirty. I know the story on Russell Mann."

Mann was the NBA star who was killed in a shooting in Orlando just a few months earlier. He was Billy's most lucrative client, and his death was a blow in more ways than one. At twenty-five, Mann never could get the demons of a brutal childhood in the Bronx out of his system and paid the ultimate price. He was one that Billy couldn't save.

"Am I one of your bad boys?" Simon asked, flashing an impish grin.

"I wouldn't call you either. You're nineteen now, so you're a man. As far as good or bad, it's up to you. Life is what you make of it."

Simon smiled. "Dad likes to say that, too."

"Just remember that it's not easy to get back on the right path once you take a wrong turn. You need to mind your business, focus on tennis, and we'll see where that takes you. Make the most of your time here. As we've discussed, the new year is going to be big for your career. And again, you're fortunate to have a good team behind you."

"I like Zander. He's a unique guy."

"Yes, he is," Billy said. "That's what people love about him."

"Dad says he's brilliant. He must be, to have all the stuff he has at this age. He's not very old."

"Glad you noticed. Your family has known him for a while, right?"

"Yeah, we used to ski together when he'd come to Denver. Sometimes we'd ride mountain bikes in the summer; he's always on a bike. I worked at the warehouse one summer, before the tennis got heavy, and used to see him pretty often."

"So, a real job?" Billy asked with a laugh.

"I guess. It was interesting seeing all the things that came through there. Some of the guys I worked with used to talk. They seemed to think everything was growing so fast that no one really knew what was going on."

"That's your father's turf. I'm guessing he has a pretty good idea of what's going on there."

"Maybe."

"Let's go back up to the house, and I'll show you some things I've been working on. Darren will be here in the morning."

Simon furrowed his brow. "Can't wait to see him."

"I'm sure that works both ways. Remember, stay focused and get better. I'll make sure you have everything you need."

"I appreciate it, Billy. Seriously. I give you some grief, but I know you're a good guy. I want to be a great player and make you proud, same as my dad and Zander."

"Make yourself proud while you're at it," Billy said. "Everything falls into place if you do that." They bumped fists and walked back up the hill together.

CHAPTER 19

Franklin Beckett never imagined leaving the Sevierville Police Department at the relatively young age of sixty-two. But he had made his retirement official at a morning news conference.

There was a large group of smiling friends and colleagues around him at the impromptu sendoff afterward at City Hall. Franklin tried to smile, too, but it was difficult.

In his thirty years with the department — the last eighteen as chief — he had always been honored to wear the uniform. And now life was moving on. *But for how long?*

Many of his colleagues stepped in to share old war stories. There were a lot to tell. Franklin was a popular chief who worked his way up through the ranks after serving in the military. A large man with a crew cut and bushy mustache, he was heroic in many ways, a true patriot.

When the subject of fighting fires back in the day came up, there was some uneasiness. Everyone knew Franklin had likely come into contact with asbestos, the cause of mesothelioma, early in his career. It often took decades for the disease to reveal itself.

And now, it had robbed Franklin of his golden years with the department. He was in a battle for his life.

Billy stood with his father and wore a non-stop smile amid the hugs, handshakes and memories. "This is nice," he said during a momentary break. "I'm really proud of you and all that you've done. A lot of other people obviously feel the same way."

Franklin nodded. His lips had a slight quiver, and the tears were beginning to well up. He dabbed at his eyes.

"Sorry to get emotional. I don't know what I'm going to do without coming down here and working with all these great people."

"I'll tell you what you're going to do," Billy said. "You're going to work with me, and you're going to love it. Everybody loves working with me. I expect to see you at the office very soon."

"Sooner is better. For everything."

Claire walked into the gathering and looked around. She smiled when she saw the Beckett boys together at the far end of the room.

"Congratulations on a job well done," she said, leaning in to hug Franklin. "It's been a great career. You've been a fine public servant."

"Condolences is more like it. Now I'm just another poor guy who's out of work."

"Not true," Billy said to Claire. "He's got a job already lined up. You're his new boss."

Franklin chuckled. "I appreciate you coming down here, Claire. It's been a while since I've seen you. You look fabulous, by the way."

"And so do you, chief. I hear you're doing well. You know I wouldn't miss this big sendoff for my favorite cop."

"I thought you were headed to the airport," Billy said.

"Soon."

"Son, you don't know how lucky you are to have this woman as your partner. Where would you be without her?"

Billy put his arm around Claire's shoulder and pulled her close. "She's special, that's for sure," he said. They looked into each other's eyes for several seconds. The chemistry between them was undeniable.

"How about some punch?" Franklin asked.

"No, thank you," Claire said. "I have to run by the house and pack a bag. I'm sorry I can't stay longer."

"You're going to Austin?"

"Quick trip. Just need to make sure everything's on track for the next leg of the tour. Ty said he's anxious to talk."

"I'll bet," Billy said. "I saw where his new single is making its way up the country charts. That's a very catchy tune."

"That boy is full of catchy tunes. New album soon."

"It's definitely a great time to strut his stuff on Austin City Limits," Billy said. "He'll get some serious mileage out of that."

"Yeah, I think the publicity will pay off big time. It's the longest-running music series in television history, and fans are tuned in all over the country. I'd expect some other nice opportunities to come from it, especially in the Lone Star State. I'm going to meet with a couple of people from the record label while I'm down there, too. Should be a productive trip."

"You've conquered Nashville and now, Texas. Hell of an agent, I'd say."

Claire winked at Billy and gave Franklin a quick kiss on the cheek. "See you both soon," she said.

The men smiled at each other as she turned and walked away.

CHAPTER 20

"**D**o you really have something for me to do, or are you just humoring me?"

Franklin was already looking ahead, as was his nature. Billy was glad to hear that. He was serious about his father's involvement at Premier and had been keeping a list of things he knew Franklin would love to tackle. He was pleased to see the interest went both ways.

"I've got several folders of cases that could use some updating," Billy said. "You know these athletes. Never a dull moment trying to keep up."

"And trying to keep them out of trouble. You've never been afraid to take on potential problems."

"Most of them are pretty solid citizens. The ones that aren't just stir up a bunch of bad publicity for themselves and for Premier. They tend to move on before long. If we can keep that from happening with a little more oversight, it's a good thing."

"You need a cop? Is that what you're saying?"

"No, I'm saying I could use a smart man who thinks like a cop. When things go wrong, I'll just blame you."

"That's funny." Franklin didn't laugh; he got misty-eyed. "You know what just came to my mind?" he said. "John."

"Why John?"

"Just talking about athletes who get off track and trying to get them straightened back out. It's not easy. You understand that better than anybody."

Billy shook his head. "Let's don't go there, Dad. I don't think there's any new ground to cover with John."

"We both know he could have been in the major leagues. He *should* have been. I think about him all the time."

"So do I. But let's just enjoy this occasion for what it is — a celebration of *you*. That's why all these people, your friends and colleagues, came today."

"And I appreciate it more than they'll ever know. I go way back with a lot of them, before I was chief, when you and your brother were just boys. I'd bring the two of you to all kinds of family events with the department. Just a lot of good memories."

Billy reached over and squeezed the back of his father's neck. "I remember." He suddenly felt himself tearing up, too.

The crowd in the conference room was beginning to thin. "Guess we can start to move out of here," Franklin said.

He shook a few more hands on his way toward the door, including Mayor Buffington's. "What a nice gesture," he said. "I really am thankful for everyone. I won't forget any of you."

"It's the least we can do, Franklin," the mayor said. "You've been the backbone of the police department for as long as I can remember. We're going to miss having you around. Good luck with everything."

They walked out into the parking lot and stopped by Franklin's truck. Someone had attached a string of festive red balloons to the antenna.

"I'll bet that was Claire," Franklin said.

"No, she would have gone with orange and white." Billy lingered for a moment. "While I'm thinking about it, Dad, let me mention something going on with Zander. It doesn't have anything to do with Premier, but I've just been wondering about it."

Franklin untied the balloons and put them inside his truck. "Okay."

"One of his drivers was murdered on a long haul out of Denver. Shot in the cab near Kansas City."

"What was it about?"

"They're not sure."

"No suspects?"

"No motive, no nothing."

"And no sports angle?" Franklin asked. "Why does this concern you?"

"It doesn't, directly. I've just been in touch with Zander more lately and was hoping I might help somehow. He's stressed about it. There wasn't a lot of information coming out, and I thought your investigative mind might be of service."

"Investigative mind, huh? I'll take that as a compliment, and I'd be happy to do anything I can to help

Zander. I'm sure there's plenty of good police work going on right now behind the scenes."

"I'm sure, too. I just wanted to mention it in case you could be of help at some point. I'll be talking to him again soon."

"Tell him to call any time. I'm pretty free right now."

"You know, he's thinking about building a distribution center on the west side of Knoxville, maybe even buying a house and spending part of the year up here. I think he's getting nostalgic in his old age."

"Would you like having him close by?"

"I'm not sure, to be honest," Billy said. "When you're around Zander, you can get involved in a lot of things you weren't counting on."

Franklin laughed. "I thought that was always part of the attraction with him."

The ex-police chief climbed into his truck, slowly circled the parking lot one last time, and drove away.

CHAPTER 21

The band was near the end of a final sound check at Moody Theater, and the anticipation was growing. Countdown to show time had begun.

An invitation to perform in the state-of-the-art concert hall was cherished by any musician, young or old. About a hundred acts appeared on stage there every year. It was an eclectic mix, cutting across all genres, and many played in front of sellout crowds of twenty-seven hundred. Everyone brought their A-game to Austin.

Ty Nelson had grown his loyal fan base in a hurry. He'd been a staple in the venerable Nashville clubs since he was old enough to drink, but everything began to change after The Songmasters. A runner-up finish at the recent national talent competition in Los Angeles had boosted his popularity in ways he never imagined. The ensuing tour and marketing blitz orchestrated by Claire, his new agent, was building momentum. It had only enhanced his reputation as a unique songwriter and picker.

Ty was in his element now. He walked to the microphone, looked out at the sound technician, and played a few licks. The band immediately launched into *Numbers Game*, one of his biggest hits. It all sounded perfect.

Ty gazed around the theater at the end and beamed. He'd always dreamed of playing a set there, and now he was just hours away from doing it. He placed his Taylor guitar on a stand and walked off stage right, where Claire was waiting in the wings.

"What do you think?" he said.

"Sounds great, and what a setting. This is an awesome venue, just like everyone said. It'll be even more awesome when it's full of people. You feel good?"

"I think we're all in kind of a daze right now." He hugged his agent. "You made it happen, Claire. The guys really appreciate everything you've done for us."

Claire smiled brightly and slung a light brown satchel over her shoulder. "I guess you're worth it."

The sound tech flashed a thumbs-up sign. Good to go. Ty's four band mates walked off stage left with a collective nod. This would be a special night. They could all feel it.

"C'mon, I want to show you something," Ty said.

He and Claire slipped out a side door, down the steps, and over to the large bronze statue at the corner of the building. The pigtailed figure, seated on a stool with his arm casually draped over a guitar, was familiar to any music lover. Willie Nelson was a legendary Texan from the tiny town of Abbott, a couple hours up I-35. Austin claimed him as one of its own.

Now approaching ninety, and still on the road, Nelson played the ACL pilot episode, in 1974, and had performed many times at Moody Theater in the decade since it opened. The building's address was 310 West Willie Nelson Boulevard.

"I wanted you to see my grandfather," Ty said. "Or maybe he'd be my great-grandfather."

"I always knew you had musical genes, but I had no idea Willie was part of the mix."

"Think there's room for another Nelson statue out here?"

Claire laughed. "Just keep up the good work. Maybe we'll see in fifty years or so."

They walked over and took a seat on a bench in the square. Ty had his show-day look — tight black t-shirt with jeans and snakeskin cowboy boots to go with the hazel eyes and long, silky hair. It was an attractive package. He was one of the current heartthrobs in country music, and like many other women, Claire had been captivated by his potential as that handsome face became more ubiquitous.

"I've missed seeing you," he said. "It's lonely out here on the road."

"Something tells me you're not real lonely. Hell, you've got at least four guys around you all the time."

"*Guys* is the operative word. I need a little female companionship."

"You're saving yourself?"

Ty started to kiss her, but she shied away. "What's wrong?" he asked.

"Nothing. I'm glad to see you, too, but I'm a little pre-occupied. I'm here on business."

"I thought you were here for *me*."

"I am. The business of Ty Nelson. I've got a meeting before the show and need to go over some notes. It's important."

"Can we get together later?"

"For a drink? Sure."

"I was hoping for more." Claire stared into the distance. "Why do I get the feeling something has changed?" he said.

"I wouldn't say that. I'm just not exactly sure where things stood to begin with. We're old friends, and I'm your agent, but what else? Occasional lovers?" She tried to take the words back. "I'm uncomfortable even talking about it right now."

Ty looked confused. "I don't want to make you uncomfortable."

"It's not you. I just don't want to put any pressure on either of us. Sometimes I feel like I'm in an awkward position. You're my *client*."

"It's never felt awkward to me," Ty said. "We know each other pretty well. We go way back. I wanted an agent that I clicked with, and we click. Man, do we click."

He looked deep into Claire's blue eyes, and she felt her resolve slipping. Maybe something more a drink later. Maybe not. The conflict was growing in her mind.

The theater door opened, and the stage manager stepped out. The man had a wireless headset pulled down around his neck and a notepad in his hand. Back to the business of making music.

"Sorry to bother you, Ty, but we've got a couple of issues here that we need you to weigh in on," he said. "Shouldn't take long."

"You guys go on," Claire said. "I need to stop by the hotel for a minute before my meeting." She patted Ty on the back. "Can't wait to see the show. Break a leg."

He offered a halfhearted smile and walked back inside.

CHAPTER 22

Billy always looked for the best way in. What were the connections, the common bonds, the personal experiences outside of sports that could bind his relationship with a client? Sometimes it was easy. Other times there wasn't much to work with, and that made the job tougher.

The agent was still trying to get a feel for Simon Shay as they stood on the dock and looked out over the Tennessee River. The early-morning fog had lifted, and bright sunshine was taking over. An unseasonably warm day was in the forecast. There would be no better opportunity to get on the water for a short cruise.

Billy grabbed the railing and pulled *Agent Orange* close to the dock. He leaned over to undo the hitch knots and work the lines through the cleats. The white houseboat was free.

"Go ahead and jump on," he said.

Wearing a black Colorado Buffaloes hoodie and sweatpants, Simon stepped across to the deck. Billy followed and opened the cabin door to let the breeze flow through. A look came over him. Calm, peaceful. He loved spending time on his boat.

"Want some coffee?" he said, walking over to the machine with a fresh pod. "Won't take long."

"No, thanks. Coffee makes me nervous. Water would be great, though."

Billy stuck the key in the ignition and let the blower run for a couple of minutes. The engine fired right up. He zipped up his windbreaker and walked around the deck to shove off before sliding the inboard/outboard into gear. It began to cut through the glassy surface of the water.

"This is how you start the day around here," Simon said. "I like it."

"I don't get out as often anymore, especially this time of year. It's usually too cold to enjoy the water. And there's not as much company as there used to be." He stood and gestured for Simon to take the wheel. "You steer while I pour myself some coffee."

Billy came back with a steaming mug and handed Simon a bottle of water. He lingered in the doorway, surveying the river while his guest continued to drive.

"We'll just do a short loop this time, down around the bend and back. Nice and easy," he said. "Darren will be at the house to pick you up in an hour or so. One day we'll go all the way up to Neyland Stadium. I'd like for you to see that."

"Vol Navy? Isn't that what they call all the boats that come on game days?"

"Yeah, there's a bunch. I used to jump in there with them whenever I could. The setting along the river on Saturdays is usually better than the football. It's fun."

Billy took a long drink of his coffee. "Back to business, how do you guys like the practice setup at the club?"

"The facilities are good, like you said, and I like the atmosphere. You know Darren. Doesn't really matter where you practice, he's going to be pushing hard. The pace is picking up, and I feel it."

"He's a good coach who knows how things work at the highest level. That's what you want. Remember, we're all working toward the same goals on Team Shay."

"Why did you invite me to come? You know I've got everything I need in Florida. I mean, you really can't beat the facilities there. Or the weather this time of year."

"That's a good question," Billy said. "We just thought you needed to clear your mind. If you can do that, you'll play your best tennis. Besides, I have a little more freedom this time of year, and I thought having you here might help both of us. The better we know each other, the better things tend to work out."

"Don't tell me you're lonely."

"It's a well-kept secret."

Simon smiled and sipped on the water as he looked out over the bow. He seemed to be settling into his new surroundings. The pressure and stress of competition had eased a bit. He felt more like a normal teenager.

"Mind if I give it some gas?" he said.

"Go ahead. Easy though."

The boat, a sixty-footer with two small staterooms and a sundeck, picked up speed and then planed off. For the moment, at least, it was the only craft visible on the river.

"You know, my parents and I used to do this in the summer at home," Simon said. "We had a pontoon boat — nothing like this — and kept it on one of the lakes. On weekends

I'd play tennis in the mornings and then we'd go out." He shook his head. "My mother loved to ride on the boat."

Billy smiled at that memory. "Mine always did, too."

Anna Beckett had been gone for almost twenty years, but she was never far from Billy's thoughts. She died tragically, on a Georgia interstate with her two sons in the car. They were headed to a baseball tournament, a routine trip on a summer weekend. Billy was driving and lost control, and Anna was thrown from the vehicle. It was the worst day of his life.

If he and Simon were looking for common bonds, perhaps that was the strongest one. They had each been shaken to the core by tragedy when they were only boys.

"I'm sorry I never got to meet your mother," Billy said. "I know she would be proud of what you're doing now. You're a man."

Simon kept his focus on the water ahead. A large cruiser was approaching, and he feathered back the throttle and prepared to cross its wake.

"Yeah, she liked tennis. But not as much as Dad."

"Wasn't he a really good player when he was young?"

"He's still a good player. He knows everything about the game. I hate to say it, but I think sometimes that he's more into this than me."

"That bothers you?"

"Not really, because I think I'll grow into it. He's giving me the best chance he knows how. He went to Zander and got him on board, and Zander got you involved. That raised everything up a level. It's up to me now. I understand that, even if it doesn't always seem like it."

"I'll be honest with you, Simon. I do wonder where your head is sometimes. Part of that is being nineteen, but in professional tennis, you have to grow up in a hurry. I've been telling you that all along. Even though the players at the very top have been around for a while, it's a young man's game, and there are a lot of hungry young men out there ready to move up. If you're going to be a world-class player — and you already are — you have to take advantage of your opportunities or you get lost in the shuffle."

"I'm sorry if I don't always seem grateful. Some days I love what I'm doing more than others."

"No need to apologize, that's normal. I do believe you've got something inside that sets you apart. I could tell the first day we met. I mean, it's not often I get to sit and watch an avalanche rescue play out."

"Yeah, but it was my fault we were there to begin with," Simon said. "I had to get my friend out of there."

"Someone with less heart might not have gotten the job done. You did what you had to then, and you'll do it now. I say that as your agent, and as your friend. I know Zander feels the same way."

Billy took a quick glance at his watch. "Let's circle back," he said. "I don't want Darren to be sitting there waiting on us. He scares me sometimes."

Simon laughed and stood up to relinquish the captain's chair. "You should be on the court with him."

Billy made the turn back into the sun and opened the throttle. "It's gonna be a good day," he said above the growing roar. "Can you feel it?"

Simon smiled broadly. "I'm starting to. Thanks for bringing me out and letting me drive. I'm still waiting on the Corvette."

CHAPTER 23

The houseboat gently nudged the dock, and Billy killed the engine. Simon tossed the bumpers over the side and jumped out to tie off. There was no sign yet of Darren Carter.

The text pinged on Billy's phone. *How are things?* It came from Zander, who was in Colorado. He was up early.

Billy smiled and tapped out a quick response. *He's learning to drive the boat. Vette next, then jet.*

The smiling clown face appeared on Billy's screen. It was Zander's favorite emoji. *What about tennis?*

Working on that. I'll call later.

"Is that Zander?" Simon asked.

"Yeah, he's just checking up on you. He's in Denver."

"I guess he's going to see my father."

"I'd say so." Billy locked the cabin door and stretched across onto the dock. "How often do you talk to your dad?"

"Maybe once a week. It used to be every day, but that got to be too intense for both of us. Now I think Dad talks more to Zander about what's going on. He's still very interested."

"They get along pretty well, don't they?"

Simon nodded. "They've been tight since my mom got sick. I really appreciate everything he's done. Dad was lost for a while, and Zander was there for him — more than a boss. He was there for both of us. He spent a lot more time in Colorado than he probably needed to."

"That's one thing about Zander — he gets involved. If he likes you, he gets really involved." Billy motioned for Simon to head up the pathway to the house. "In your case, he's *super* involved. You're lucky."

"I know I told you, but I feel the pressure to win, for him and Dad. And you."

"You don't need to put any more pressure on yourself than is already there. This business has plenty. The key is being able to manage it, turn pressure into a positive. Expectations will crush you if you let them. Or they can fuel you – help you reach your potential. You could be the best player in the world one day."

The men walked into the house. Simon had stacked his racquets and tennis bag by the door and stopped to take inventory. He grabbed a couple of water bottles to fill.

"Sometimes I wonder how I got here," he said. "My dad gets most of the credit, I guess. He made big sacrifices. We really didn't have much money when the tennis got serious, but he kept trying to figure out a way to get me to Florida. That was his dream, and he somehow came up with the funds to make it happen."

"I guess that's where Zander came in. He appreciates dreamers."

"He's been pretty funny really. We had to teach him a lot about tennis."

"Yeah, but he's a quick study. If he's passionate about something, even tennis, he gets up to speed in a hurry. Then you have to get out of his way."

"I've noticed that."

"Well, it has all worked out pretty well to this point. As you said, it's up to you now. The sky's the limit, so get out there and fly."

There was a knock at the door, and Darren Carter peeked through the glass. Billy waved him in.

The coach seemed to be in a peppy mood. "You ready to hit some balls? I'm anxious to see what you've got this morning."

"I'm ready," Simon said. "Gonna wear your ass out."

"That's what I want to hear. Billy, nice place you've got here. The change of scenery was a good idea. I think the young master is raising his game in Tennessee. He's no bludger."

"Bludger?"

"Lazy man. He's working hard."

"Too bad you missed the boat ride," Simon said. "I got in some driving time. Getting some practice for Zander's yacht."

"That's a little different deal," Billy said. "Big boat on big water."

"Simon, do you know what time it is in Melbourne right now?" Carter asked.

"Sometime tomorrow."

"Fourteen hours ahead."

"Why do you ask?"

"I just want you to start getting in that mindset. We're building toward your first Grand Slam. Put yourself in the moment. We'll be Down Under before you know it. You'll be standing there across the net from your first opponent. You'll always remember it."

"Are you excited, coach?" Billy asked.

The stony exterior didn't betray any emotions. "Can barely contain myself, mate. Haven't been home in a couple of years."

"To Melbourne?"

Carter nodded. "I miss it. The city is a mecca for sports, entertainment, the arts. And the food is unbelievable. You say you've never been there, Billy?"

"Never had a chance. I'd love to see the Open, but it's so damn far and January is always a crazy month for me. Lots of football meetings with players making final decisions on agents. And I always have a coach or two going through job interviews. I'll get there someday, maybe to watch this guy do his thing."

"I wish you and Dad were coming along this year," Simon said.

"I think we're leaving that to Zander and your coach here. The fewer distractions your first time, the better. We'll be watching, though. Seems like every year at that tournament there's a young, unseeded player that goes deep into the draw. Maybe that's you this year."

"Well, enough standing around here dreaming," Carter said. "You said you're gonna do something with my arse. Let's get on with it."

PART II

CHAPTER 24

Special Agent in Charge Sean McGuire was growing impatient as he sat across from his informant. Glen Chapman was dead to rights, yet he was still trying to spin his way out of this mess. He was negotiating for more time.

Chapman considered himself a worthy adversary when it came to tactics. He'd learned in the military that no matter how sound the strategy, no matter how honorable the intentions, the situation on the ground dictated the course of events. And the ground shifted often.

You had to be nimble in the pursuit of your interests — something the Army surely was not. Chapman would have to see about the DEA and its operatives.

"You need me to crack this case," he said. "Hell, you weren't even aware of what was going on. I know the ins and outs of the operation, how it works and who's involved. Everything."

McGuire clenched his teeth. With his ice-blue eyes, square jaw, and broad shoulders, he looked more like a film star than the head of a DEA task force. But he was a cop through and through, and he was used to playing these games with con men.

"You think you can get caught with a van full of illegal cash and weed and somehow walk away? That's not going to happen."

"I'm opening other doors for you."

"No, you're not. We're still waiting to see if what you're saying leads anywhere. I'm not sure that it will. So far, all you've accomplished is stringing this out."

"It takes some time to line everything up. No one else can give you this information. No one else has it."

"Glen, you're playing both sides of this," McGuire said, "and it has to stop. You know you're on a tight rein here. If you don't come clean and help us, and soon, you're going to prison for several years. Simple as that. The only reason you're sitting here right now is that we believe there's more than meets the eye."

"I don't know what you mean."

"Let's just throw it out there. You never give us much about who's running the organization, how it fits together. It's just empty promises. We need more, and we need it now."

"I told you that it's a group of guys. Old friends. The whole thing started as a lark."

"It clearly ceased being a lark a long time ago. Millions of dollars are floating around in this cesspool that you've all created. You're up to your neck in trouble, and there's only one way out. Give us what we want."

Chapman's eyes darted about the room. He knew he might be playing a losing hand, but he couldn't fold now.

"You know all that cash I had? There's a lot more where that came from. I know about duffle bags, stuffed full, just sitting there in the mountains, waiting on somebody to come along and pick them up. I'm not lying."

"Then let's bring this to a close. We've got plenty of manpower and more than enough evidence to make a case. We've got weed running out our ears in this state."

"I'm not talking about weed."

McGuire perked up. *Was this another ploy?* "Go ahead," he said.

"I'm just saying that cannabis is the backbone of the business. But it's not the only revenue stream. The business has grown."

"So ... *what?* Cocaine? Heroin? Meth?"

"Blow."

McGuire leaned back in his chair and rubbed his chin. "That's a new twist. I'm not sure I believe you, Glen. You're playing more games."

"It's the truth, but you can believe whatever you want. I'm just telling you there's more to this operation."

"And what's your role in it? Cocaine doesn't come from a growhouse in Colorado."

"I still move the product and collect the cash. For me it's the same. Just smaller packages."

McGuire stared at his informant with a wry smile. "Wait," he said, and he got up and walked out of the room. When he returned five minutes later, McGuire was accompanied by another man. They stood and looked down at Chapman.

"This is our friend, Glen," McGuire said. "He's going to fill you in on what's happening at Good Budz. And then he's going to find you a job there. We need an extra set of eyes and ears."

Chapman frowned and shook his head. "I don't do the hiring. And I damn sure don't bring undercover agents onto the property. I don't bring *anybody* onto the property. That's one of the rules."

"I got the impression that you're a rule breaker. Or do you just make your own?"

Chapman smiled but said nothing.

"You've raised this to another level, if what you're saying is true," McGuire said. "You've bought yourself time. But the clock is ticking on that deal you accepted. Just remember, there's a prison cell waiting for you. We can throw you in there anytime."

McGuire waved the other agent out of the room, pulled out his chair, and sat back down directly in front of Chapman. "I want to hear more," he said. "Right now."

CHAPTER 25

Michael Shay was waiting when the boss touched down. This was one meeting he wasn't looking forward to.

Authorities in Missouri had completed their initial investigation of the murdered trucker. Only one promising lead had materialized: A security camera at the travel center had captured a fleeting glimpse of someone near the Freightliner cab just moments after Mack Luttrell had walked away. The partially obscured view didn't show if that person climbed aboard, but the truck pulled away seconds later.

Authorities had gone through the stolen rig, checked the contents in the trailer against the manifest, talked to Luttrell, the primary driver. And nothing was coming up to explain why J.T. McClanahan would have been targeted. It seemed like a random act of violence.

The cops did know that McClanahan had lied about being assigned to make the trip to Detroit. He had once been a struggling independent driver, as he claimed, but he hadn't officially been behind the wheel in years. And he wasn't from Nebraska. Nor was there any evidence that he ever made frequent runs up and down the East Coast.

"What the hell is going on here, Michael?"

The pointed question was the first thing out of Zander's mouth. Michael had picked him up at Centennial Airport, and they made the short drive over to the AAF facility in Aurora.

The usual niceties between the men were absent this morning. Zander was all business. He didn't like the negative publicity the murder had created for his company, and he didn't like the lack of answers he had been getting. The whole affair couldn't be over soon enough.

"Why was this man on one of our trucks?" he said. "I want to know that before I leave here."

"We've all been asking that same question. I've talked to everyone at the warehouse who had anything to do with this shipment. So far, nothing."

"And nothing was missing from the trailer?"

"Doesn't look like it. We sent everything on its way."

"What about Mack?" Zander asked. "Our HR people tell me he's a veteran driver with a spotless record, a respectable guy. What does he say about this?"

"It seemed like any other long haul to him, until this J.T. character showed up. He said the guy was different. Mack blames himself for not looking closer at the situation. One thing he did say was that Mr. McClanahan talked a lot about Miami. Seemed to know what was going on in the city. Even went on and on about some unsolved murder that had made the news."

"What kind of murder?"

"It involved three local truckers there outside Miami. They were tied up in the trailer of their rig and shot in the head. One survived. They're still looking for the killers."

"Ironic, maybe, but *Miami?* What does that have to do with anything?"

"No idea. Seems like a long shot, but the cops are looking into it."

The men walked through the warehouse to the loading bay where the AAF truck had departed. Number twelve. Zander just wanted to see it.

He went outside onto the dock and scanned the area like he was trying to envision the scene that night. The wheels inside his head were always turning.

"Mr. McClanahan walked up in the darkness from that area over there?" he said, pointing to the left. "Did he leave a car in the lot?"

"We never found one. It's like he just showed up on the property. Security didn't notice him, unfortunately."

"That's a hole that needs to be closed." Zander shook his head. "This company has never experienced an incident like this. So why now? It's a one-off, a freak occurrence, or something else?"

"We're adjusting some procedures with the drivers and with the security people. But at the moment, with nothing else to go on, yes, it looks like a one-off. We're simply at a loss to explain how a strange guy gets in a cab with one of our experienced drivers, takes off with the truck when the driver stops for breakfast, and then gets killed behind the wheel a few miles down the road. About the only thing we know for sure is that he didn't kill himself."

"I guess it's possible that J.T. didn't take the truck on his own volition. Maybe somebody got in at the travel center and forced him to drive away."

"Their security footage was unclear about that. We'll just have to see the final report."

Zander took a deep breath and walked back inside. "I guess Simon told you that I stopped in Bradenton a few days back."

"He did say you and Billy were there. I believe he was destroying racquets and acting like a brat at the time. Sorry about that."

Zander chuckled, and his dark mood broke for a minute. He had a soft spot for Simon.

"That boy has spirit," he said. "Too much at times, but better too much than not enough. He gets that from *you*, right?"

"Maybe. His mother had some fire, too. She rode him hard and kept him in line. Her being gone is part of the problem."

"I don't doubt it."

"I know that Simon is spending the holidays at Billy's. I'll miss him, but it's probably for the best. I really appreciate all that you gentlemen are doing for him."

"You can thank Billy for that decision. You know how he is. If he thinks he can help the cause, he'll do about anything."

"Having Simon around isn't always easy," Michael said. "He tends to drift off course."

"I texted Billy this morning. He said Simon was driving his boat, so they're apparently getting along fine. Billy knows how to handle the young bucks."

"That's what you always said. By the way, I arranged to have a car sitting out front for you when you're ready to leave her. I think you'll like it."

"Don't tell me it's a big truck."

"Not this time. It's a little smaller and sportier."

"You're just trying to make me feel better?"

"I hope so," Michael said. "I believe Tom Skiles, our security director, is waiting in your office now, as you requested. Anything more I can do for you before our meeting?"

"No, I've seen enough for the moment. I'll stay the night downtown in Denver and drive back out here tomorrow, and we'll talk again. I'm pissed off about this whole thing. I said I want to know why J.T. McClanahan was on our truck before I leave Colorado, and I mean it. I hope you know more in the morning."

"Like I said — "

Zander held up his hand, and his expression hardened again. "Find out. I'll see you at the meeting."

CHAPTER 26

Michael had pulled out of the Grand Hyatt parking garage and was about to turn onto Welton Street when his cell phone rang. Glen Chapman.

"I need to see you," Chapman said.

"This isn't a good time. The boss is in town, and he still has a lot of questions. So do I."

"The cops haven't figured out who killed your driver?"

"No, and we don't need anything complicating the situation," Michael said. "I just want to lay low. This may take some time to work through."

"It's already complicated on this end. That's why I'm calling. There was a problem with our last shipment."

"What kind of problem?"

"The customer says the order was incomplete."

"What do you mean? It was loaded just the way your people prepared it. It took longer to get there, obviously, but nothing was different about anything on that trailer. I'm sure of that."

"Something was missing, and it's a huge problem."

"You're going to have to tell me more than that," Michael said. "Are we talking about the usual? It's been routine. Nothing could be missing."

Chapman hesitated. "There was something else, and it was in there when the wing was sealed. I know exactly how it was situated. How could it have just disappeared?"

"What are we talking about?"

"Cocaine. Five kilos. Bricks wrapped in brown paper."

"Are you serious? You put cocaine on my truck without telling me? That's an absolute game changer. I've told you that, Glen."

"I need to know what happened to it. That's all that's important right now. I'm suddenly in a very difficult position."

"I have no idea what happened to your cocaine. Who knew it was there to begin with, and who would have been able to break down that assembly on the fly and just take it? It defies logic. Maybe your customer is lying."

"He's not. I'm sure."

"What am I supposed to do about it?" Michael asked. "We had an agreement, and now you're telling me you're not playing by our rules. You're bringing Schedule II drugs into this. We get busted with that, and we're going to prison for a while."

"You get busted smuggling several hundred pounds of marijuana across state lines, and you're going to prison, too."

"How long has this been going on without my knowledge?"

"This was the first time."

"Why didn't you say something?"

Chapman hesitated again. "I wanted to make sure we could set things up and connect with these people without any problems. And now we have a huge problem."

"They received the other just fine?"

"They said it was perfect, and that's the only saving grace. But I have to make them whole, and I have to do it in a hurry."

"I don't want to be part of that," Michael said. "You owe me my cut. You figure out how to make things right on your own."

"We're in this together, and I need your help."

"Are you crazy, Glen? I just told you that my boss — the guy that owns the whole damn shipping line — is in town. And he ain't happy. A man was killed on one of our trucks, and we don't know why. And now you're telling me *this*. We'd be fools to just carry on like nothing happened. It's a major concern now."

"You'll have more concerns if I can't work this out."

"You don't need a truck for this. You've got a plane. It wasn't a huge amount, so take your profits and work another deal. Take care of it."

"I still need answers."

"While you're answering questions, tell me why this driver was killed. Better yet, who killed him?"

"I've got two more," Chapman said. "Who the hell *was* this guy? And why was he on this particular truck?"

"I can tell you that no one at AAF had any knowledge of him before he climbed aboard. Our regular driver had never seen him before. It's like the guy just showed up out of thin air."

"But *why*? Makes me think he might figure into my missing package."

"Tell me how. This is all too strange."

"Meanwhile, we still have business that needs to get done."

"I'll decide when," Michael said.

"That's not the way this works. I decide, and you make it happen. That's why you've been getting those stacks of cash. Once you join the fray, you have to see it through to the end. Those are the rules of engagement."

"Glen, we're not talking about war here."

"Like hell we aren't."

The sound of desperation in Chapman's voice was growing. The man had nerves of steel, but now he seemed unhinged. *Reckless.*

For the first time, Michael began to feel the pressure building. The drug money had been a life-changing bonus. *But was it still worth the risk?* He worried that he could be dragged under, and there would be collateral damage, perhaps even to his son and his tennis career. Nothing could jeopardize that.

"I have people breathing down my neck," Chapman said. "They're getting impatient."

"I thought this was *your* operation."

"I'm not going to get into it with you. It's my job to put the shipment together, and your job is to make sure it arrives just like it left. That's the arrangement, and you should never discuss it with anyone else. You'll get us both killed."

"I don't like the way this conversation is going," Michael said. There was a long pause. "I'll tell you what, I'll meet you at the airstrip on Friday, and we can discuss this face to face. My boss should be out of here by then."

Chapman thought about it for a few seconds. "I have a small group scheduled to jump that afternoon. It's about time; we're struggling to fill the slots."

"Business isn't good?"

"Not the skydiving business. Takes a lot to operate, and that's why I need all the outside revenue I can generate. You come at two and you can join us. We'll talk afterward."

Michael took a deep breath and exhaled with a clear sign of exasperation. "Okay." He ended the call and sped back to his office.

CHAPTER 27

Khai Le was weighing his options. He had let his friend walk away after a huge loss for the operation, but how to best recoup? There was still time to make things right. And that included making Chapman pay if necessary.

The questions wouldn't go away. *Had Chapman been telling the truth? If not, had he covered all his bases in spinning a very elaborate lie?*

Khai was sitting in the waiting area next to the receptionist's desk when the shipping manager walked briskly past. "Mr. Shay, there's a gentleman here to see you," the woman said.

Michael stopped in his tracks with a look of mild annoyance. Khai stood to introduce himself. "I'm sorry to bother you, Mr. Shay," he said. "I just hoped we could talk for a few minutes."

Michael glanced at his watch. "Can you tell me what it's about? I'm in the middle of something, and I'm pressed for time."

"It's about Glen Chapman."

Michael's eyes grew larger. "Come in," he said, motioning the visitor into his office. "No calls, Karen." The door closed behind them.

"Please, have a seat," Michael said. "Forgive me for being short, but let's get right to it. Who are you?"

"I'm a business partner of Mr. Chapman's. You do know him, right?"

Michael sat down behind his desk and leaned forward. "I wasn't aware that Mr. Chapman — Glen — had a business partner. Are you into skydiving?"

"No. Actually, we're in another line of work. We have several business partners."

"Okay. Is there a problem?"

"I understand he's been doing some deals with your shipping company here," Khai said. "You do *ship* things, right? All over the country? Or maybe Glen has just been doing business with *you*. Maybe no one else is aware."

"I'm not sure I follow, Mr. Le."

"You can call me Khai." His manner was pleasant yet direct. "Just between us, I know you've been moving some of our freight on your trucks. Glen has told me that. In fact, he convinced me that it was a good idea to partner with AAF, to the extent possible. Has it been good for you?"

Michael wasn't sure how to answer. "What do you want?"

"All I want for the moment is some honesty on your part, Michael. I have a suspicion that things aren't quite right in our business dealings. And that makes me wonder about all sorts of other things."

"I don't want any trouble."

"You most certainly do not. That's why we need to reach an understanding here."

"Go on."

"Tell me about your relationship with Glen."

Michael proceeded cautiously. "I got to know him a while back through his skydiving company," he said. "I was kind of looking for something new to get into at the time, and he showed me how."

"Are we talking skydiving, or something else?"

"No, just that. We've done a lot of jumps together."

"Then you understand that Glen has a fearless streak that can drift into foolishness at times. That can get him in trouble."

"I haven't seen that side of him. We're usually just trying to have some fun jumping out of airplanes. I'm an adventurous guy myself."

"Would *smuggling* be adventurous?"

Michael didn't answer.

"Smuggling large quantities of marijuana on your trucks? Of course, it would. It would also be a major source of new income for a man who's already doing reasonably well for himself but could use some extra funds. Am I right?"

Michael shook his head. "Again, what do you want?"

"The two of you went from skydiving together to smuggling my product all over the place. Your trucks expand our reach with bigger shipments. A great idea, until something goes wrong. Until someone gets greedy. Or until someone gets killed. Do you understand where I'm going with this conversation?"

"Not really."

"What I'm saying is that something has gone wrong. Someone has gotten greedy. And we don't want anyone else getting killed. The rest of us have to be aware."

"What's your point?" Michael asked.

"What I want to know right now is how the shipments line up. How many times have you put my product on your trucks? How many times have you and Glen worked together?"

"I don't know off the top of my head. Several, I'd say. It started small and has steadily grown. When we came up with using the wing, it opened up more possibilities."

"That's very clever, and I heard it was your idea. What would your boss think of that? Would he think that's clever?"

"I don't think there's any reason to go there," Michael said. "Zander Fleming would blow up your whole operation. In a heartbeat."

Khai nodded and smiled. "I'm not concerned about that. Tell me, sir, are you aware of anything else mixed in with our product?"

"Such as?"

"Smaller packages. Cocaine, perhaps? I keep hearing that Glen has gotten more involved with a source I know."

"No, definitely not. That would cross a red line for me. Moving weed across state lines is one thing; moving coke is another."

"I agree completely. It's a different can of worms, so to speak. That's why I'm concerned when these rumors keep coming up."

Khai stood and gazed out at the parking lot. "When was the last time you heard from Glen?"

"Recently."

"And what did he want?"

"He was ready to prepare another shipment. I told him now isn't a good time, but he didn't want to take no for an answer."

"Where did you leave the conversation?" Khai asked.

Michael took a deep swallow and pursed his lips. "I'm supposed to see him on Friday. We're doing a jump together. Then we're going to talk."

"You'll see Glen at the airstrip? You'll get on his airplane together?"

"Yes."

"One other thing," Khai said. "Do you know Glen's girlfriend?"

"Gina? She was around most of the times I've been with him at the airfield. Drives a Suburban with the Blue Yonder trailer."

"Is that the skydiving equipment?"

"Yes. She looks after all that and likes to talk a lot. Other than that, I don't really know much about her. I don't even know her last name."

Khai nodded and turned to leave. "It's Simpson." He stopped at the door and extended his hand with a wry smile.

"Thank you for your time, Mr. Shay. I'm hoping we can find a way to keep working together, but you never know. Let's stay in touch."

CHAPTER 28

The door to the apartment opened slowly, and Gina Simpson stood before them with a dazed expression. Her dirty-blond hair was disheveled, and the tight Broncos t-shirt and jeans looked like she had slept in them. She could have just awakened from a deep sleep, or an all-night bender.

"Can I help you?" Gina said, apparently unfazed by the odd couple on her doorstep.

"My name is James," the smaller man said, and motioned to his oversized friend, "and this is Phillip. Sorry to bother you, but we've driven past a few times and noticed the cargo trailer beside the building. Is that yours?"

"No, but it stays here. It belongs to a friend. Why?"

"Blue Yonder. Isn't that a skydiving company?"

"It is."

"Are you a skydiver?"

Gina had a unique laugh; it was more of a cackle. She seemed to be coming back to life. "Do I look like a skydiver? Come to think of it, what *does* a skydiver look like? Your friend here damn sure don't look like one. Don't know if a parachute could hold Phillip."

Khai and Big Butch looked at each other with bemusement.

"We'd be interested in knowing more," Khai said. "How much does it cost to jump out of an airplane these days?"

"Well, I've got some brochures inside. You know you don't just strap on a chute and go skydiving. Right?"

"I have my D license, so I know the drill. I'm new in Denver and just looking around to see what's out there. Phillip is helping me."

"Well, my name is Gina. Why don't you gentlemen come in and have some coffee, and we'll talk about it."

"We don't want to bother you, Gina."

"Too late for that. Since we're all standing here on my porch, and I'm still a little hazy, might as well drink coffee. I could use some after last night."

The men walked into the small living room and took a seat on the couch while Gina went to the kitchen. She returned a few minutes later and filled three Styrofoam cups from a pot of steaming brew.

"Sorry, but my coffee mugs are dirty. I only have two anyway. Here are those brochures. Prices are on the back."

Khai glanced quickly at the information, while Big Butch just sipped from his cup with a detached stare.

"You said your friend owns Blue Yonder?" Khai asked.

"Yeah, Glen is crazy into skydiving. I just kind of help him with the business, take care of the chutes and keep the reservations straight. This Southern girl ain't jumping out of no airplane with him, though."

"How long has Glen been doing this?"

"I don't know exactly. His ex-wife got him into it and then bailed. He's got a plane and a pilot who flies when Glen does the jumps. He'd rather be jumping than flying. He's still in the marijuana business, too. Isn't that the perfect combo — getting high and jumping out of planes?"

"Marijuana, huh?"

"I don't guess I should talk about that, but it's all over the state now. *Recreational?* I never knew smoking weed was recreation. Colorado is where all that began."

"There's obviously a lot of money involved."

"Honey, more than you can imagine. It's the wild, wild West out there. There's edibles and hash and hash oil and whatever else gets you stoned. We've even decriminalized those trippy little mushrooms. Got more people driving around in an absolute stupor in this state … I'm surprised there aren't wrecks on every corner. The banks won't work with the growers, so cash is everywhere. Glen is always trying to figure out what to do with it." Gina giggled. "Don't guess I should talk about that either."

"Don't worry, we're not from the government, or criminals." Khai smiled and took another drink of his coffee. "We just saw your trailer and were curious. You were saying you bring all the equipment to the plane?"

"Yeah, whenever they need it. There's an airfield and a drop zone outside town. We're still trying to build the business, get more people to take the plunge, so to speak. Sometimes it's people like you and sometimes it's beginners, just people looking for a one-time adventure. They do tandem jumps with Glen or whatever. I pack the chutes and off everybody goes."

"*You* pack them?"

"Yeah, I'm the official parachute rigger — Federal Aviation Agency senior parachute rigger, to be exact. Took the course and passed the tests. Been doing it for years. That's how I first got to know Glen."

Khai chuckled and looked over at Big Butch. "Seems odd to pack chutes for other people when you don't sky-dive yourself. You do the rigging and then deliver them to the airfield?"

"That's right," she said. "They're all sorted out and in their place in the trailer. When I show up at the plane, everything is ready to go. It makes things easy for Glen. He trusts me, and he should. I'm good."

"I'm sure he does, Gina." Khai leaned in close. "Let me ask you something else. Did Glen happen to mention anything about losing some money lately? A big chunk of money?"

Gina set her cup on the table and frowned. "What kind of question is that?" she said. "You're not being straight with me, mister. Who are you?"

"To be honest, I'm a business acquaintance of Glen's and am concerned about his welfare. I'm afraid he's gotten himself into some trouble. He's in way over his head, it appears, and needs help."

"I don't know what you're talking about."

"For some reason, Gina, I believe you do." Khai nodded to Big Butch, who suddenly seemed interested in the conversation. He pulled a long knife from a shoulder holster under his jacket. "And if you don't talk to me, I'm going to have my friend Phillip here cut you into pieces. It'll ruin a perfectly good day."

Gina took a deep breath and exhaled slowly. "What do you want to know?"

"That's more like it," Khai said. He stood up and closed the front door. "I want to know what happened to three hundred grand of my money."

"*Your* money? You run the operation Glen works for?"

"Answer the question."

"I just know what Glen tells me. Are you talking about Texas?"

"Yes."

"He said he ran into a problem coming back."

"What kind of problem?"

"He said he got pulled over, and it took him a while to work things out. He was torn up about it. I've never seen him like that."

"Pulled over? By the cops? Or someone else?"

"Cops. Somewhere in New Mexico, not far from the Colorado line. That's all he'd tell me."

"They just let him drive away? With duffels of money and weed in the back?"

"If you say so. I don't know anything more about it; I really don't. He's been a mess since he got back."

"Have you noticed Glen getting more actively involved with the marijuana?" Khai asked. "I mean, transporting it from place to place?"

"He's come by for the trailer more than he used to if that means anything. I don't know what he's using it for."

"You do know that he's using his plane for deliveries sometimes?"

Gina looked away. "Sometimes. He doesn't fly as much anymore. I don't think he enjoys it like he used to. He's never been a very good pilot, to be honest."

"Do you know whether he's had skydiving customers booked on the days he got the trailer?"

"I can't say how that lines up exactly. Glen usually calls me to meet him at the airstrip with the chutes when he needs them."

Khai rubbed his chin and smiled. The light had come on in his head. "Sounds like what you're telling me is Glen isn't a thief," he said. "He's a snitch."

Gina was quiet now. She watched Khai carefully as he walked to the windows and closed all the blinds.

"You've been a delight," he said, putting a hand on her shoulder. "Where's the key to the trailer?"

CHAPTER 29

"**M**ind if I drop by for a minute?"

The request seemed innocent enough, but Billy was quick to notice when Claire sounded stressed. Her voice rose an octave.

"Sure," he said. "I have a Zoom meeting coming up later, but I've got time. Cassie never takes long."

"Cassie Haynes? I haven't heard that name lately. What's the latest from Las Vegas?"

"Her next fight is a few weeks away, and she and her brother are just going about their business to get ready. She's one of the odd clients who doesn't need a consultation every couple of days. In fact, she rarely has much at all to say. I have to prod her."

"Quiet fighters — we need more clients like that. Kidding, of course. Cassie is one of a kind."

"What's up?"

"I just got back from Texas and wanted to talk about it."

"About Ty?" Billy asked.

"Yes, mostly."

"Would you rather that I meet you at the office later?"

"I'm already headed your way from the airport. I brought you a gift. If you've got time now …"

"C'mon. I'll see you when you get here."

Billy was standing outside on the veranda when Claire pulled into the driveway. They often hashed out problems at his house, or on his boat. She loved the river and thought the atmosphere was conducive for clear, collaborative thinking.

Billy could see that Claire had something in her hand as she approached. "I brought you some barbeque sauce," she said, handing over the jar with the distinctive red crown above a white J on the label.

"The Jank," he said with a laugh. "*Too awesome to describe* — isn't that what Texans say? Thank you. I'll smoke some brisket and share it with you soon." Billy motioned for her to sit. "Tell me about the Austin City Limits show. Was it everything you expected?"

"I loved the city and the theater, loved the performance. First-class all the way. It'll definitely be a popular episode when it airs."

"Ty and the band were hot?"

"They just have a great energy right now. They're even better than I thought when we started putting the tour together, and I expected a lot."

Billy could tell Claire's facial expressions didn't quite match her words. "What's the problem?"

"Frankly, I don't know how happy Ty was with me when I left. And it makes me wonder how happy he's going to be with Premier moving forward."

"I don't get it."

"I think you do. We've talked about the perils of getting intimately involved with clients. This falls into that category. I made a mistake, and those tend to spill over into business pretty quick."

Billy knew another heart-to-heart conversation was coming on. He and Claire had helped each other through all sorts of crises, personal and professional, through the years. There was no one easier to discuss matters of the heart with than his business partner.

"Mistake?" he said.

"Not really that. We just didn't leave on the best of terms."

"Isn't he happy with the job you're doing?"

"He's happy with everything about the band and his career. But he wants more."

"You obviously have concerns about that."

"I don't know, and that's the real problem. He's younger and the timing just doesn't seem right." She turned and looked off in the distance. "But I like him a lot. You know what I mean?"

Billy smiled and rubbed his chin. He knew.

"Funny we're on this topic," he said. "I just spoke with Holly Grace earlier. She's coming through Knoxville on her way back to Florida. I think we may get together this evening."

"Getting together, huh?"

"I told her we'd do dinner somewhere, maybe Stock & Barrel. She's been on the road for about a month. We just need to catch up and talk a little strategy. Business with a personal touch, remember?"

"I remember. Does it feel like a mistake?"

"Not yet."

Billy heard a car door slam and looked around the corner. Simon was coming in after his afternoon workout. Carter had dropped him off.

"You don't have to keep bumming rides," Billy said. "Tennis pros shouldn't have to do that. I told you we'd get you a car if you like. No problem at all."

"No, I'm good so far. Unless you want to give me the blue one in the garage."

Billy didn't respond.

"Hi, Claire," Simon said, breaking out that high-wattage smile. "Good to see you. You look great today."

"Such a charmer," she said. "You look like a champ yourself, young man."

"Working on it."

Simon picked up his tennis bag and went inside. He had the downstairs to himself. Carter would bring some takeout food for dinner later, talk tennis and maybe watch a movie. That was the new routine, and they all hoped it would pay off before long.

"Claire, I'd like to give you some smart advice," Billy said, "but I don't have any. You're good at what you do, and it's easy for people to take a real liking to you. Especially men. Happens a lot."

"I didn't figure you'd pull out the agent handbook for answers. I just wanted you to know, in case I have a rough patch with Ty. I'm not sure exactly what he expected to start with, but I'd hate to lose the account."

"And the relationship?"

"Yes. But it's important for Premier to keep the momentum going on the entertainment side. Ty is our bell cow right now. His success opens other doors for us. It's the same as the sports side was with Jarvis Thompson. We need him to hang with us."

"He's just on the road a lot right now," Billy said. "It's the first big tour and he's lonely, hard as it is to believe about a man that looks and sings like that."

"He doesn't have to be. I'm certainly not standing in the way of his, uh, romantic interests."

"Apparently you are. He wants to be with *you*."

Claire's flashed a radiant smile, lightening the mood. "These young and foolish stars. What are we going to do with them?"

"They're everywhere," Billy said. "Got one of those staying here, too."

He stood up and checked the time. The virtual meeting with Cassie Hayes needed to happen soon.

"I'm sure this will all work out fine, Claire," he said. *Famous last words*, she thought. But she always was glad to hear Billy's take on things. He understood her better than anyone.

"I'll let you know when the Austin City Limits show is scheduled to air here," she said. "May be a little while. Hopefully the tour will keep building momentum in the meantime."

Claire started toward her car and then turned back to Billy. "Good luck with Holly."

CHAPTER 30

The white Audi made its way down the driveway, and Holly Grace pulled in beside Claire's red BMW. She quickly stepped out of the car with a broad smile.

Holly was a professional golfer who lived in Fort Lauderdale. Tall and blond, she had become a poster girl for the LPGA Tour after breaking through with her first tournament victory. That elevated her in the eyes of serious golf fans, and it made her more than just another pretty face on a tour with a rapidly growing number of those.

Holly was already more than just another client to Billy. They had been getting closer for a while, although usually from a distance. They spent much of their time on the road, going in different directions, but Billy's guidance and reassurance was always just a call away.

Claire was a little uneasy about the connection, for reasons that weren't always clear in her mind. Her experience with Ty Nelson had made the feeling worse for the moment.

"Billy and I were just talking about you," she said. "And here you are."

"Yeah, I'm working my way home after a hectic couple of weeks. I'm glad to stop and have dinner with the world's greatest agent — with all due respect. How's he doing?"

"He just went upstairs to start a Zoom call, but I don't think he'll be long. He's expecting you."

"I'm a little earlier than I thought. Traffic wasn't as bad coming into town, and I was driving pretty fast."

"Couldn't wait to get here?" Claire asked with a smirk. "I understand. We're all in a hurry to see the world's greatest agent. I just got back in town myself. Spent a couple of days in Texas."

"Texas? You guys are always going somewhere."

"You know what they say about agents — if you're not going somewhere, you're going nowhere."

"I hadn't heard that, but I guess it's true. I'll just go inside and wait. Good to see you again."

Claire offered a wave and headed out as Holly went in and began to size up the place. She hadn't had an opportunity to spend much time in the house and was intrigued. She stopped first in the great room to look around.

There was a wall of framed photos of Billy and his clients. They all looked so happy. Holly was prominently in the mix, holding her championship trophy with her arm around her agent. That was a memorable day.

Just got here, she texted.

Within a few seconds, Billy walked into the hallway at the top of the stairs and looked down at her. "Still waiting," he said with a big smile. "Be there soon. Have something to drink."

Holly went behind the bar and opened the refrigerator. She grabbed a bottle of Perrier and gazed out at the river as she poured herself a glass. Billy had turned her on to the sparkling water, and now she was hooked.

She could see Billy's packed travel bag and laptop in a chair, right where he had tossed them after walking in from his Florida trip. There was a folded *Miami Herald* on top; he still enjoyed buying newspapers whenever he was on the road.

The door to the downstairs opened, and Simon appeared to be in a hurry. He was clearly surprised to see the dazzling stranger in front of him.

"I'm sorry, I didn't know anyone else was here," he said, stopping abruptly. "I'm Simon."

"Hi, I'm Holly. Are you looking for Billy?"

"Umm, not really." He collected himself and tried again. "Actually, I do need to talk to him."

"He's upstairs on a call. Are you a client of his? You look like an athlete."

"Tennis player. And you? You look familiar."

"Golfer."

Simon nodded with a smile, and the two stood there awkwardly before Billy bounced down the steps. He gave Holly a quick hug. "Still waiting to get started," he said. "I see you've met Simon." They all smiled together.

"Sorry to bother you," Simon said, "but I left my phone at the club. I think I know where it is, but … not sure what to do. Darren was going to go a couple of places before coming back out. Maybe he could swing by there? Could you call him?"

"Tell you what," Billy said. He quickly walked into the kitchen and pulled a key out of a drawer. "Take the car to get your phone."

"The *blue* car?"

Billy smiled. "And why don't you take Holly here with you if she's up for it. You guys can get to know each other a little better while I deal with this. I always like for the Premier team to work together. I should be free by the time you get back."

"Are you sure?" Simon asked.

"Hell, you've been talking about it since you got here. You do have a driver's license, right?"

"Sure do." He looked over at Holly. "I'm game if you are. Do you trust me?"

"I think so."

"You sure?" Billy asked. She nodded again.

"All right then," the agent said, before turning to walk upstairs. "I'll see you back here soon. Be careful."

CHAPTER 31

Simon turned the key on the marina blue Sting Ray, and a deep growl belched from the side pipes. He looked over at Holly with eyebrows raised.

"Are we safe?" she said with a nervous laugh.

"Of course. I've driven about everything you can think of back home — snowmobiles to big trucks. Had some friends who were into old muscle cars, but not like this one. This is a real beauty. *Classic*, Billy says."

"Can't say I've ever ridden in a car like this."

"Yeah, I looked it up online. Nineteen sixty-three, with the split rear window and side pipes ... it's rare. With the low mileage, this one would probably bring six figures. A friend of ours wants to buy it, but Billy won't sell."

Simon depressed the clutch and grabbed the shifter handle to get a feel for the action. "Wow, Hurst four-speed."

"Is that good?" Holly asked.

"That's good, the whole package. It's old-school Chevy power and performance. My father would love it."

Simon eased the car out of the garage and slowly made his way up the driveway. The trip to the racquet club and back would usually take a half-hour or so if traffic weren't bad.

"Where do you live?" he asked.

"Fort Lauderdale now, originally from Atlanta. I've been out doing some endorsement work while the LPGA Tour takes a little break. Billy is sharp about lining up that stuff. The reception has been great everywhere I've been."

"I bet. How long have you worked with him?"

"A few years now. He's really helped me in a lot of ways. What about you?"

"We first met about a year ago. Kind of getting to know him better here lately. I like him a lot. He's a cool guy."

"Yes, he is," Holly said. "And you're … how old?"

"Nineteen. Young and innocent. Can't even have a drink, legally."

He blushed when she said Simon reminded her of her little brother. That wasn't what he wanted to hear.

Simon turned onto the winding road through the neighborhood and punched the gas. The tires barked briefly, and the acceleration pressed their heads back against the seats.

"Amazing how a sixty-year-old car can get up and go," he said, shifting through the gears. "This car is more than three times as old as me."

Holly smiled and seemed more interested. "Where are you from?"

"Eagle, Colorado. It's near Vail."

"I have a good friend on tour from that area. Beautiful country."

"It's ski country."

"I'll bet you're a good skier."

"I grew up skiing," Simon said, "but I crossed over to snowboarding a few years ago. Probably could be doing that now instead of playing tennis."

"Really? Sounds like fun, but I'm guessing tennis is a little more lucrative."

"It can be. My dad is really into tennis; he wanted me to attend an academy and work my way up. So that's what I did. I live in Florida, too, on the Gulf. Bradenton."

"You're staying at Billy's place for the holidays, right?" Holly asked. "How's that going?"

"Better. I'm getting ready to go to Australia, just trying to get my game razor sharp, and Billy invited me to stay for a few weeks. He thought it would help me. He's really into the mental stuff — focus and all that — and I think he's right. Being here has helped. Hopefully it's going to be a good year for me." His smile was captivating. "And for you."

"I hope so."

They turned onto the main road. Traffic was light, and the racquet club soon came into view. Simon pulled into the parking lot and jumped out of the car. He had a young man's energy, always ready to spring into action.

The man at the front desk nodded when he saw the player approaching. "Bet you're looking for this," he said, holding up Simon's phone. "It was in your locker, with the door open. Billy had called about it."

"Must have had my mind on something else. Thank you. See you tomorrow."

Simon was still tapping the screen when he got to the car, trying to see what he might have missed in the last hour or so. With the phone back in his possession, there was one less thing to worry about.

He folded himself back into the driver's seat; he felt like a pilot in the cockpit of a vintage plane.

"Back in touch with the world?" Holly asked. The gaze of her cool blue eyes almost took his breath. *Big sister?* The thought never entered his mind.

"Yeah," he said. "I've already got a bunch of messages. I start getting nervous without my phone. Teenagers, right?" He started the car. "Need anything while we're out?"

"Don't think so."

"You sure? I don't mind driving around and showing off Billy's car." He flashed a mischievous grin. "And you, of course."

"Did you say you're just nineteen?" she said with a giggle. "It's been nice to talk, but Billy's probably finished and waiting on us by now. We're supposed to be going out for dinner."

"Let's get on back to the river then."

Feeling a sudden adrenaline rush, Simon mashed the gas and the Sting Ray fishtailed out of the parking lot. Too much gas. The rear end broke loose in some gravel that had accumulated in the intersection, turning the car sideways in the face of oncoming traffic. Simon tried to straighten it but overcorrected, and the situation only got worse.

He would remember the terrible sounds of that sequence — squealing rubber, Holly gasping as she tried to brace herself, the crush of fiberglass and metal. The rest was a blur. The car had pitched hard to the left and shot across the centerline before contacting a power pole at the passenger door — Holly's door.

They were both in a state of shock as they sat there, then a painful cry. Holly slumped over holding her right arm, unable to move. Other motorists were already stopping to see if they could help.

"Are you okay?" Simon shouted, desperately reaching out to her.

"My arm ... it feels broken," Holly moaned. "I think my leg is hurt, too." She bowed her head and immediately began to sob.

Simon jumped out in a panic to assess what he had done. The classic Corvette was still resting against the pole, with heavy damage all along the right side. Jagged pieces of debris were scattered about. It was a sickening sight, likely a total loss, but Simon was uninjured.

How much damage had been done to his passenger remained to be seen.

CHAPTER 32

Simon was pacing back and forth in the waiting area of the University of Tennessee Medical Center. He'd made a lot of dumb mistakes in his young life, but this one turned his stomach.

He could barely make eye contact with his agent when Billy rushed through the sliding doors and confronted him.

"What happened, Simon?"

"I can't believe it. I'm so sorry. Holly is hurt."

"How bad?"

Simon was close to tears as he rubbed his face. He tried to keep from melting down. "It's her arm. She thought it was broken, and her leg was hurting, too. It's all my fault. So stupid."

Billy's face turned ashen. He was used to dealing with all manner of problems with athletes, from the criminal to the merely ridiculous, but this was unique. Two clients who just met involved in a traffic accident together. His treasured Corvette totaled. It was beyond his imagination.

Simon had called him on the way to the hospital but hadn't been coherent. All Billy knew when he raced out of the house was there was a crash, and an ambulance was coming.

"Where did this happen?" Billy asked.

"Right near the club. Everything just happened so fast."

"Are *you* all right?"

Simon closed his eyes and pressed against his skull with both hands. "I think so."

The ER doctor came around the corner and stopped when he saw the men. He was Dr. Patel, according to the badge on his lab coat.

"How is she, doctor?" Simon asked.

"She's resting, and we'll be releasing her before too long."

Billy stepped forward. "How bad is she hurt?"

"I can't really get into the details with you," the doctor said. "I just wanted you to know that she's going to be okay, and we'll have her out of here as soon as possible. We appreciate your patience."

"My name is Billy Beckett, and I'm Holly's agent. I'm sure she told you she's a professional golfer."

The doctor managed a slight smile. "Oh, she mentioned her career a few times. She's not a very happy golfer right now."

"She was just at my house before this happened. Surely you can tell me something generally about her condition. She doesn't have any family in the area. We're really worried about her."

"I'll just tell you the break is near her right elbow. There's also a contusion on her right leg. It's painful but should heal on its own in good time."

"Break?"

"Afraid so."

"Will she be able to play again?" Simon asked.

"Not for a while; she'll have some rehab ahead of her. It'll take some getting used to, but I'm not an orthopedic surgeon, or a golfer, so I can't give you specifics. I'm sure she'll be working with some specialists down in South Florida. That's where she's from, right?"

"Yes," Billy said as he watched Simon go to a corner of the waiting area and collapse into a chair. "Thank you for taking good care of her. Just have the nurse call me when Holly's ready. I'll make sure she gets taken care of."

"Well, good luck. I'm sorry, but it could have been worse. Hope that's a little consolation."

Billy took a deep breath and sat down beside Simon. He was mad at the kid, and increasingly mad at himself. It was a struggle to control his emotions.

"I've ruined Holly's career and your car all at once," Simon said. "Your car. Your beautiful car." He shook his head. "I've ruined everything."

"What happened to cause the accident?"

"It was stupid. I gave it too much gas and lost control — that simple."

"Do you know where the hauler took it?"

Simon handed him a business card that had been given to him. "I can't stay here, Billy. I need to get my stuff together and leave."

"And go where?"

"Back to Florida. Colorado. Doesn't matter. I just can't stay here any longer, not after *this*. I don't even care about tennis right now."

The silence lingered for several seconds. Billy wasn't sure what to say, but he was trying to be measured. It was times like this when his life experiences — all the heartache and setbacks — made a real difference.

"You're not going to run away from this, Simon," he said. "I think we can all agree what you did was foolish. *Stupid*, as you say. But I want you to stay."

Simon was taken aback. "Why?"

"Because I believe in you and what we're trying to accomplish. That road was always going to be rough, and you've certainly made it rougher. But this is my fault, too. I'm the one that suggested you drive a car that you weren't familiar with — and that you take Holly with you. I'm really more to blame than you."

"You were just doing me a favor. This is totally on *me*."

"Either way, we'll get past it. Try to calm down."

Billy couldn't believe what he was hearing from himself. Two promising careers, not just one, were affected here. He could easily have gone ballistic, and he was amazed that he wasn't doing just that.

"I'll be there for Holly, as long as it takes," he said. "She'll be fine. I'll worry about my car later. I have very good insurance."

"I can never face her again."

"Well, I can't promise that she'll ever want to ride with you again. But Holly's a forgiving person. She just needs time to get well and back on the golf course. We'll take it one step at a time."

CHAPTER 33

The repeated knocks on the door went unanswered. Glen Chapman tapped his foot impatiently on the porch as he called her cell phone. Voicemail, again.

He stepped back to look around the corner. The trailer was there, but Gina's Suburban was gone.

Chapman returned to his truck and backed up to the trailer. He had tried all morning to touch base with her about delivering the equipment, to no avail. It wasn't like his girlfriend to miss his calls, especially when she knew customers would be waiting at the airfield. She had taken the reservations herself. That was worrisome.

Chapman went ahead and hitched up the trailer. He leaned in the passenger door to get his keychain from the console and walked back to the front. The apartment was dark and quiet as he stepped inside. A quick look around revealed nothing.

He'd have to take care of this adventure himself, and he was pressed for time.

***

The airfield was out in Clear Creek County, about a half-hour west of Denver. A couple that appeared to be in their mid-thirties was already waiting near the plane, talking to the jump pilot, when Chapman arrived. The woman was there to take video of her husband.

Another Blue Yonder newcomer was scheduled to jump with the group. Michael Shay, if he showed, would round out the foursome.

"Beautiful day," Chapman said as he walked to the back of the trailer and unlocked it. He always had a look of excitement on his face when he was about to take to the skies. "You ready?"

"I am," the man said, "but she's worried about me." He smiled. "Mostly because of the plane."

The Cessna looked old and tired from a distance, and it grew less attractive upon closer inspection. The original color scheme — white with accents of orange and brown — had begun to fade long ago. The interior was simply an open space with a pilot's seat and controls in the left front corner.

Looks could be deceiving. The Cessna 182 was a workhorse that had been in production for more than sixty years. Chapman's was a 1980 Skylane model modified to accommodate up to four skydivers and the pilot — all crammed onto what was essentially a steady platform in the sky. With help from his ex-wife's parents, Chapman had bought it from a friend for one hundred fifty thousand dollars, and it had more than paid for itself.

"You don't like my plane?" Chapman asked.

"You're sure it'll fly?" the nervous woman responded.

"All day long. What's your name?"

"Beverly. Beverly and Sam."

"Beverly, you don't need to worry. You're safe here on the ground, and Sam has a great life insurance policy, right?" They all laughed.

Michael Shay was pulling into the grass parking area. The last jumper pulled in right behind him. Marcus, the pilot, had taken his seat on the plane and was going through his pre-flight routine. They would soon be ready to fly.

Chapman stepped out of the cargo trailer with parachute packs in hand. He checked the IDs and licenses of the jumpers he hadn't met and handed them each a twenty-pound pack. He was glad it was an experienced group. That always made the process smoother.

"Who packed these?" Madison, the last man to arrive, asked. "I always have to ask."

"We've got one of the best parachute riggers around. Her name is Gina. She's usually here to see us off but not today."

Chapman turned to Michael. "You've got your own gear, right?"

Michael gave the thumbs-up sign and began to fasten a GoPro camera to his helmet. "I'd like to get some shots of that Flying Star again, if we could," he said.

"We'll have Marcus drop us at about twelve. I've got my camera, too," Chapman said.

Michael sidled up to Chapman. "Looks like you're in a little better frame of mind today. Did your missing package show up?"

"No, it hasn't. We'll talk about it here shortly. I've got another thing or two I want to run by you. But first, let's enjoy a little rush."

Chapman was the last to strap on his gear, and the group moved toward the plane. "Which one will *you* be coming down?" Beverly said to her husband before parting.

"He's the black and white chute," Chapman said. "He'll be looking good."

The skydivers climbed aboard and began to prepare for the moment they would step out the door. The group was suddenly quiet and focused as the plane began its slow ascent into a crystal-clear Colorado sky.

Chapman tapped them all on the helmet when the pilot reached twelve thousand feet. Michael smiled and was out the door. Sam and Madison quickly followed. Chapman jumped last.

They quickly came together to join hands for the star formation during the minute-long freefall. And then they let go.

It was always breathtaking to see the chutes open from ground level, and Beverly leaned back to get her husband floating down on video. One … two … three …

I think something's wrong, she thought to herself. *Where's the other one?*

Chapman's primary chute was flapping in the breeze; it hadn't opened properly. The lines connecting the harness and canopy were tangled. He began to spin as he plunged toward earth at one hundred fifty miles per hour.

The others could see he was in trouble, but Chapman didn't panic. In thousands of jumps, only once had he needed to employ the emergency chute. It had been a memorable rush, but no had been done harm done.

He was able to put that aside and keep jumping, always mindful of the odds: fifteen fatal skydiving accidents in over three million jumps in the U.S. the previous year. Many of those were operator error on the landings.

What had gone wrong here? Were the odds still in his favor?

Chapman pulled the emergency cord. The freefall continued, and his eyes connected with his friend's, one last time. Michael yelled out helplessly. *Glen!*

The other skydivers craned their necks to see, until it was too late. He had disappeared below them.

CHAPTER 34

hai Le watched intently from a service road near the drop zone. If he harbored any remorse, it didn't show. As far as he was concerned, his old friend had brought disaster on himself.

The inevitable crash.

"You really do know how to rig a parachute," Khai said, sounding envious. "Don't feel guilty. It was him or you. You did what you had to, and you did it well."

Gina slumped in the passenger seat of the SUV. The shock was only beginning to set in; she wasn't yet able to cry. She had been convinced until those final moments that the second chute would open and save her boy-friend's life. He had always been a survivor. He would walk away from yet another death-defying ordeal.

When it failed, she bowed her head. "Forgive me, Lord," she said, and leered at the man beside her. "You're a son of a bitch!"

Khai Le was not the same man he used to be — the calm and calculating player simply intent on carving out a space in the growing cannabis market. The game had changed dramatically in recent months, and so had he. There was a vile air that enveloped him now. He more closely resembled a vindictive mafia boss, willing to do anything to protect his turf and livelihood.

Khai started the car and glanced behind him. Big Butch was stretched out in the back seat, quiet and emotionless. It was hard to tell what impact Chapman's death had on him. Butch had also been swept up in the fatalistic mindset that was running rampant through the organization.

"It's going to be a circus over there in a few minutes," Khai said. "The question now is what to do with Miss Gina here. The authorities are going to be looking for her. She's responsible for a murder."

Gina glared at Khai with a look of disbelief. "I've never seen such evil." She tried to catch her breath. "I did what you asked."

"This isn't over. Now that Glen is gone, I want to know everything. Who was he working with? How much was he stealing from me?"

"Stealing?"

"Product, cash, information. Anything. I want to know."

Gina covered her face with her hands. She couldn't surrender without a fight. "What's to keep you from killing me after I tell you?" she said, as Khai pulled back onto the road.

"I'm not a killer, but I'm not really sure about Butch here. He handles security threats in ways he sees fit. You really don't have much leverage in this situation."

"Are you sure?"

"What do you mean?"

"If I said that Glen was working with the DEA, would you believe me?"

"DEA, as in Drug Enforcement Administration. The big boys? You know something about that?"

She took a deep breath and nodded.

"Why would Glen share that information with you?"

"He was looser than you imagined, especially during certain times, when he was higher than a kite. And he had to have an explanation for some of the things that were going on."

"Like what?"

"Stuffing money into the walls at my place. Bringing in duffel bags of weed to hide. He was planning for a future without you and your business."

"If he was an informant, why hasn't the DEA brought down our organization? Glen knew everything about it. Why haven't the authorities just stormed in and arrested everybody? Why would they wait?"

"I'll tell you this much: When Glen was pulled over and that cop saw what he had, that was the first thing out of his mouth. He wanted to talk to someone from the DEA."

"And he told you this?"

"He told me everything." She looked Khai in the eye. "I'll talk if I have some kind of security. Job security."

Khai laughed. "You want a *job*?"

"Without Glen or his business interests, I have nothing now. What I know might keep your ship from sinking. I need to be on a lifeboat."

"This was a different world when I brought Glen in. I don't trust you."

"Then you'll just have to wonder," Gina said.

"Okay, make me a believer. Tell me about the plot against me."

"Glen was stringing the authorities along for as long as he could. He hadn't given everyone up yet. He hadn't given *you* up. But it was coming."

"You're saying they don't know."

"They probably know, but they're waiting. Have you been approached by strangers asking questions? Of course not. You wouldn't be here now if you had."

"Why should I believe you?"

"It just makes sense. But everything may have changed with what you did today."

"You mean what *you* did."

Khai clenched his jaw as he thought things over. "I'm going to take you back to your car now," he said. "Don't make me regret this decision."

***

Khai pulled to a stop beside the Suburban and made eye contact with Butch in the rear-view mirror. A sinister smile broke out on both men's faces.

Before Gina could take her next breath, Butch pulled a plastic bag down over her head. She flailed wildly as he leaned over the seat and held her in a chokehold with one of his massive arms while pulling the drawstring tight. Her muffled screams and the flailing lasted only a few seconds.

"Let's move," Khai said.

Butch opened the car door and picked up Gina's lifeless body. He carried it across to the big SUV and placed it behind the steering wheel. Khai removed the bag from her head, dropped her key fob in the console, and started the engine. The hose that ran from the exhaust was wedged into place by the passenger window.

Khai admired the scene for a moment before closing the driver's door. There was still a chance to salvage the operation and keep the machine running. It was his legacy. That was all that mattered.

CHAPTER 35

When it came to women, Billy had often been his own worst enemy. His lack of trust had grown out of failed relationships and utter deceit, but it was up to him to make things right. He just never seemed capable of loving completely.

With Holly, he had the perfect companion. She was beautiful and talented, and he knew she loved him. And still, he couldn't fully commit. That was on *him*.

Billy stood inside the main terminal and tried to be upbeat as she moved toward the security line.

There wasn't much to be upbeat about. Holly was flying home to Fort Lauderdale with her arm in a temporary cast. She already had an appointment with an orthopedic surgeon who advised golfers and other professional athletes. She dreaded the rehab that would follow and feared for her professional future.

It was hard to know when Holly would be fit to play again, much less rejoin the tour and compete against the best players in the world.

"Keep an eye on my car," she said. There was a detached quality in her words, but at least she was talking. After the last few days, Billy counted that as progress.

"It's already in the garage and will be right there when you come back," he said. "You'll be back soon."

Holly shook her head. "I don't know. I may have it shipped to me." The days since the accident hadn't eased the disappointment. In fact, it had only grown as she came to realize the challenges in getting her career back on track.

"I still can't believe I'm standing here with a damn cast on my arm," she said. "Everything was so good ... I should have kept right on driving, all the way to Florida." It sounded like she was going to choke up again. "I just wanted to see you."

Guilt continued to gnaw at Billy's conscience — as a lover and as her agent. Holly's decision to sequester herself at a downtown hotel after the accident left him even more remorseful. He was walking that line again. And now here they were in another airport, unsure of where things stood as they were about to part company.

"The orthopedic people I've been talking to are encouraged," Billy said. "They think you'll be firing at the flags again before you know it. I'd like to connect you with one of the doctors in Miami. He sees all kinds of professional athletes and — "

"Please, Billy. I know you're trying to help, but just give me some space. Let me work through this."

"Okay."

"Really, I just need to step back and not think about you and me for a while. Or Simon."

"For what it's worth, he couldn't feel any worse. He's devastated."

Holly swallowed hard and didn't make eye contact. He could tell she was still fuming inside.

"Good," she said. "As for you, I don't have much use for an agent right now. And you're not much of a companion either when we're over eight hundred miles apart. I really don't know where to go with this."

"You know I'm always there for you. Anything you want or need; all you do is call. It's times like these when an agent is most valuable. I promise that you'll come out of this better than ever. Your star will continue to rise."

"You can't promise that. You can't promise anything. Even if this sets me back just a few months, who knows what kind of player I'll be then? It's a mental thing as much as physical. You know what you always say about golfers: we think too much."

There was a trace of a smile on Holly's lips, but it quickly disappeared. "I've got plenty to think about now."

"Believe me, you're going to be a top priority," Billy said.

"You're saying that I wasn't one already?" She turned and headed toward the security line.

"Wait, wait. You know better." He pulled her close and gave her a long hug that brought tears to her eyes. "I'm going to come down to see you, maybe next week. And we're going to get through this and be stronger. I promise."

"There you go again making promises you can't keep."

"Do you remember when I first told you that you'd be a star on the LPGA Tour? You didn't believe me because you didn't believe in yourself. I saw something in you."

"You say that to all your clients."

"I tell them that they have to believe in themselves to be successful, which is true, but you're different, even among professionals. You're a champion. You're smart. You're charming and funny. And you're gorgeous. You're one of the most marketable women in golf. None of that has changed."

Holly wiped her eyes and took a deep breath. "I have to go."

Billy squeezed her left hand until she finally pulled away. "You know you're really sexy with that cast," he said, and gave her one of those looks to remember him by.

Holly couldn't help but smile.

CHAPTER 36

"**I** just got a text from Simon. He's in Colorado."

Darren Carter stood in Billy's doorway and shook his head in dismay. He had driven out to the river with the bad news — Simon had gone home and probably wasn't coming back. It wasn't totally unexpected, at least by Carter.

The coach had been distressed by their workouts since the accident. Simon's heart wasn't into tennis, and no amount of cajoling was going to change that. The whole plan — and Simon's career — was in danger of blowing up.

"If I had to guess, I'd say he won't be going to Australia either," Carter said. "I don't know what you can do about any of this, but you're his agent and I just wanted to let you know before I leave. I'm planning to fly back to Florida this afternoon. I believe I've done all I can here."

Billy was thinking the same thing, at least for the moment. "Come in," he said. "Let me call Zander."

They sat down at the kitchen table, and Billy put the call on speaker as it rang. As far as he knew, Zander was working in Florida and probably busy. But this couldn't wait.

"I'm guessing you've already heard that Simon left Knoxville," Billy said.

"I just talked to Michael. He's not happy. He blames you."

"Blames me for what?"

"For letting Simon take your car out and wreck it, I guess. He thinks you should have known better."

"Well, he's not wrong about that. But we can't undo the damage now. The question is whether Simon is just going to cut and run; looks like he already has. I have to admit, I'm thinking the same thing at this point."

"That you're out as his agent?"

There was a long silence. "Darren is sitting here with me," Billy said. "Simon texted him this morning."

"Did Darren talk to him?"

"No, but he got the idea that Simon isn't coming back. Darren is planning to go back to Florida today. He's on speaker with you now."

"Darren, will you wait until you hear from me before you do anything?" Zander asked. "If we all bail at once, this thing is over. And I'm afraid we'll all regret it. Let me talk to Simon, for his sake, before you leave there. You're still on retainer."

"Zander, this isn't about money," Carter said. "You know my thoughts on Simon. I like coaching him — he's a spectacular talent, and I like his spirit. You go along for weeks, and everything is great. You think you're getting through. You can see his potential — it's unlimited. And then ... balls up."

"With all due respect to Holly and her pain, a car accident where nobody is seriously injured shouldn't derail the kid's playing career. I mean, he's climbed into the top hundred in the world rankings. *And he's just nineteen.* A few years down the road, this will all be a distant memory. At least, it should be."

"I agree with that, but I've seen a lot of promising careers go in the dunny for no good reason," Carter said. "As far as Simon, you never know what teenagers will do."

There was another long silence. All three of the men were weighing their options.

"Zander, let me call Michael," Billy said. "We've never really had a clear understanding, the two of us. I know this is Simon's career we're talking about, but his father is central to the discussion. After I talk to him, I'll call you back and let you know where I stand. I've got a lot of other things going on right now, and I can't afford to waste time."

"Fair enough."

"I hate to say it, but maybe it's time for me to let go of this."

"I'll tell you what, Billy. If we can work this out, I'll come to Tennessee again and pick you up, and we'll go to Denver together. Call it a last-ditch effort. Maybe we can just clear the air on everything."

"Maybe," Billy said. "The more I think about it, there's really no reason for Darren to stay in Knoxville while this goes on. It's the holidays, and he has family in Florida. He can just head home, and we'll see what plays out. Simon probably won't come back here anyway, regardless."

***

Michael Shay answered quickly at his home in Aurora. "What is it, Billy?" He sounded angry.

"I hear that Simon's there," Billy said. "He didn't bother to tell me his plans before he left."

"*Plans?* Hell, he apparently doesn't have any plans, at least as far as tennis is concerned. I'm really disappointed about all of it."

"Is he there now?"

"No, he got his snowboard and headed off to Vail. That's how Simon handles stress; he goes to the mountains."

"Hopefully he'll clear his head and figure out he has a bright future ahead of him. I just wish he'd told me he was leaving. We had a few things lined up here, just to keep his name fresh in people's minds. That's important when you're building your reputation."

"He's building quite a reputation, all right. I'm sorry to say it, Billy, but a lot of this is on you. You shouldn't have given him the keys to your car."

"I take responsibility for that."

"I don't mean to be a prick. I hope Holly Grace is doing okay, and I'm sorry as hell that Simon has put her through this. I'm sorry about your car. But there's a lot of stress on this end, too. It takes a toll."

"Stress on *you?*"

Michael took a deep breath. "I know you brought Simon up to your place to help get him ready for Australia. And I know he really respects you. That's why he left; he knows he disappointed you."

"I thought we had talked that out," Billy said. "I told him I didn't blame him. Holly's situation is weighing on him, big time, but she'll work through it. She's tough, and she's going to be okay; I'll make sure of it. It'll just take a little while."

"Simon just doesn't let go of things easily. He's still a kid in a lot of ways and has that frustration pent-up inside. I wish he channeled it better."

"I know you've talked to Zander. What if he and I come out to Denver and try to get things back on track? I've got a small window in my schedule, and I'd be happy to try. I want to help. Maybe I can't with Simon – he wouldn't be the first – but I'd at least like to try."

Michael's sigh was audible on the other end. "I'm sorry for the trouble, Billy. There doesn't seem to be any shortage of that right now."

"Again, are we talking about you or your son?"

"Both, I guess. If you and Zander are committed to getting things back on track, I'm willing to listen and do what I can. I'll make sure Simon is, too."

CHAPTER 37

The AAF jet landed at McGhee Tyson Airport and taxied toward the executive hangar. Billy waited inside with his father for the engines to shut down and the stairs to drop.

After a few minutes, Zander emerged. He was wearing a dark business suit instead of his usual casual attire. Billy couldn't remember the last time he saw him that way.

"I appreciate you gentlemen joining me," Zander said, greeting them with a handshake and a rueful smile. "It's really good to see you again, Franklin. Been a while, but Billy has kept me up to speed on how things are going. You look great."

"Thank you, Zander. I'm excited to go along — beautiful plane, by the way. Hopefully, I might bring something to the process."

"Just bring your bags for now, and we'll throw them on and get out of here. Maybe we can kill two birds with one stone on this trip."

The Gulfstream was soon back in the air and bound for Denver. It was less than a three-hour flight from

Knoxville. There was much to consider, and the mood in the cabin was subdued.

Franklin was already thinking about the circumstances surrounding J.T. McClanahan's death. He had been looking into the details for the last few days. As a former detective and police chief, perhaps he could shed a new light on the investigation. Zander figured it couldn't hurt to take a second look from an internal point of view, separate from what his security people had already done.

"Let me ask you something, Zander," Franklin said. "Has there been any more mention by the authorities of the double murder in Florida that this gentleman was talking about?"

"No, that was just an aside from our other driver. He thought it was a strange topic of conversation, but a lot was strange about Mr. McClanahan. There's been nothing more to connect the two. It was a real event — I actually read about it — and was obviously top of mind for this guy at that moment in time. Just sounded to me like another double homicide in Miami. The state police in Missouri didn't find any connection."

"But they never made an arrest down there?"

"No."

"I'm sure the authorities went through the trailer to see if anything stood out. Was it locked when the driver was found?"

"I believe it was unlocked. I understand nothing was taken, and we went ahead and delivered the cargo."

"Would Mr. McClanahan have had a key?"

"I'm not sure. Mack said he locked the trailer before they left Aurora."

"So J.T. was found slumped over the wheel in the cab, like he'd been surprised by someone."

"Or was just made to sit there. And then shot."

"But someone was able to open the trailer without using force. And that person may not have been the driver."

"What are you thinking, Franklin?"

"Just trying to understand the lay of the land, so to speak. The obvious question is whether something in the trailer could have been valuable to J.T. and no one was aware of it."

"Or valuable to someone else," Billy said. "And they had maybe an hour to get to it."

"The cops combed through the manifest and didn't come up with anything unusual. Pretty mundane stuff, and nothing was missing. We move freight for a lot of the same companies over and over. Michael Shay cleared the list and then sent everything on its way."

"Could I see a copy of the manifest?" Franklin asked.

"Of course, as soon as we get to Aurora."

"What if J.T. was a middleman in some kind of scheme?" Billy asked. "Is it possible that he was just supposed to divert the shipment and things went terribly wrong?"

"Divert it for someone else?"

"Maybe, but he didn't know where Mack was going to stop that morning. Whatever was supposed to happen, it looks like J.T. was going to handle it himself."

"He didn't get very far."

"Maybe someone just saw a chance to rob him there at the truck stop and made him drive away."

"Rob him of *what*? Mack said he didn't have anything with him but a backpack. And the security footage wasn't clear, even though it looked like someone could have gotten on board."

"It had to be about the cargo. Something in the trailer was valuable."

"Valuable enough to kill a man in cold blood?"

Everyone sat in silence for a minute. Zander then turned to his friend, whose primary concern on the trip was getting a certain tennis pro back on the court.

"Billy, I've been thinking about Simon," he said, "and I'm almost inclined to close the book on this. If it weren't for his dad, and for you, I probably would. It's been interesting, but I don't need the extra drama or the aggravation. I'm especially not in the mood for it now."

"You don't need to do anything on my account," Billy said. "I can represent Simon, with or without you. Or we can all just go about our business without him. I don't think it'll take me long to make a call on that."

Franklin couldn't help but smile. "What is it about the troublemakers, son, that seems to draw you in?"

"To be clear, I like clients who stick to the plan, go home, and then get up the next day and do it all over again. Professionals. No drama. I'll admit that some of my clients tend to be more, uh, adventurous than others."

"I wouldn't call Simon a troublemaker," Zander said. "He's had some bad luck. And, of course, he's created some bad luck for himself, too. I hate to have to keep defending him, but he's a kid. Kids drift a little more easily."

"Well, hopefully he's not involved in anything worse than a little snowboard therapy right now. There was an avalanche the last time I came out here to see him. And if I recall correctly, he brought that on himself, too."

"I'd forgotten that."

"In the grand scheme of things, Simon hasn't really lost anything more than some preparation time as far as getting ready for the new season."

"He's lost his coach for the moment."

"Yeah, but Darren will be ready and waiting in Florida. He's still more than willing to go to Australia and see what happens; that's the last thing he told me."

Zander folded his arms across his chest and looked out at the thickening clouds before turning back to Billy. "I think you should go, too," he said.

The agent didn't respond, which was a positive sign. Zander could tell he was thinking about it.

CHAPTER 38

Simon backed up the GoPro footage and watched it again. He'd heard and read about the accident, and now the principal characters were here, right in front of him.

Glen Chapman had been a good friend to his father, helped pick up Michael's spirits when they were low. But the relationship had become a bit strained in recent months based on Michael's own off-handed comments. There was tension.

And now, this chilling video.

Simon watched the sequence again. His father beside Chapman, holding hands in formation on the freefall with the two other men. The joy on all their faces. The release to employ the parachutes. And within seconds, the horror of Chapman plummeting to earth.

Simon backed it up again. He was trying to understand.

Michael Shay had tucked away the small camera in a desk drawer at his condo. It was the same camera that Simon had worn the day of the avalanche, and he was beginning to think it was just bad luck.

He tapped the screen to access the media box. The footage with Jenny Riddick was there, along with several other action clips that Simon remembered well.

But it was a face frozen in the display grid that caught his attention. He tapped the screen again and watched as his father escorted Glen Chapman into this very room. The conversation started.

By the time Chapman walked out again, Simon was stunned.

He let out a deep sigh and slipped the camera back into the drawer. He knew Billy and Zander were on their way. Before he had time to digest what he'd just heard, the doorbell rang.

Simon answered with a somber greeting. "Happy holidays. Come in."

"Happy holidays to you," Zander said. "I didn't realize you were planning to do Christmas in Colorado this year."

"I just thought my dad needed some company. So here I am."

"Why didn't you tell me you were leaving?" Billy asked. "You haven't answered my calls, or my texts."

Simon turned and walked away. "I'm sorry."

"Another apology? You need to get past that. And here's a thought: Stop doing things you need to apologize for."

"Did you come all the way out here just to beat up on me? I don't need it."

"That's not it," Zander said. "We think you need to get back to work. Keep moving forward."

"So, go back to Florida and … what? Just pick up again like nothing happened?"

"To be honest, I just wanted to see if we could salvage our business relationship," Billy said. "I've said about all I can say about the accident. Life goes on. Maybe you need another agent, someone who can get through to you. Or if you're quitting tennis, maybe you don't need an agent at all."

"And you may not need me either," Zander said.

The men looked at each other and back at Simon. He motioned them into the den.

"Where's your father?" Zander asked.

"He's supposed to be on his way. I know he invited you here."

"Actually, we invited ourselves and he was kind enough to agree," Billy said. "This may be the last time we get together like this, and I just wanted to be sure."

"Sure of what?"

"Sure I've done all I can and am ready to move on. I don't like to leave clients hanging, but if you're not committed to your career, trying to become the best tennis player on the planet, you don't need somebody like me. And I, in turn, don't need you."

Simon seemed surprised. "I thought you were a good guy."

"I am a good guy, but that doesn't seem to mean much to you. So, again, I'm here on business. This is a fork in the road for us, Simon. Let's make a decision, get it settled, and move on."

The door opened and Michael walked in. He seemed out of breath and his face was pale. "Sorry I'm late," he said.

Simon frowned as he studied his father. "You look … strange. Did you have to talk to the police again?" Michael nodded.

"I'm sorry about your friend," Zander said. "What a horrible accident. Do they know what happened yet?"

"They're still piecing it together. Today I heard that maybe it wasn't an accident, and I'm trying to understand. It's a shock, to say the least."

They all sat in stunned silence. Michael took a deep breath and shook his head. "Son, how about getting everybody something to drink. Bring that pitcher of water in the refrigerator and some glasses."

"In a minute," Simon said. "Let me hear the rest. They think Glen was *murdered*? By who?"

"There's a story out there that investigators have evidence the chutes were tampered with. And the person who packed them is dead, too. She apparently committed suicide after Glen Chapman died."

"*She?*"

"Glen's girlfriend. She was found unconscious in her SUV. Looks like carbon monoxide poisoning."

"What reason would she have had?"

"That's a question for the cops right now … I don't know. Her name was Gina, and she used to come out to the airfield when we'd go up. Seemed like she and Glen got along well."

"I don't know what to say," Zander said. "That's crazy."

Michael ran his fingers through his thick brown hair and watched his son go into the kitchen. "I know you're here to talk about Simon, so let's put that to the side for now. I don't want to think about it."

"I'm sorry," Billy said. "What's your take on Simon? Am I missing something? Is there anything more I can do?"

"I don't know. I'm afraid this may have to run its course. That's the way things tend to go with my son."

"It may have to run without me then. I have a lot of other things going on, clients who are counting on me."

"I understand, and I apologize for what I said to you earlier. The accident wasn't your fault; it was Simon's."

"We're trying to get past that," Zander said.

"One thing I can tell you – he isn't the same without you guys behind him. He needs that kind of emotional support. Billy, I could tell the difference in just the short time he was at your place. He was on top of his game and really happy until the accident."

Simon walked back into the room with the pitcher and a stack of cups.

"Simon let's get real here," Michael said. "A lot of people are invested in you. I think your mother would be disappointed if you don't show more toughness. You can't let a little adversity ruin your career. Or even *detour* it."

"You're just thinking about yourself. This whole thing has been more about you than me. Don't bring Mother into it."

"You've worked so hard. Most kids would do anything to be in your position. I know I would have."

"Again, it's all about *you*."

Michael turned to his guests. "You see what I'm up against here. Simon doesn't understand yet that you have to toughen up and do whatever it takes to get ahead.

That's the way life is; that's the way *tennis* is. If he doesn't have it in him, we'll let you gentlemen get on with your business."

"We're going out to AAF," Zander said. "Billy's father is there now. I'd like for you to join us if we're all finished here."

Billy sat up and leaned in close to his client. "Simple question, Simon: *Do you want it?* If you do, you'll be on the plane with us tomorrow. You'll go back to Florida and put everything else aside to get ready for the next tournament, the next challenge. That's the sacrifice champions make, day after day. They keep working to get better."

"And if I don't?"

"Then we'll say goodbye right now."

CHAPTER 39

Franklin was studying papers on a desk in the AAF offices when the men returned. His reading glasses were perched at the end of his nose, almost touching his mustache, and there was a bemused expression on his face.

The look reminded Billy of bygone days when his father was bursting with energy and enthusiasm. Franklin always enjoyed the challenge of solving a case, large or small. It was the essence of police work.

"Find anything interesting, Franklin?" Zander asked as they walked through the office door. He leaned over the big man's shoulder while Billy took a seat.

"I'm not sure yet. I've been looking at the shipping manifest from that day. I also thought it might be a good idea to compare it to the previous one to Detroit, and the next one back to Denver. Your people have been very helpful in getting together information."

"Let me get Michael in here. I want him to be part of the discussion. Just a minute."

Zander stepped out and went down the hall.

Franklin turned to Billy. "Did you get anywhere with Simon?"

"Looks like we may have a breakthrough," Billy said. "He'll be flying back with us tomorrow."

"That's good news. Great news, actually."

"The bad news is that Michael's friend, the one who died skydiving with him, may have had his chute tampered with. That's what is being reported."

Franklin looked up with eyebrows raised. "What?"

"I'll tell you later. It's a strange story. Police are still trying to get a handle on it."

Zander stepped back into the office, with Michael right behind him. "Questions?" he said.

"I'm still wondering about the trailer being unlocked when police found it," Franklin said. "I understand there was only one key, and your driver, Mack, had it. He's sure the trailer was locked, and the key supposedly never left his possession."

"That's right," Michael said. "Mack had the only key. I spoke with him on the road this morning."

"Are there extras here?"

"I'm sure there are."

"Do you have complete faith in what Mack has told you?"

"I don't know him personally, but I don't have any reason to doubt him. I guess anything is possible at this point."

Franklin nodded. "I notice a lot of the same companies on both manifests. I remember somebody saying that before. It's fairly typical on these routes, right?"

"Yeah, we've created a solid pipeline between Denver and the Great Lakes. Some cargo will end up as far north as Traverse City. We truck a lot of goods back to the Rockies through Detroit also."

"What about Airflex? Are you familiar with that one?"

Zander glanced over at Michael, who furrowed his brow. "That's a manufacturer of airplane parts just down I-70 here. They make mostly specialty stuff for vintage aircraft."

"Like a wing assembly?"

"Sure. And a lot of other things."

"Why do you ask?" Zander asked.

"I noticed that there was a wing assembly on both of your last shipments to Detroit." Franklin pulled out another sheet and scanned down the list. "They were headed to a company with a Mount Clemens address. And it looks like there was a wing assembly — maybe the same thing — that came back to Denver on the next AAF truck."

"I don't understand," Zander said.

"It just seems unusual for something like that to keep making thirteen-hundred-mile trips back and forth."

"Like I mentioned, Airflex does a lot of specialty work," Michael said. "They have business connections all over the country. They've been a good customer of ours."

"What's the suggestion?" Zander asked.

"Not sure. Just caught my eye."

"Anything else?" Michael asked.

Franklin rubbed his chin. "There was mention, by Mack, I believe, that J.T. had been on his phone a lot that morning. Maybe spent some time texting with somebody. Did they ever find out who he was texting with?"

"Not that I'm aware of."

"So, Mack was mistaken? Or could J.T. have been using another phone? Maybe a burner phone?"

"I guess it's possible."

"I'm sure they've checked," Zander said, "but I'll talk to the lead investigator again; I've gotten to know him. What else, Franklin?"

"I've got a few other thoughts, but nothing to share at this time. If I could spend an hour or so here in the morning before we leave, that would be ideal. We can talk more on the plane."

"Again, I respect your experience and appreciate you giving everything a look," Zander said. "Frankly, I don't know how much of a priority this case is for the authorities at this point."

"Unsolved murders fade over time, but they never go away. I'm sure people are going to be working the angles for a while."

"I just want to make sure as a company that we've done our due diligence before we move on. Nothing like this should ever happen again. And it won't if I have anything to do with it. But I need to understand it first."

The men all rose at once to leave. "On a more pleasant topic, dinner's on me," Zander said. "There's a place on 3rd Avenue that's one of my favorites. La Merise. It's a French bistro with an awesome menu and great atmosphere. I think you'll really like it."

"I appreciate the offer, Zander, but I'm going to have to pass," Michael said. "I need to get on home."

"Not even a glass of Cabernet?"

"It's been a really long day. I want to make sure Simon's head is right before he goes out of here with you guys tomorrow. I know it really means a lot to him, you coming, even if he doesn't show it. Hopefully we're all going in a much better direction from here on."

The group walked into the parking lot and over to the black SUV that Zander was driving. Franklin took a long look around the property as he opened the rear passenger door.

"One last question for today, Michael," he said. "What was the name of your skydiving friend's business?"

CHAPTER 40

Simon was waiting in the living room when his father returned. He had a tennis racquet in his left hand and was deftly dribbling a yellow ball with the edge of the frame on the hardwood floor. It had been a nervous habit for years.

Michael slipped in the front door with a look of relief. "I'm glad this is settled," he said. "There's no need to look back. You've got everything out in front of you — great career, great life. Don't ever forget that. It's time to get on with things."

"What about you? What's out in front of *you?*"

"What do you mean?"

"I'm talking about Glen Chapman," Simon said. "I know."

Michael took a deep breath and pivoted toward the kitchen. His words trailed behind him. "You may think you know something, but you don't."

Simon was about to snap. He reached back and fired a tennis ball into the bookcase across the room, sending a family portrait on the shelf crashing to the floor. His father stopped in his tracks.

"I've seen the video," Simon said. "I know something is going on. And it sounds like it's been going on for a while."

"*Video?* What are you talking about, son?"

"With Chapman. *Here.* He came to visit, and you recorded it. He was sitting *right here.* You were afraid of him. Isn't that why the camera was on?"

Michael's chin dropped to his chest. He had forgotten.

"It was in the drawer with the skydiving footage," Simon said. "Pretty stupid. I'm surprised it didn't end up with the cops. How long have you been involved in this?"

"It's not like you think. Glen and I were doing some business together. You need to worry about you and not me. I'm fine."

"You've been smuggling drugs, using AAF trucks. *Trafficking.* I can't believe it. And I know Zander wouldn't believe it. You'd be in deep shit. You *are* in deep shit."

"It's over now. Chapman is gone and so is this problem."

"And you had nothing to do with that?"

"Of course not."

"I'm sure he had friends who are still interested. Why would you get involved in the first place?"

Michael shook his head and sat down at the kitchen table. He was caught completely off guard. He rubbed his cheeks and tried to decide how to respond.

"You want me to be honest? It was all about the money," he said. "Easy money. Glen made it easy for me."

"And you see where it got him. He's dead, and we don't really know the reason why. There's a good chance it had something to do with drugs. And you were right there beside him."

"I told you that it's over."

"I don't believe you. You know how smart Zander is. He'll eventually figure out what was happening with his trucks. Now he's got Billy's father helping him figure it out. It'll come back to you."

"All I was doing was finding room for some cargo. Simple as that. I wasn't involved in anything that happened before or after it was loaded."

"I heard you on the video. He was telling you to do more. *Higher. Bigger. Faster.* You were smuggling, and you sounded ready to push it even further. I'm sure you would have if Glen hadn't died. Hadn't been *murdered*. Is that where you're headed?"

"Simon, you need to forget all that. Get your stuff together and be ready to leave in the morning. Keep your head in the tennis world, where it belongs. Nothing else should matter."

"Just go off and play tennis while my father gets deeper into trouble?"

"Everything here will work out like it's supposed to. Stay focused and go about your business. You have a huge year ahead of you."

Simon could only stare at his father in disbelief. "What would Mother say?"

"She would understand that everything I've done is for you."

"For *me*? Don't say that."

"I just had to make sure you were taken care of. I never had that chance when I was your age. I never got to train at an elite academy in Florida. I never got to see how far I could go. You have that chance."

"Because of drug money?"

"No, but it guaranteed some things. You have a team around you now, and you're on your way. You'll be able to go as far as your talent takes you. That's all I ever wanted."

Michael pulled his son close. "I know it's hard to understand right now," he said, "but some day you will. Please, just go back to Florida and turn your full attention to the game. It's time to move forward."

CHAPTER 41

Michael was up early after a restless night and scrambling to get his act together. He was afraid of what the morning might bring. *Questions from his son. Questions from his boss. Questions from Franklin Beckett.* The situation could easily spin out of his control.

Simon was still asleep in his room; he had thrown his stuff together late and sequestered himself to avoid any more confrontations with his father. They were supposed to meet the men in Aurora in a couple of hours. Soon he'd be back in Florida, trying to put everything but tennis out of his mind. It was a lot to ask of a volatile teenager.

There was a knock at the front door. Michael walked into the room with his cup of coffee, expecting to see Zander or Billy. Instead, Khai Le was smiling on the doorstep.

Michael slipped outside and closed the door behind him with an incredulous glare. "What in the hell are you doing here?"

"We need to talk. Again."

"Talk? My son is here, and we're getting ready to leave for the office. Now isn't the time. There's no good time for you to come here. Please leave."

Michael turned to go back in, but Khai grabbed his arm. "I know you were with Glen Chapman when he died."

"That's right. And I heard it wasn't an accident. I'm afraid to ask what you know about that."

"I know that Glen put us in a very bad position. And I mean you, too."

Michael's brow furrowed. "I don't know what you're talking about."

"I have reason to believe our friend was an informant. Understand? He was setting us all up for a big fall. I had to head that off in any way possible. I may have saved you as well."

"*Saved* me?"

"There's no evidence that has come to light that you were involved in anything. *Yet.* Glen always had a soft spot in his heart for his skydiving buddies. Maybe he never would have said anything. Or maybe he already did, and we don't know."

The sun was just beginning to rise, and Michael looked around like he was waiting for trouble to come out of the dawn. "I'm finished with this," he said. "I'm out."

"I'm afraid it's not that easy, Michael. You're part of the organization now. Glen was using you, and I'm just now learning about some of the details. Just because he's gone doesn't mean you can walk away and be done with it. He left behind some outstanding debts that need to be settled. We still need your contribution."

Michael turned and towered over Khai. "I told you. I'm out."

"Perhaps I need to call my friend over here right now and clear this up." He nodded toward the car in the parking lot, where Big Butch was waiting. "Maybe we can even go inside and discuss it with your son."

"Leave him out of this. Please. He's leaving town this morning."

"I'm going to be straight with you right now, Michael. Glen was stealing from my organization. He had stockpiled product and intended to use your trucks to move it. At the same time, he was stringing along the feds, promising that he'd help shut down our operation."

"Why do you think that?"

Khai rubbed his chin. "You remember talking about Gina, his girlfriend? Unfortunately, she got caught in the middle of this."

"What did she tell you?"

"That Glen was playing both sides. He was lining his own pockets while promising to build a case against his friends. Glen had to know that was untenable, and that it was only a matter of time before everything came crashing down."

"And so, you killed her?"

"She killed herself. She just couldn't live with the guilt of sabotaging her boyfriend. I know you've heard about that."

Michael opened the door slightly and looked inside. Still no sign of Simon.

"I'm sure you don't want to get your son mixed up in this," Khai said. "It wouldn't be good for his career."

"He has no knowledge of anything. He certainly doesn't know anything about *you* or your organization. Let's keep it that way. Please."

"Just understand that we have a mutual interest now. We're still going to use your trucks, but it's going to be different. It's going to be bigger. We may need to liquidate in a hurry."

"Why would you want to ramp up operations when you know the feds are on the trail? That makes no sense."

"There's a lot about this story that doesn't make sense," Khai said, "but I know how it works. Sometimes the best moves are the ones that are counterintuitive. You just lay low until you hear back from me. And make sure you look after your son."

Michael walked back inside in a daze. He could feel the walls closing in. All the time and money he'd invested in Simon's career were in danger of going to waste. He was in danger of going to prison.

He flinched when he heard the voice. "Who was that?" Simon was standing at the top of the stairs. His racquet bag was slung over his shoulder, and his suitcase was on the floor beside him.

"Nobody. It's nothing to worry about."

Simon walked to the window and opened the blinds. He watched the man walk to his SUV in the parking lot. "I know better than that. Are those men drug traffickers, too?"

"Please don't use that term. I told you it's nothing."

"I've known people around here who have gotten involved, over their heads. Either them, or family, or friends. They say it's easy to get in but not easy to get out."

"That's enough, Simon."

"They're going to keep coming around here. You know that." He looked deep into his father's brown eyes. "I'm worried about you. I don't see how I can just walk away and forget about what's going on."

"You have to. If you say anything about any of this, I don't know what will happen. Please, let me work it out."

Simon clenched his jaw and turned to walk up the steps. "Can I trust you, son?" Michael said. There was no response.

CHAPTER 42

Khai slid back into the white SUV and tried to collect himself. "I think we're going to be okay," he said. "We can control Michael. He's still in."

Big Butch was sticking his phone in his pocket. He shook his head. "I don't know, man. I'm hearing bad things."

"What?"

"It's the autopsy report on Chapman's girlfriend. Says she didn't die from carbon monoxide poisoning. Not a suicide. Already a lot of chatter in the department, and soon it'll spread like wildfire through the media."

"It's speculation."

"It's not speculation, and it's going to bring even more attention and resources to all of this. It'll hit close to home for everybody, especially me."

"There's no hard evidence."

Butch raised his eyebrows. He knew the range of possibilities. "We'll see," he said. "Bottom line, I'm the one on the hook."

"Don't jump to conclusions. You're still in the clear. No one knows what happened."

"One person does." Butch stared intently at Khai. "That worries me. All of this worries me."

"*Worries* you? I didn't think detectives worried about anything."

"They do if they're smart. And there's more on another front. I'm also hearing this morning that the guy who was shot on the truck may not have been a stranger to everybody. He and Michael Shay may have known each other."

"From where? And when?"

"I don't know yet."

Khai tried to process the information. "Our friend here may have set up that whole caper? Is that what you're telling me?"

"I'm sure he didn't plan for it to end like it did. He was just moving our product and taking a cut. And then …"

"What was the plan?"

"I don't know," Butch said, "but people get greedy. Maybe he and Glen were doing a deal on the side, and it blew up. I blame Glen."

"Doesn't explain who killed the guy."

"It'll come out. Just takes time."

Khai started the car and glanced back toward Michael's condo. "Things don't look good for him. He's about to find out that it can all go to hell in a hurry."

Butch stared straight out the windshield. "It already has. I should never have gotten sucked in either."

"Your job is to protect the Trust, and that's all you've been asked to do. I've paid you well."

"You hired me as security, not to get rid of people."

"None of us saw this coming," Khai said. "The idea was to get rich without hurting anyone. I didn't want to kill Glen; we were all friends. I had to protect what we built. He forced my hand."

"That's what happens when it starts raining money. People get greedy, other people get hurt. Some get killed."

"It just takes one rat to spoil the whole thing. Glen Chapman." Khai shook his head. "And he may still be a problem. You remember what Gina said about a letter? That Glen had spelled out everything about the Trust just in case something happened to him? That was his insurance policy."

"You thought that was bullshit. We looked everywhere for it at her place."

"Now, I'm not sure," Khai said. "Where would it be? She made it sound like somebody else knew where to find it."

"Either way, we've got serious problems. The feds are on the trail. We may be under surveillance right now. I think we need to start making plans."

Khai looked around nervously and sped out of the parking lot.

CHAPTER 43

Zander had arranged to see another tract of land in Knoxville, so he decided to stay the night downtown. He and Simon would fly back to Florida in the morning, after a quick look at the potential building site.

The whole experience in Colorado had been emotionally draining for Simon. The teenager was quiet and spent most of the flight with his head back and his eyes closed. His fellow passengers were simply glad he was on board. They hoped his spirits would improve once he got back to Florida.

Simon and Zander parted company with the Becketts at the airport and drove on to their hotel. The Tennessean was a luxury property on Henley Street, not far from World's Fair Park and the university. A friend of Billy's was the general manager and had set the men up with executive suites for the night.

Zander figured that he and Simon would stay close for dinner, maybe eat downstairs, but Simon wasn't in the mood. He said he wanted to order from the room service menu and watch a movie.

"You sure?" Zander asked.

Simon nodded. "Just call me when you're ready to get out of here in the morning."

Zander sat at the desk in his room and pondered his options as he flipped through the local news stations on television. He preferred having company to share a good meal, conversation, perhaps a bottle of fine wine. He scrolled down the list of favorites on his phone and smiled.

"Hello, Claire," he said. "I'm still in Knoxville and was just wondering if you might be free tonight."

"Well, hello Zander. I'm actually at the office and was getting ready to go home. I just spoke briefly to Billy on the phone. Sounds like your trip was productive."

"We'll see. Hopefully we at least got the young man back on track. We're here at The Tennessean, but he doesn't feel like going out for dinner. Would you be interested in keeping me company? I'd love to sit down and catch up ... it's been a while. My treat, of course."

"That's an offer I can't refuse," Claire said. Her sultry voice was mesmerizing to Zander. "I can be there in twenty minutes. If you want to meet downstairs, I'll just pull in and we can go wherever you like. Lots of good options close by."

"Your call. You're the connoisseur."

"Let me think about it on the way. Thanks for calling, Zander. I look forward to seeing you."

Zander congratulated himself for a great idea. He suddenly had new energy as he bounced into the bathroom and splashed some cold water on his face. He looked at himself in the mirror and smiled. The thought of spending time with Claire was a stimulating development.

The red BMW stopped in front of the hotel, and Zander walked out from the lobby with a broad smile. Just seeing her under the lights — the blazing hair and exquisite face — made him freeze to savor the moment.

He slid into the passenger seat and leaned over to give Claire a quick kiss on the cheek. "Thanks for coming," he said. "What's your pleasure?"

She laughed. "We're talking *dinner*, right?"

"Of course."

"How about Lonesome Dove? Don't know if you remember, but it's in that cool building down in the Old City. Unique atmosphere and menu. Urban Western cuisine, they call it. Too heavy?"

"Absolutely not. I'm hungry, so let's go."

***

The restaurant had lived up to its billing, and so did the company. It was hard for Zander to take his eyes off Claire; he felt like he'd been transported back, almost two decades ago.

She was the dream girl in college — beautiful, charismatic, and smart as a whip — but was already spoken for. She and James Bosken were married right out of law school, and the relationship endured for years. Until recently. Claire was a single woman again.

Zander's experiment with marriage was brief. Peg was a Florida girl with a fierce independent streak, and they parted after little more than a year. Zander vowed to never put himself in that position again.

He became more popular, it seemed, as his wealth grew, but he continued to tread lightly on the dating scene. Claire … she was *different*.

There wasn't much time to reflect on the evening before Zander had to say goodbye. The hotel was only five minutes away.

"I don't suppose you'd like to show me around a little before we call it a night?" he said.

"You want to drive around town?"

"Sure, if you're not in a hurry. I really haven't had a chance to take in the city in quite a while. It has a new look and feel."

"The Market Square area is really popular now. The music scene and theaters in the city are better. You know all about the university and the river backdrop, which I don't suppose we really appreciated as much back in the day. You know I love Nashville, but this has been a good place to live."

"Tell me more."

They revived old memories as Claire looped through the city a few times. Finally, she pulled back into the hotel drive and stopped at the curb near the lobby. They sat there for a few seconds in silence. Zander didn't want the evening to end, and it seemed to him that Claire didn't either.

"How do you like the Knoxville vibe?" she said.

"I liked it from the car; maybe we can get out into it more next time I'm in town. There's a lot going on besides football at Neyland Stadium. I hope my company is part of the new development in the city. That's the plan."

"I hope so, too. I know Billy would really enjoy seeing more of you. You guys have always been good together."

"He's like a brother to me. The brother I never had."

"Yeah, he's a great guy. I've never met anybody quite like him. Guess the old UT connections have held up well through the years. Most of them anyway."

Zander nodded. "Whatever happened to James? I mean, it's none of my business."

"It's all right. James is still a big-time defense attorney in town, probably the biggest. We just kind of lost our way."

"For what it's worth, you know Billy and I never liked him. We always thought you could do better."

Claire giggled. "Did you have anyone in mind?"

Zander beamed, one last time, and opened his door. For a fleeting moment, he felt like he should invite her up to his suite for a nightcap.

"Thanks again for sharing the evening with me, Claire," he said, stepping out of the car. "I hope to see you again soon."

CHAPTER 44

Billy had tried to reach her several times after getting home from Colorado, but his calls kept going to voice mail. Finally, Holly picked up.

"You're persistent, if nothing else," she said.

"Agents are supposed to be persistent. Why aren't you answering? I might have something important to tell you."

"Do you?"

"Yes. I'm coming down to Florida in a few days. I'll be in Bradenton on Monday and plan to drive across to Fort Lauderdale to see you on Tuesday, if that works."

"I thought you were going to tell me something important."

Billy let out a deep sigh. "C'mon, Holly, let's be serious. I know things aren't great right now, but you won't be down for long. You're a strong woman."

"I don't feel strong right now."

"I know the medical people are taking good care of you. You said you liked the specialist."

"I like him pretty well, in fact. He asked me out to dinner."

"Is that right? Are you going?"

"Already did. It's the first time my mind has been on something other than this damn cast."

"How is your arm?"

"Just great. I'm able to putt on my living room rug and everything. Should be winning tournaments in no time."

"I detect sarcasm," Billy said, "but that's an improvement from where we were when you left. I'd call that progress."

"Maybe. Britt has really been helpful."

"Britt?"

"Dr. Stearns. He's drawn up a regimen to keep me active until I can start hitting balls again. He's a scratch golfer, so he understands."

"I used to play golf."

Holly didn't laugh. "Anyway, you're saying you want to meet here on Tuesday? After, I assume, you've stopped to see my friend, Simon?"

"I guess you could call it a meeting. I just want to see you. I told you I'd be down soon."

"Did I mention that I don't have much use for an agent right now?"

"I remember, but you didn't mean it. And I'm not thinking of business so much on this trip."

"What are you thinking of?"

"I'm thinking of you and me."

"That's a real change. Guess all I had to do was be involved in a car crash to get your full attention. Guilt goes a long way."

"That's not fair. I'm juggling a lot of balls, like always. Everything in your career was going along just like we planned, and you know it. You're an LPGA star now."

"I'm not talking about my career. I'm talking about *us*. How's that going?"

"Seriously, how long do you intend to punish me?"

"I don't know. We'll see."

There was a long pause on the line. "Well, maybe I should wait to come down," Billy said. "I've got some more ideas, but they can wait until you're feeling better. I'm sure Britt will take good care of you in the meantime."

"I've had a few ideas myself lately." There was that dreaded pause again. "I'm thinking maybe we should make a clean break."

"*Clean break?* You can't be serious."

"You're a hell of an agent, Billy," she said. "In all honesty, you've done an amazing job helping me get where I am professionally. I never thought these things were possible until you came along and convinced me. You deserve a huge amount of credit, and I know most of your clients would say the same thing about you. On the personal side, though, I'm just not sure I can do it anymore."

"All because of this accident?"

"No, I was already struggling with our relationship. The time off has just given me more time to think. We're apart and moving in different directions emotionally; I know you've struggled with that in the past. I really like you a lot. In fact, I think I told you once that I loved you. Remember? We just never got much beyond that."

Billy was almost speechless. "I understand everything seems up in the air right now," he said. "But let's don't overthink it and lose perspective. You need to get healthy and get on with your career. And I need to continue making sure that everyone knows what an amazing athlete you are."

"I need more than that."

"What are you asking me to do?"

"I don't know. For starters, you could arrange to have my car shipped down to me."

Billy's heart sank. He was usually able to dig his way out with women. Not this time.

"Listen, I need to go," Holly said. "Maybe we can talk again in a few days, but I doubt anything will be different. Goodbye, Billy."

With that, she was gone.

CHAPTER 45

There was a noticeable difference in the atmosphere at the Branson Academy. Billy could feel it the moment he sat down in the courtside bleacher.

Simon had just taken a break and gone to the locker room. Darren Carter was walking over to Billy. The coach was actually smiling. That was the best validation the agent could ask for.

"Good to see you again, Billy," Carter said. "Didn't know how this would turn out, but things are good. You should be pleased."

"Looks like we're kind of back into the old routine."

"Yes, and no. I think Simon is coming out of that funk he's been in."

"I can tell from here. The chemistry is totally different than my last visit, for both of you. What happened?"

"Well, it took a few days after he got back, but we've had some of the best workouts I've been involved with. It's not the same as tournament matches, so you can't read too much into it. But something has changed. The light has come on. What did you do?"

"Nothing that I know of to help his tennis. We just reached an understanding. I told him if he wasn't going to be serious about the game that he didn't need me. He didn't need to come back here."

"Well, he's looking like a serious player. No tantrums, no distractions. He's been focused like a laser, and the talent speaks for itself. I hate to say this — and I'll only tell *you* — but I'm starting to think Simon might win some matches in Melbourne. If this form holds, he's capable of doing some real damage on the big stage. But don't quote me on that."

Simon walked out of the locker room in the distance with a water bottle in his hand and a towel draped over his shoulder. He started toward the men. "Five minutes," Carter said. The coach winked at Billy and began gathering practice balls on the court.

Billy was admittedly excited and intrigued by Carter's assessment. He smiled when Simon sat down beside him. "It's good to see you out here again," he said. "Darren says your game is really taking off."

"I'm trying to mix in a little more serve and volley, just change things up and take advantage of my strengths. I've been working hard. I'm glad he noticed."

"I'm glad to see it myself. That makes this whole trip worthwhile."

"Doing the Florida loop?"

"Yeah, I'll be going on to Miami to see Jarvis Thompson. The Dolphins are at the end of the regular season, and we've got some things to talk about. He's had another great year, and so has the team."

"He's one of the best receivers in the NFL now."

"No doubt."

"What about Holly? I'm afraid to ask."

"Not sure about that. She's not real anxious to see me, but you don't need to worry about it anymore. Leave that to me."

"You've been a good friend, Billy, and I know it hasn't been easy. In all honesty, you're probably a better agent than I deserve. I know sports is big business and all, but it doesn't seem that way with you. It feels personal."

Billy wasn't sure what to say. He rarely heard Simon relate in that way. Hopefully it was another sign of reflection and maturity.

"I appreciate you saying that, Simon. Let's just start fresh right here. One of the most exciting players in tennis is about to have a breakout year, and we're all going to enjoy it. No looking back."

"Two minutes," Carter said.

Simon toweled off his face and hands. "I just want to tell you again that I appreciated you and Zander coming out to Colorado. I might have stayed there if you hadn't. That would have been a mistake. A big mistake. This is where I belong."

Billy nodded and slid out of the bleacher. "I agree. You've got too much going for you to stop now, or even slow down. It's all right there for the taking."

"My father likes to say that."

"What have you heard from him since you got back? It seemed like he had a lot on his mind when we left."

"I don't know … I told him not to call. I don't want to talk to him."

Billy pursed his lips. "Why is that?"

"I'm just going to lean on Darren and the people here. They're the ones that matter now. They're the ones who are going to help me get where I want to go with my game." Simon stood and started to walk toward the court. "And I know I can count on you and Zander."

"One last thing I want to mention to you," Billy said. "I wasn't totally sure when I first got here, but I am now."

"What is it?"

"I'm going to rearrange my schedule for the first of the year. Claire will look after things for a week or so."

"Why?"

"Because I'll be in Australia watching one of my favorite clients kick ass. And hopefully I'll be there more than a couple of days."

A huge smile broke out on Simon's face. He could see his reflection in Billy's sunglasses. "That's awesome, man." They bumped fists, and he yelled over at his coach. "Hey, Darren, Billy says he's going to Melbourne."

"That's a ripper," Carter said. "Team Shay, all the way." He pointed back to the court. "Let's keep the pedal down, mate. Back at it."

"Lunch is on me," Billy said, and he walked toward the gate as Simon jogged to the other end of the court. There was a little extra bounce in the player's step. He danced along the baseline and twirled his racquet like a young man whose confidence was surging. The smile was still in place.

Billy could hear the *thwack!* of Simon's ground-strokes behind him as he reached the parking lot. He slid into his Lexus and pulled out his phone. He felt better about his mission again, about making a difference in his clients' lives.

Maybe the air had cleared a bit in Fort Lauderdale, too.

"I'm going to head your way tomorrow," he said, "if you're up to seeing me. Hopefully we're past the *clean break* thoughts and ready to get back to business."

Holly needed a couple of seconds to respond, even though she obviously had prepared. "I've been thinking a lot about it, Billy. Since I think you're a great agent — and I've always said that — let's just keep it that way. Let's stick to business."

CHAPTER 46

Franklin had been fueled the last few weeks by adrenaline. Preparing for his tenure to end as Sevierville police chief, and then trying to find a niche working with Billy, had kept him going.

But the trip to Colorado had taken more out of him than he realized. He was feeling the effects of his battle against cancer. The disease was relentless; it never took time off.

He could hear the carport door shut and leaned back in his office chair. "Who is it?" he said. There were footsteps in the hallway, and Billy's face suddenly appeared at the door.

"Hello, Dad. How is everything?"

"I'm a little tired, son, but mostly good. I didn't expect to see you back so soon. How was Florida?"

"Not very Christmas-y, I'd say. December in the Sunshine State never feels quite right."

"Not if you're from the Smoky Mountains."

The holidays were challenging at the Beckett household; they hadn't been the same since Anna died. The loss of John only compounded the grief. Franklin and Billy grew tighter with each passing year, but Christmas was still painful. Sadness was the prevailing spirit of the season.

And now, this year, Franklin's illness loomed like another black cloud over both of their lives.

"Tell me what's going on," Franklin said. "Simon is back in line?"

"Better than that. I've never seen him more focused. His coach thinks he might even win a match or two in Australia. I told him I was going to make the trip."

"I'll bet he liked hearing that. It's easy to see he really enjoys being around you."

Billy nodded. "Just spreading joy everywhere I go."

"You get down to Miami, too?"

"Yeah, Jarvis is doing well. If there was ever a success story in the NFL, he's it. He's come such a long way given his upbringing. The dreads are gone, he's wearing Miami Vice suits, and their fan base loves him. He's the kind of guy the whole franchise — the whole city — can rally around." Billy laughed. "Things are so good that we can almost joke about the kidnapping now. Almost."

"What about Holly?"

"I didn't get a chance to see her on this trip. We talked for a minute; she's working on her rehab. We'll try to get together sometime soon."

Franklin shrugged. "Son, would you mind bringing me some water? There's a pitcher in the refrigerator."

Billy cocked his head and looked closer at his father. "You feeling all right? You're a little pale."

"I'm fine. Just tired."

Billy went down the hall and into the kitchen of the modest brick ranch. He opened the cabinet door. The same glasses were still in the same places above the sink, lined up the same way. Some things never changed.

He poured from the Brita pitcher and took the glass to Franklin.

"The doctors say you're doing good, right? I'm not going to go halfway around the world if you're having any problems. I mean it."

"You go about your business. I'm as good as can be expected at this point. Some days are tough, but most days I feel like I'm winning the fight. I just need to stay busy, keep my mind occupied."

"I've got lots of ways to do that," Billy said.

"I know you do. Speaking of, I talked with Zander yesterday."

"About the investigation?"

"I passed along a few more thoughts, and there was still a question or two. That's about all I have to offer. For some reason, I think they'll get a break before long."

"I'm sure Zander liked hearing that. Anything you can share with me?"

"Not yet, son."

"Well, I'm going to the office to try to knock out some of the work that has been piling up. December is like the calm before the storm. Claire won't be happy when the lightning and thunder start rolling in, and I'm not here. She's got plenty going on herself."

"I'll say it again: you're a very lucky man to have her. Zander was just saying that, too."

"Everybody loves Claire. I get it."

"Have you ever thought about … you know, getting closer to her?"

Billy chuckled. "It doesn't seem like we're close enough? I talk to her almost every day."

"You know what I mean. She's single now. You're single."

"I know, but I've got enough problems with women without adding another one with my business partner. My relationship with Claire is just fine the way it is. We work well together. I don't want to ruin that."

"I understand. It's not like you don't have any female companionship. You *do* have some, right?"

"When did you get so interested in my love life?"

"I guess I just have more time to think about stuff like that now. I hate to see you wasting your prime years, son. I may never get to hold another grandchild the way things are going."

Billy had never given it much thought, but suddenly it made sense. Carrying on the family name was up to him. And Franklin might not be around long enough to see how that turns out.

"I'll keep you posted," Billy said. "How's that?"

"Fair enough. Doesn't sound like Holly is the one."

"No, I think we're going to keep things on a business level moving forward. That's fine. It's simpler that way."

"She's a beautiful girl."

"Yes, she is." Billy turned and started back toward the kitchen. "Anyway, I just wanted to stop by and check on you. I'm glad to hear you're staying in touch with Zander. I know he appreciates whatever insights you might have."

"Hopefully he'll get that resolved soon and move on. I know how protective he is of his company's image. An incident like that eats at any good CEO, even though the general public has long forgotten about it."

"He's built a monster of a business. Everyone at school knew he was headed for big things, but it's one of those be-careful-what-you-wish-for deals. AAF has so many moving parts, and Zander is a control freak, so there's always major tension trying to keep everything on the right path."

"Kind of like your business."

"In a weird sort of way."

"Is Zander still going to Australia?" Franklin asked.

"I don't know. He was hedging the last time we talked about it, mostly because of the investigation and some other things that have come up. He didn't feel like he could be out of the country, but I think he's feeling better about things. I haven't told him yet that I'm planning to go."

"It sounds like a good opportunity for both of you to get away. Call it a business trip and make the most of it. Long way to go, but it should be fun."

"We'll see. How much fun depends on Simon. It could be the start of a big year for him, or a disappointment. Hopefully it's a year to remember."

PART III

CHAPTER 47

"**W**hat time is it, Simon?"

The teenager looked across the aisle and smiled. "We're on West Coast time, now. Seventeen hours ahead in Melbourne. Tomorrow afternoon, maybe three o'clock?"

"No," his coach said. "It's time for a toast."

The men laughed, and Carter and Billy each poured a splash of Jack Daniel's in their glass and raised them toward the center of attention. Simon reciprocated with his orange juice.

"Here's to a productive … *two weeks?*" Carter asked. "Let's say two weeks. We're going to be positive about this. People are going to know who Simon Shay is by the time we're back in the States."

He turned up his glass and then licked his lips. "Tennessee whiskey. Great stuff. You got me hooked, mate."

"Hear, hear," Billy said.

The Qantas flight from LAX to Melbourne had just planed off moments earlier. It would take the Boeing 787-9 Dreamliner about sixteen hours to reach the land Down Under.

Team Shay was stationed along row three in first class — Billy and Carter in two center seats, with Simon on their left flank by a window. The trip had been in the works for months, and finally they were on their way. The excitement was palpable.

For Billy, the stress of leaving behind unfinished work was beginning to subside. He had touched base with all the clients who needed his immediate attention and put together a to-do list for Claire. He was now focused on one task: getting Simon comfortable and competitive. That was his job in Australia.

"We haven't had a chance to talk much lately," Billy said to Carter. "Last time you thought our man over there might win a match or two. You still have good vibes?"

"I'm making no predictions, but this is bringing back a lot of memories. I've been thinking about the first time with Lleyton Hewitt."

Simon had his ear buds in hand, ready to drift off, but the conversation caught his attention and he leaned across the aisle to listen. It wasn't often that his coach shared personal reflections.

"Nineteen ninety-seven," Carter said. "Simon, you may be too young to remember. Hell, what am I saying? You weren't even born yet."

Simon had a twinkle in his eye. "Go ahead anyway. Tell me about the old days, grandpa."

Carter laughed and poured another splash from the airline bottle. He was loosening up in a hurry. "Well, Lleyton had drawn Sergi Bruguera, a tall Spaniard who was a major champion. Tough draw. First match of his first tournament — not even sixteen; you're an old man by comparison — and Lleyton was nervous as a cat. Bruguera had won the French back-to-back a few years before that and was a top-ten player. Nobody knew who this skinny kid from Adelaide was."

"And he pulled off the upset?" Simon asked.

"No, he lost in four sets. Won the first set and then got smoked."

Billy laughed out loud. "I thought you were going to give us something uplifting. How does *that* help?"

"It's a lesson about perseverance. That was the start of something big. Three years later Lleyton was number one in the world. He never won the Open but made the final in 2005. We weren't still together then … Lleyton did all right without me. He ended up winning thirty singles championships, couple of Grand Slams, made a pile of money, married a beautiful girl, had three kids. These days he and Bec are like a royal couple in Australia."

"He still lives in Melbourne?" Simon asked.

"Lives large. They've got a twelve-million-dollar mansion in Toorak, luxury car collection, all the toys. We're still good friends. I wouldn't be surprised if he pays us a visit when we get there."

"Well, there you go, Simon," Billy said. "The moral of that story is that once you get rid of Darren, your career will take off."

"No, that's not it, mate. It's about grinding; Lleyton was a grinder. Even if he didn't have his best stuff, he was still going to be hard to beat. Everyone knew it, and they respected him for it. That's what we're looking for now. Respect."

Carter held up his glass and signaled to the flight attendant for another. "Two's my limit on business trips," he said. "I got plenty of time to sleep on this one. By the way, I'm sorry Zander couldn't make it out with us."

"Me too, but he knew it would be hard to get away right now. Hopefully he won't be too far behind us. I think he was looking forward to going to Australia more than anybody."

Carter chuckled. "Did I ever tell you how we hooked up to begin with?"

Billy shook his head and poured the rest of his whiskey into the glass. "Don't believe you did."

"Well, I'm at home down in Naples and the phone rings. There's that voice:" He tried to put a little Southern drawl into it. "*You wanna coach again?* I hadn't worked with a touring pro in a couple of years, and I didn't know this guy from Adam. Two days later Zander is knocking on my door. We sat down and had a drink, and the next thing I know I'm up in Bradenton working with this kid."

"Who told Zander about you?"

"I don't remember exactly, but he had done his homework. Zander's a beauty. Knows what he wants and gets right to the point. We hit it off pretty good from the start, even though he's a country boy and didn't know diddly about tennis. He was the first to admit it. But he knew what he wanted. He wanted this young man over here to be great, to be a champion. I know his father wants that, too. Bad."

The men looked over at Simon. He had already tuned out. His eyes were closed, and he was listening to music — probably one of those bands Billy had never heard of.

"Michael deserves a lot of credit; he put it all in motion," Carter said. "He should be sitting here with us right now."

"That's interesting, Darren. I don't believe I've heard you open up like this before."

"Must be the Jack."

"I don't guess it had occurred to me that you probably know what's in Simon's head better than any of us. You've spent far more time with him. His success is in a large part due to you and your influence."

"I've been hard on him, and I know he doesn't always appreciate it. Like most kids, there's a rebellious streak that comes out when things aren't going his way. He's a bit of a larrikin."

"What's a larrikin?" Billy asked.

"He's mischievous but has a good heart. I believe in Simon. His success means a lot to me."

Billy nodded, pressed back against the headrest, and stretched his legs for the long flight. They were all fully invested at this point.

CHAPTER 48

Michael Shay glanced at the clock on the dash and allowed himself a moment to smile. He realized his son was on his way.

There was an early meeting at the office, but Michael first wanted to collect his thoughts. While he was at it, he'd give thanks that, occasionally, the stars lined up right.

He felt like he should be celebrating, anticipating the first victory. But he needed to keep things in perspective. Just stepping onto the court at Rod Laver Arena was, after all, a win for any nineteen-year-old. Hell, Simon could still be sulking at home, sabotaging his career with his stubbornness. Where did he get *that?*

Michael's thoughts turned to Ellen, and his eyes got misty. His beautiful wife loved tennis, but not the way he did. She didn't fully understand the promise it held for their family. It all would have come into focus by now.

Ellen would be so proud, Simon earning his place on one of the great stages in the sport. The three of them would have been together today, Australia bound. Everything would have been different.

Michael snapped back to reality and was about to pull out of the garage when he noticed the white SUV in his rear-view mirror. It was parked behind him in the driveway. He got out of his car and walked back.

Khai Le lowered the heavily tinted glass and scowled. Big Butch was in the backseat.

"What are you doing here?" Michael said.

"I want you to take a ride with us. We need to talk."

"I'm tired of hearing that. I'm going to work. We don't have anything to talk about that hasn't already been said."

"I think we do." Khai looked back at Butch and shook his head. "We can do this hard or easy. Please get in. Now."

Michael hesitated briefly before stepping out and locking his car. He wasn't afraid for his safety. Not yet. But he needed to lower Khai's temperature if possible.

He slid into the passenger seat of the SUV without another word. Khai eyed him closely and pulled away.

Michael had gotten used to the man's threatening aura, but he felt a greater sense of desperation was suddenly at play. The game had reached crunch time.

"We've had a little more time to sort this mess out," Khai said. "None of it looks good from where I'm sitting. We've got a lot of people in the organization getting nervous."

"Why do you keep coming back to me? I had a limited role ... I'm just moving freight, minding my own business. You have all this other stuff going on that doesn't have anything to do with me. I'm out, remember?"

"You're up to your neck in this, Michael. *Just moving freight?* You were trafficking marijuana. It was easy money, and you got greedy. If *we* go down, *you* go down."

Michael began wringing his hands. "I said all along that I didn't want to know what was going on. I told Glen that."

"You're going to act innocent? You don't get paid in this world for being innocent. Let me ask you something: Do you even know how many pounds of weed you were moving each time?"

"No, it didn't matter. There's pot all over Colorado."

"You weren't doing business in the state. That's why Glen approached you to begin with. Your company has a long reach, and a solid reputation."

"We just put the assembly on the trucks and delivered it where it needed to go. Simple as that."

"Every bit of it, every ounce, was supposed to be money in my pocket. That's where Glen lost sight of things. He started skimming for himself. I know now that it had been going on for a while. I'm sure it added up to quite a bonus, right?"

"I don't know about that. I thought he was the boss."

"You know what else I heard? You were doing more than trafficking weed. You and Glen had a little side hustle going. More than a little, in fact. Am I right?" There was no response. "It wasn't simple at all, was it? That's what led to the shooting on your truck."

Michael slumped back in the seat and rubbed his face. "I don't know where you got this."

Khai pounded the dash with his fist. "How did he approach you about the shipments the last time you talked about it? What did he say?"

"He wanted to turn up the volume on the whole operation. Wanted bigger shipments. I thought he was calling the shots. I didn't know— "

"You didn't know shit about anything, did you? Is that what you expect me to believe? You didn't know this last shipment was all Glen's doing. It was my product — except for the cocaine. And that got away somehow."

"How do you know about that?"

"I talked to some people we know in Detroit. Word travels fast in small circles like this. What happened to the blow?"

Michael took a deep breath and exhaled. "I didn't even know it existed until Glen told me. I told him from the start that I didn't want any part of trafficking cocaine. I didn't want any trouble. I just wanted my cut, and that was it."

"The problem is there *was* trouble. One of your drivers was killed. You think that was by accident, Michael? Just a random act of violence? You know better. And so do I."

"I don't know who killed him. And I don't know why. It has caused me nothing but trouble with my boss."

"You'd have more trouble if he knew you were using the company trucks to run drugs. You'd be in jail. You've been pushing your luck for a long time now. I think it's finally caught up to you."

"What are you going to do?" Michael asked.

"That's the question right now, isn't it? Butch, should we just let Michael go and see how things go? That would be extremely charitable since I don't know how much time we have before things blow up. People used to think I was charitable. That's why they took advantage of me."

"I don't like any of this," Butch said. "We might be better off if we just cut ties. Everybody goes their own way."

Khai looked at his bodyguard in amazement. "You think you can just walk away, too? You know that's not going to happen. You're just as involved in this as our friend Michael here and all the rest. I don't trust anybody right now."

"I didn't mean it that way. It's just that we're running out of time."

"Let me be clear," Khai said. "I won't be the only one holding the bag if everything goes south. We started this together, and that's the way we'll finish it."

Michael began shaking his head. "Don't do something you'll regret. Maybe I can help make this right."

"I think I heard Glen say that once. You know what? He never made things right. He only made things worse — getting you involved, getting another pilot involved, getting cocaine dealers involved. Foolish decisions. He lost my money, and then he turned on me." Khai gritted his teeth. "His luck was running out, right down to the minute he pulled that ripcord, and the chute didn't open."

"So now what?"

"The way I see it, you're just a liability, Michael. You're a potential government witness against me now."

"I haven't talked to anyone."

"But you will if that's what it takes to keep your ass out of prison. I know you'd rather be watching your son play tennis."

"You don't want to kill me," Michael said. "You already have enough trouble. I've done everything you asked. I'm never going to say anything to anybody."

"I've never asked anything of you, have I? But Glen did. Let's be clear, that's how we got here. You went down that road with him, and now you're at a dead end. I thought you were smarter than that."

"Please, I want out of this. My son needs me."

"Then let's get it all out here on the table," Khai said. "You need to tell me everything."

CHAPTER 49

The SUV sped off, almost before Michael's feet hit the pavement. He pressed his hands against his head, as if trying to keep it from exploding. *Lucky to be alive*, he thought. But he knew he'd never be rid of Khai Le.

Michael shuffled toward his condo. Before he reached the porch, the phone rang in his jacket pocket. He looked at the screen; there was no caller ID number.

"This is Michael," he said, trying to regroup.

"Mr. Shay, my name is Sean McGuire," came the reply. "I'm a special agent with the DEA task force in Denver, and I have some questions for you."

The words took Michael's breath. He closed the door behind him and dropped into a chair. "What can I do for you?"

"It's more a matter of what I can do for *you*. I understand that you're in a bit of trouble. You need a lifeline."

"I'm not sure what you mean, sir."

"You knew Glen Chapman. Correct?"

"I used to see him occasionally. I supported his skydiving business."

"You were with him the day he died. Correct?"

"Yes. I just happened to be part of that group. I've spoken with the authorities about it, more than once."

"Did you support other business activities of Mr. Chapman?" McGuire asked.

"I'm sorry, but I'm not following here."

"We're trying to flesh out some details of his death, and the case is taking some unusual turns. Of course, the whole story is unusual. Skydiving deaths are few and far between, thankfully. Am I right?"

"Yes."

"I guess you heard on the news that Mr. Chapman's girlfriend may have had something to do with his parachute malfunctioning. She was the one who packed the chutes for the business. Of course, she's now dead, too, so we can't talk to her."

"I am aware of all that," Michael said. "But …"

"We're learning a lot about what was going on in his life — friends, enemies, business acquaintances, all of that. I'd like to try to explain it to you in person, put everything in perspective and see where you and your company might fit in. Can we meet today?"

Anything involving the DEA was serious. Michael knew that. *Why didn't they just show up at his door and arrest him?* That was the obvious question.

"Do I have a choice?"

"Yes and no. I'm trying to be cordial."

Michael glanced at his watch and sighed. "I can come by your office if you like. Two hours?"

"Thank you for your cooperation, Mr. Shay. I look forward to meeting you. My office is in Centennial, by the way. I'll text the address."

Michael disconnected the call and rubbed the phone on his chin. He stared at himself in the mirror. More wrinkles, more gray in his hair. He seemed to be show-ing his age more by the hour.

If he was on the DEA's radar, they had to know about the marijuana shipments. *Or maybe something worse.* Then again, maybe they were just fishing for information.

Michael weighed his options. If worse came to worst, he could claim Chapman had threatened him, and he went along under duress. He might offer to testify against Khai Le for leniency, but he'd likely still go to jail. His life and career would be ruined.

This was the beginning of the end.

The phone rang again in his hand as he stood there con-templating his fate. He was afraid to even look at the screen.

Zander.

"Good morning," his boss said. "I have an idea that I think you're going to like."

Michael tried to compose himself. "*Idea?* What about?"

"I've been kicking it around, waiting to see how my schedule clears. I don't think there's much more we can do. So, how would you like to go to the Open?"

Michael didn't see that coming. His world was spin-ning, and he needed to get a grip. "The *Australian* Open?"

"Yes, that little tournament your son is getting ready to play in. Remember? I'm making the trip tomorrow and thought you might want to join me."

"I don't know what to say. We weren't planning on that. I didn't think it was possible."

"Neither did I, but now it is. I've pulled a few strings, and I'd be glad to have you along if you want to go. We talked about this way back at the start."

"I had given up on that idea."

"Have you spoken to Simon?" Zander asked.

"No, he hasn't called. I know there's a lot going on and don't want to bother him."

"Well, I'm sure he'd be glad to see your smiling face in the stands, cheering him on. All you have to do is get to L.A. by tomorrow morning; we'll meet there and fly commercial to Melbourne. I'll take care of the accommodations."

Michael's mind was racing. "Again, Zander, I don't know what to say. I'm blown away by the offer, but not sure …"

"Not sure about *what*? I'm giving you the green light to see your son play in his first Grand Slam tournament. And what better place than Australia?"

There was a noticeable sigh on the line. "It sounds awesome, but … have you discussed it with Simon?"

"No, I thought it would be a nice surprise. But if you don't want to go …"

"It's just that I made other plans when I knew I wouldn't be making the trip."

"Cancel them."

"I don't think I can. It's a strange situation. I really appreciate the offer, but ..."

"Michael, is there something wrong? To be honest, I can't believe you're telling me this."

"I can't either. But I can't go."

There was a long delay. "Okay, then. I'll hook up with Billy and Darren, and hopefully we'll see your son at his best. Don't ever say you didn't have the chance."

Michael was almost kicking himself by the time he hung up. But he knew he didn't have the option of suddenly leaving town, much less leaving the country.

He couldn't imagine the day getting much worse.

CHAPTER 50

Simon unloaded a sizzling forehand down the line and leaped in the air with delight. His coach nodded as he walked off the indoor practice court. Final preparations were over.

"Meet us outside," Carter said. "Half hour."

When Simon stepped out into the VIP area, he could see the men across the way. Carter and Billy were smiling as they stood beside the exotic black sports car. Ferrari.

Simon approached slowly with his racquet bag draped across his shoulder. He'd never seen a car like it. Few others there had either. Even in this crowd, it was a star attraction.

"Here you go, Simon," Carter said. "This is what a lot of talent and hard work, not to mention cash, can get you in this sport."

"Is that Lleyton Hewitt's car?"

"Yep," Billy said. "It's an SF90 Stradale. Think you could keep it on the road?"

"Stra-*dolly*?"

"It means 'street,' I've learned, and it's a rare car, to say the least. Almost a thousand horsepower. Scary."

"Looks like it belongs on a racetrack, not the street."

"Lleyton said he just had it delivered a couple days ago. I think he's afraid to drive it. I've been out here talking to him while you were practicing. Great guy."

"I told you," Carter said. "He's a popular bloke around here."

Simon nodded and walked around the car admiringly. "Where is he?"

"Somebody grabbed him a few minutes ago and took him inside," Billy said. "He said he wants to meet you when he gets back."

"I'd like that, but I think I'm going back to the hotel and rest. I'm feeling the heat."

"It's a blast of summer in the middle of winter," Carter said.

"This is summer on steroids."

"The world is turned upside down here. Takes some getting used to, and that's why players usually come over early. That and the time difference. Young guys like you usually adjust quickly."

"I'll be fine. Can you drive me to the hotel, Billy?"

"Sure. Let's go."

"I'm going to wait on Lleyton," Carter said. "I'll be along soon."

***

Crown Melbourne was a sprawling resort and casino complex located on the south bank of the Yarra River. In recent years it had become a popular spot for players during the Open, many of whom used to seek rental properties farther from the stadium. Billy had reserved a suite in Crown Towers months earlier for Simon and his coach; he booked himself a room in Crown Promenade.

Everything about the unfolding scene in Australia was an eye-opening experience, but Simon was focused. It looked to his agent like the maturing process was moving quickly. They had come a long way since the accident involving Holly; it was hardly mentioned anymore. Simon was all about tennis.

"You ready to play?" Billy asked as the player plopped down on the couch and unfolded the case of his iPad Pro.

"Ready to win."

The odds were against him. There were one hundred twenty-eight players in the draw of Grand Slam tournaments. Simon was among the ninety-six who were unseeded. He would be an underdog in his first match with veteran Dominique Alfaro of Spain.

"I've been looking into Alfaro," Billy said. "He's a typical Spaniard, better on clay than hardcourts. The faster surface here should work to your advantage."

Simon couldn't help but laugh. "You're scouting the opposition for me now? Thanks."

"You're welcome. Since I've come all the way over here, I might as well be multi-tasking. I just thought I'd mention that you're in position to get off to a good start. You're bigger and stronger, have a better serve, and young legs. And you're a lefty."

"You make it sound like I'm the favorite."

"You would be if people knew you like I do. Be confident. Always."

"Don't worry, Darren's got a plan that's going to work. You'll see. Then you can start breaking down the next opponent."

"Already working on it," Billy said.

Simon smiled and scanned through the email messages on his tablet. Nothing seemed to grab his attention. "What time is it in Colorado?" he said.

"Looks like about eight in the evening."

Simon jumped off the couch and grabbed a bottle of water from the refrigerator. They had cases of water stacked up beside it. "I'm going to call my father." He walked into his bedroom and closed the door behind him.

"Okay," Billy said to himself.

The door to the suite opened and Carter ambled in with that natural Aussie swagger. He pulled out a chair at the table across from Billy.

"You look pretty pleased, considering how you usually look," the agent said. "Is that confidence I'm seeing?"

"Dead set. But you never know in this game, especially with a kid who's never been here. Simon seems to be in a good place mentally."

"Looks that way to me, too."

"You have dinner plans?" Carter asked.

"Nothing yet. I'm just waiting to see what Simon wants to do. I'm guessing he'll lay low, maybe eat in."

"He likes to be by himself before a tournament starts. There's a lot to think about here."

"I told Zander that I'd pick him up at the airport and we'll probably grab an early bite. How long will it take me to drive out there?"

"A half-hour if traffic isn't brutal. Believe it or not, I'm going out in high society for a bit. The Hewitts were kind enough to invite me over for hors d'oeuvres at the palace. I'll be back here early. I still want Lleyton to meet Simon, but we'll worry about it later, after he wins his first match."

"How sure are you?"

"He's going to beat Alfaro if his head is right. Simon just has too much firepower. After that match, it gets dicey."

"You win the first one and who knows? Simon could get on a roll. There's something to be said about being young and naive."

"Ignorance is bliss, right?"

"Seen it with clients many times over. They just go out and win, for no particular reason except they haven't learned to be afraid yet."

"I'll bet you have," Carter said. "How are you liking Australia, mate?"

"It's beautiful — everything you said it would be. I'm glad to be here. I just hope we can stick around for a little while."

The bedroom door opened, and Simon walked out. Something had changed. His face showed a detachment that hadn't been present just a few minutes earlier.

"Did you get your father?" Billy asked.

"Yeah, we talked."

"Didn't talk long. I assume he's fired up about tomorrow."

"I guess."

"Zander said he offered to bring Michael along. Apparently, he had plans he couldn't change."

"That's what he told me, too."

"Zander should be landing shortly. He has a villa rented over in Crown Cove and has invited me to come and stay with him. I may do that and let you boys focus on the job at hand."

"I believe we're as ready as we can be," Carter said with a smile. He got up and started toward his room. "I want Simon to leave here with no regrets."

CHAPTER 51

Billy immediately looked over at Simon, who was sitting on the couch, staring blankly at the television screen with his arms folded across his chest.

"Something's wrong," Billy said.

The response was barely more than a whisper. "What do you mean?"

"I mean that a half-hour ago you were fired up and ready to take on the world. After talking to your father, not so much. What's up with that?"

Simon took a deep breath and exhaled slowly. Still no eye contact. "Don't worry about it, Billy."

"What did he say?"

"He wishes he were here. That's all."

"Sounds like he had a chance to be here. Zander was going to make it happen. I'm still not understanding."

"It's complicated."

"How complicated could it be? You're his son, and he's put everything into your career, giving you a chance to make it big. And now here you are. Win or lose, you've arrived." Billy hesitated. "It had to be something major to keep him away."

"I said don't worry about it."

Simon got up and walked to the window. He was clearly conflicted by the thoughts running through his head.

Since his mother's death, he and his father had walked an emotional tightrope. Ellen had always kept her boys in line; she was the guiding light in the family. Without her, and with Simon living in Florida, Michael had become more and more unpredictable. Tennis was the strongest bond between them, but even that had become fraught.

Simon got wind of drug use a while back during a trip home. He didn't read too much into it. Colorado catered to that lifestyle, and many of his friends' parents were casual users. But trafficking was another matter entirely.

Simon didn't understand how Michael's adventurism could go *that* far. He thought he would have too much respect for Zander to undermine him that way. He thought his father would have too much respect for *him*.

"Just between you and me, I'm worried about him," Simon said. "He's in trouble."

"What kind of trouble?"

"I don't want to get into it, especially right now."

"And I don't want to pry, Simon, but whatever it is has you upset. And this isn't a good time to be upset. Did he tell you he's in trouble?"

"No, but I know."

Billy's eyes narrowed, and he put a hand on Simon's shoulder. "It's my job to try to smooth out problems that come up. Any problems. What can I do to help?"

Billy could tell that Simon was growing more frustrated. He had seen plenty of that from the teenager, but this was different. There was an overriding sorrow.

"There's nothing you can do," Simon said. "At this point, I'm not sure there's anything he can do either."

"Tell me about it. It won't help to keep it to yourself. You know by now that you can trust me. I want to put your mind at ease as best I can."

"Would it help if I said he's involved with some bad guys? Probably not."

"Tell me what you mean."

"I think he's gotten himself into a situation that he can't get out of. He should have known better."

"Bad guys? In what way?"

Simon sat up and wrung his hands. "Drugs," he said. "He's been helping them move drugs."

"On the *trucks*?"

Simon nodded. "Yes."

Billy was taken aback, but not totally shocked. The scourge of illegal drugs had derailed the lives and careers of other clients and their families. The death of Russell Mann, the NBA star, was only the most glaring example.

But he didn't see this coming with Michael. The Shays lived a life of relative privilege.

"I can't believe we're talking about this," Simon said.

Billy shook his head. "I can't either, but there's nothing you can do now, except go out and win tennis matches. That may sound cold, but that's why you're here. It's how a pro handles his business."

"I know I owe it to everybody — my father, you, Zander."

"We've talked about that. You owe it to yourself, and no one else. Do your best here and deal with problems at home when you get back. You know I'll help you in any way I can when the time comes."

Simon stood and forced a smile. "I know you will, and I appreciate it." He started to walk away before stopping. "I don't want Zander to know about this," he said. "You can't tell him."

"If Michael has been running drugs on the company's trucks, it's going to come out. Zander has a right to know. It's his company."

"And that's the hardest part. Everything he's done for me and my father … I don't know what to say. I don't want to hurt Zander, but I don't want to get my father in trouble either."

Billy stood and tried to clear his head. Distractions were the last thing he wanted to hear about on the eve of the tournament. And this was a major distraction that could soon grow into something far worse.

"This puts me in a really bad position," he said. "Zander is my friend. We're always straight with each other."

"Zander is my friend, too, but this is different. I think my father is beginning to understand that everything is going to come out. Just not now." Simon slumped into a chair. "I shouldn't have told you."

"Why *did* you?"

"I don't know. I guess I trust you. I believe you'll say and do the right thing."

Billy knelt and looked Simon squarely in the eye. "I'm glad you did. Just focus on your job and control the things you can, which doesn't include family business nine thousand miles away. That's what your father would want you to do right now."

"What are *you* going to do?"

"I haven't decided," Billy said. "I'll promise you this: I won't say anything as long as you're still alive in this tournament. I want us all to enjoy the moment. After that, I don't know."

CHAPTER 52

Sean McGuire leaned forward in his chair and reached out to shake Michael's hand. He didn't bother to stand. The agent wore a grim look on his face, the kind that was reserved for men in legal jeopardy.

"Have a seat, Mr. Shay," he said. "I appreciate you coming down to talk with me. As I told you on the phone, we've got a lot of loose ends to tie up regarding your friend, Mr. Chapman. We'd like to get those resolved as soon as possible."

"I told you that we were acquaintances more than friends."

McGuire smiled and leaned back in his chair. "Be that as it may, you were right next to him on the day he died. Was there anything unusual about his behavior?"

"I didn't notice. We went skydiving together fairly often, and I just happened to be there … *that day*."

"And you're distribution manager of the AAF Transport facility up in Aurora? I know it's a growing company, getting out to a lot of places. You oversee shipping operations there?"

"That's right. Why?"

"Just want to make sure I have everything straight. I understand one of your drivers was killed recently in a shooting in Missouri. The truck had left that morning from your facility."

"He wasn't one of our drivers, but he was on one of our trucks. He took it when the driver stopped for breakfast."

"I've read the report," McGuire said. "Didn't make a whole lot of sense, to be honest. Seemed to be more questions than answers in the final analysis. How would he have been cleared to be on that truck to begin with?"

"If you don't mind me asking, sir, what does the DEA have to do with this? There were no drugs involved to my knowledge."

"Are you sure?"

"Yes. There was nothing to suggest it that I've heard of."

"As of now, we have nothing to do with that case. It just came to my attention when we started looking into you, Mr. Shay."

"You're looking into *me*? Why?"

"We try to look at everything during the course of an investigation. Call it due diligence. Certain facts just present themselves."

Michael's brow furrowed. *How did I get dragged into this?* If it was indeed a fishing expedition by the feds, he suddenly felt like chum in the water, and he was afraid the sharks were moving in.

"Do you know a man named Khai Le?" McGuire asked. The agent pulled a black-and-white photo from a folder and held it up in front of Michael.

"I don't believe so. Who is he?"

"He used to be a marijuana grower involved with the caregiver program in Colorado. He may be much more than that now."

"I don't know him."

"Okay. Do you know why he was seen leaving the parking lot of your condo complex earlier today?"

The threat was becoming clearer now. Michael stood and tried to sound indignant. "Agent McGuire, am I being charged with something here? If I am, I'd like to have my attorney present."

McGuire smiled. "No charges today, Mr. Shay. Like I said, we're just hearing and seeing a lot of things and trying to run them to ground. Seems like some of them lead to you."

"I've told you the truth as far as my knowledge goes. If you have further questions about our operations at AAF, I suggest you speak to my boss. He should be the one to address them."

"Mr. Fleming? He owns the line, correct?"

"Yes. Zander Fleming. I believe you'll find that he's a fine corporate citizen and has done everything possible to try to get to the bottom of what happened in the unfortunate incident you described. Zander wants answers as much as you do."

"I'm sure he does. But for the moment, let's go back to Glen Chapman. You probably knew him as well as anyone, apart from the woman who allegedly orchestrated his death. What reason do you suppose Gina Simpson would have had to want her boyfriend to crash to the ground like that?"

"I've answered these questions already," Michael said. "I didn't know Gina, except in the brief encounters we had at the airfield. She and Glen seemed to get along fine. Beyond that, I know nothing about their relationship."

"Did you know that Mr. Chapman was part of Khai Le's organization?"

"I did not."

"Nothing more you'd like to share with us regarding these gentlemen?"

"I've told you everything I know. If you'd like to continue this line of questioning, I'd really like to call my attorney."

McGuire pushed back his chair and abruptly stood up. "No need for that today," he said. "Thank you for your time, Mr. Shay. We'll stay in touch."

Michael seemed confused as he walked out of the office and turned the corner toward the elevator. McGuire stood at the window at the end of the hallway and watched him move quickly through the parking lot and slide into his SUV.

There was a black travel bag in the passenger floorboard. Michael pulled it up into the seat beside him, unzipped the bag, and took a quick look inside before driving away.

CHAPTER 53

Agent Amy Stafford was already waiting to talk to her boss when he walked back to his office.

"What do you make of Mr. Shay?" Stafford asked.

"He's up to his eyeballs in this. I could tell when I mentioned Khai Le's name. It's one thing to be buddies with a drug runner like Glen Chapman. It's another to be working with the man in charge of the whole operation."

"You think Shay's company is part of this?"

"Of course. And I'd bet that shooting on their truck in Missouri is related. Just don't know how exactly."

"What about Shay's boss?"

"I don't know. AAF has trucking routes all over the country. They have unlimited reach; there's the potential to smuggle about anything in any direction if it's done well. But that doesn't mean Mr. Fleming knows what's been going on in this case. He has a golden reputation in the business community."

"You think Shay's acting on his own?"

"That's my guess. He can set the rules at the Aurora office, and the payoff is pretty lucrative." McGuire leaned back in his chair. "I'm starting to believe that he's as big a player as Chapman was in this operation. They were friends at first, and then it got more serious."

"And Shay was able to connect the dots with AAF trucks."

"That's my guess. What about Chapman's girlfriend? Anything new about her death? She's an important piece of this puzzle."

"Nothing the last time I talked to the Denver detectives," Stafford said. "They know it wasn't a suicide but are still looking for a connection to who killed her. No one seemed to have a real reason."

"What are the chances that it's Khai Le, or someone who works for him?"

"Reasonably good, I'd say. If he knew that Chapman was cooperating with us, he had motive to shut him down. Staging a parachute accident without a trace is a tough thing to do, but Gina Simpson made it possible. From everything we know, she was very good with chutes. It's pretty creative, you have to admit."

"And then he tries to cover that by staging her death as a suicide? I don't know … seems a bit much. It's far-fetched."

"Money and drugs make for outside-the-box narratives. Khai Le is immersed in that world. Who knows what could happen next if we don't get this shut down?"

"That's a big part of the problem right now," McGuire said. "We've given this too much time to unfold, in my view, but that's what the higher-ups wanted."

"It's not my place to say but seems like there's a disconnect when you start putting agencies together in these task forces."

"I wouldn't disagree. Regardless, I don't think we can afford to let it go on much longer. We need to take some people off the streets."

"Michael Shay?"

"He's on the list," McGuire said. "These people are going to turn on each other, try to cut a deal like they always do. I don't care if they're old friends or not. Every day we're finding out more about their network. It's all starting to crack."

"And maybe that's a reason to wait just a little longer."

"I'm still intrigued by Chapman. The guy was riding around with three hundred grand in cash, and enough weed to bring in another hundred. That was just one trip out of town."

"Out of *state*," Stafford said. "Big difference. It really adds up fast when you're doing business in places that don't have legal weed. And when you have an airplane …"

"People are out there just dying to get their hands on it. From the growers' standpoint, a million here and a million there and soon you're talking real money. These guys could have stayed under the radar, but they couldn't resist chasing the big bucks."

"How much longer?" Stafford said.

"I'll talk to our task force friends this afternoon. In the meantime, let's have a chat with Butch Fleenor."

"Khai Le's bodyguard?"

"Make a big show of it. That should draw some attention from his cohorts."

"He's been in the mix all along. Let's see whether he's feeling any heat."

CHAPTER 54

Big Butch seemed cool and collected when the agents brought him in. The former detective knew the drill. If he was feeling pressure to admit his role in any kind of murder plot, it didn't show.

McGuire was waiting in a conference room when Butch was led in. The big man took a seat and folded his arms while Stafford stepped outside. "You're interrupting my pleasant day," he said.

"Funny. Michael Shay said the same thing earlier," McGuire said.

"Michael Shay?"

"You don't know him? He was friends with Glen Chapman."

"Look, I didn't know Glen Chapman, either."

"You don't work for Khai Le?"

"No."

"Then clarify your role at Good Budz for us. Were you a security guard for the business, or a bodyguard for the owner? Or did you just hang out and test new strains?"

"I did whatever was needed. It was a caregiver business, and since the banks still turn their backs on those folks, there was a lot of cash floating around. All the dispensaries have security people around them; they have to. You know that."

"Apparently Good Budz has outgrown its mission as a caregiver, noble as that was. There's a lot more product moving under the table. Isn't that right, Mr. Fleenor?"

Butch smirked. "I don't know about that. How they conduct their business isn't my concern. I'm there to protect the proceeds and the product."

"You're still there? I thought you had quit."

"I'm no longer there in an official capacity."

"If we saw you riding in a car with Khai Le, say, this morning, that would just be a social occasion? Just two friends out for a ride in Michael Shay's parking lot?"

Butch shook his head and exhaled a deep breath.

Stafford knocked on the door and entered the room. She handed McGuire an envelope. The special agent pulled out the contents, looked it over for a minute, and slid it back in with a slight smile.

"You were there to protect Khai Le's interests?" he said.

"Mostly."

"And you'd go to great lengths to do so? Correct?"

"That was my job, but I didn't do anything illegal. It was mostly routine security."

"Of course. Would *murder* be routine?"

"I haven't murdered anyone. You're just fishing here."

"Looks like we may have hooked something. It was just brought to my attention that we have some new lab results in the death of Gina Simpson. DNA evidence from the scene." McGuire scanned the document again.

"I can tell you it's not good news for anyone who might have been close to Ms. Simpson in that car. How close were you, Butch?"

"No clue who she was. I do remember reading the name somewhere. Why would I be involved with her?"

"Maybe to cover up something else. Another murder perhaps?"

"I'm sure you're aware I understand the game you're playing here. I'm not going to play along. I've said all I'm going to say without counsel."

McGuire chuckled to himself. "As a former detective, you surely remember when something small would turn up and break a case wide open. Something out of left field."

Big Butch rolled his eyes. "What's your point?"

"How far would you go to protect your boss? If the evidence showed your involvement in a murder scheme, would you go down all alone? Or would you want everyone who was responsible to share in the guilt?"

"What are we talking about? I remember reading somewhere Gina Simpson killed herself."

"Did she?"

Butch declined to answer.

"What if I told you evidence had come to light that proves she was murdered? And what if I told you there was a match on a DNA sample that was found on her body?" McGuire asked. "Who do you suppose the killer is? Someone you know?"

The big man began to wring his hands. The steely resolve was waning. The agent could see it on Butch's face.

"Let's start over," McGuire said. "Tell me how you came in contact with Ms. Simpson. And don't tell me you were looking for skydiving lessons."

Butch stared at the wall.

"You don't think Khai Le is just going to let you run free when you can incriminate him in this murder, do you? You're a marked man. I'm sure that would cross the mind of a former detective."

"Are you charging me with something? If you are, I want to call my attorney. If not, I'll be on my way."

"Just to be clear, we've been speaking to some other colleagues of Mr. Le. Seems like there are bad feelings running through the whole operation. A lot of these people don't seem to like each other anymore. Some of them don't like you, Butch."

"I've said all I'm going to say here."

"Okay. We'll just throw you back into the shark tank. You're free to go."

"Just like that?"

McGuire opened the door and extended his arm toward the hallway. Butch's shoulder brushed his as he walked past.

The agent smiled and tossed the envelope into the trash.

CHAPTER 55

The relative excitement of Rod Laver Arena seemed distant as Simon warmed up for his first-round match against Dominique Alfaro. There were a few hundred fans in the stands on the outer court. It was easy to hear the sneakers squeak and the sound of individual voices all around.

For all intents and purposes, the scene was a world away from the big stadium where the more glamorous battles would be waged over the fortnight, with almost fifteen thousand in attendance. *Keep winning and work your way into the limelight.* That's what every unseeded player was dreaming of.

Billy and Zander settled into their seats in the grandstands along the sideline, just behind Carter. The coach had arrived earlier with his game face firmly in place. He said little as he leaned forward in his dark sunglasses and watched Simon's every move. The warm-up routine was always a tense time for coaches, who were intimately connected to their player yet powerless as they envisioned how a match would play out.

Billy felt the same way, but different thoughts were going through his mind. *Was Simon capable of putting it all aside? Could he forget his father and take care of the business at hand?* There was no way to know.

Zander hovered over Carter's shoulder and whispered, "Waddya think, coach?" Carter nodded, which was a good sign, but said nothing.

Zander leaned back again. "I can't believe we're here," he said to Billy. "We're actually sitting here together on the other side of the world getting ready to watch a damn tennis match. That never would have occurred to me when I was growing up in Jonesborough. I'm not sure which I knew less about — Australia or tennis."

Billy laughed, but his nerves were jangled. There was a certain kind of anxiety whenever he watched clients perform; didn't matter what the venue was. It was as if the outcome partially reflected on him professionally.

This time he felt more of a burden on his shoulders. He feared the worst.

The first swing of the match was encouraging. Simon blasted a serve that caught the line for an ace. The teenager's demeanor and energy impressed Billy. He seemed loose. There was something liberating about it.

Simon went on to win the first game, and his serve wasn't seriously challenged in the entire opening set. When he closed it out, 6-4, he jogged to his seat with confidence.

One set in the bank, two more to go.

"I like what I'm seeing," Zander said. "It's everything we imagined with this kid. He's got plenty of game."

"Long way to go," Billy said. "I'd expect Alfaro to dig in."

The Spaniard began to show his veteran savvy in the second set, moving out to an early lead that allowed him to even the match. But the youngster was not to be denied.

Using an attacking style that took Alfaro by surprise, he reeled off eight of the next ten games to seize control. The 6-4, 4-6, 6-3, 6-2 victory would raise a few eyebrows around the complex and beyond.

The fans, perhaps short on numbers but not enthusiasm, hailed Simon with a rousing ovation as he walked to the middle of the court. He acknowledged them with short bows and his racquet held high. The first big test had been passed with typical flair.

Carter was standing with a broad smile. He turned and shook hands with the men behind him. "What did I tell you?" he asked.

"Nicely done," Billy said. "He was well prepared."

"I'm going down. We'll catch up to you gentlemen later. There's more work to do."

"Absolutely. Give him our best."

Billy and Zander sat back down to digest what they had seen. The agent was feeling relief mostly. Simon had been mentally tough enough to win his first match in a major championship.

"That was great," Zander said. "My only regret is that his father wasn't here to see it. Michael should be here."

"Yes, he should." Billy left it at that.

"Want to get some lunch?"

"It's lunchtime? I can barely figure out what day it is."

"I thought we might go for a drive down Great Ocean Road, if you're up for it."

"Great Ocean Road. I like the sound of that."

"May take an hour or so each way. Darren said the scenery is spectacular. We'll stop and eat somewhere interesting."

"How are we getting there?"

"You'll see."

CHAPTER 56

Billy could only stop and stare when he walked out the door at Crown Cove and saw the Bentley Continental GT waiting at the valet stand. "We're taking a pink convertible?" he asked. "Wow!"

"Rose quartz, actually," Zander said. "I think it works on this car." He walked to the front and admired the classic lines. "It's like a flawless diamond. I've always wanted to drive a Bentley."

"I don't guess it ever occurred to me."

The valet opened both doors and the men slid in gingerly, like they were afraid they might soil the cream-colored leather interior with the contrast stitching and seat piping.

"I'd be afraid to know what this costs," Billy said.

"Two-twenty-*ish*, but who's counting? Not as bad if you rent by the day. I thought a couple of Tennessee boys should see the south of Australia in style. Might be a long ride if we go slow, and we want to be comfortable. Hope you don't mind."

Billy's eyes sparkled. "Go as slow as you like, my friend. I believe I could sit in this seat for the rest of my life." He laid his head back and chuckled. "This is theater of the absurd."

"Ain't it, though?"

"You've been in a very good mood since you got here."

"It got better this morning," Zander said. "Seeing Simon play like that made the long flight worth it. Now we can just cheer on our man and enjoy ourselves."

"Sounds like you're saying it's all gravy now."

"No, I'm not. I just think we finally got a glimpse of what Simon is capable of — winning at majors. He played a helluva match against a good opponent. He can win again – keep going. I really believe it now."

"It's going to take more to beat Laskaris. The crowd will be bigger — and a lot more involved in the match."

Neval "Wild Thing" Laskaris was a native son Down Under, known by tennis fans as much for his colorful antics during matches as his considerable talent. The contest was scheduled for Margaret Court Arena, which seated more than seven thousand fans and was one of the three venues at the complex with retractable roofs. It would likely be packed.

Another upset and Simon might find himself playing in Laver Arena.

Zander slipped on his sunglasses and started the engine. The Bentley barely made a sound. The men looked at each other and smiled, and Zander eased down the drive.

For a minute or two, Billy almost forgot about Michael Shay. He couldn't be sure about what Simon had said — that his father was involved with drug traffickers — but he knew Zander needed to know. Soon.

"What a day," Zander said. "All we need now is a couple of beautiful Aussie women to enjoy the ride with us. Perhaps Miranda Kerr and Margot Robbie. I should have called."

"You *almost* thought of everything."

"It's a shame Claire couldn't make the trip."

"*Claire?* I'm sure she would have been glad to come. Someone had to mind the store."

Billy held up his phone. "Why don't we give her a call," he said. "Maybe she's eating breakfast."

"At four in the morning? I'm pretty sure she's asleep."

"Okay, we'll try her on the way back. Funny that you'd bring her up."

"I'll be honest with you; I wouldn't mind spending some time with Claire. She's special, and I don't have anyone special right now."

"Normally, I'd say you might have to stand in line. But she likes you. Just remember that I don't want her too distracted. It's hard to say where her head is right now anyway."

"Because of her musician friend?"

"Musician *client*. Because of him and everything else. She has a lot going on in her life."

"Rightly so. Smart and beautiful women should be busy. And successful."

Zander opened up the throttle, pushing the men back in their seats a bit. The wind whipped their hair, and everything seemed perfect. It could have been fresh out of a Bentley commercial.

"Slow is good, but fast is good, too," Billy said.

"Twelve cylinders, baby. Sounds different now, doesn't it? Six hundred horsepower."

"And dripping with British sophistication, even though it's a Volkswagen subsidiary. Where did you come up with this anyway?"

"Had a little talk with the dealer in Melbourne. Told him we wanted to go for a drive, and we got to be fast friends. This is actually his personal demo car."

"That East Tennessee charm pays off again?"

"Of course."

"Where are we going?"

"Down to Torquay. It's about an hour's drive and is supposed to have some of the best surf beaches in the country. Great scenery, they say. There's a town called Lorne where we can get some fish and chips on the beach. I don't know if we'll make it all the way to Apollo Beach … we'll see how we feel. No rush."

"No rush indeed. Sounds like you've done your homework."

"Surprised?"

"No."

***

The scenery lived up to the billing, and so did the battered hoki and fries. The men were content as they walked back up the beach to the car. They decided to skip Apollo Beach and just enjoy the setting sun on the ride back to Melbourne.

But first, Billy had something to get off his chest. He stopped on the sidewalk. "We need to talk about Michael Shay," he said.

"That came out of left field. What about Michael?"

"I have some concerns about him."

"So, do I. He passed up a chance to be here, after everything it took to get to this point. Something has to be wrong."

"Legal troubles?"

Zander frowned. "Why would you think that?"

"I don't know … just seemed like it would take something extraordinary to keep him away."

"What kind of legal troubles?"

"Let me withdraw the question, your honor. No need to be a buzzkill. It's been a great day."

"Unless it's life or death, let's talk about Michael later."

Billy was already questioning himself for bringing it up. He said he wouldn't as long as Simon was still alive in the tournament.

"It's not life or death," he said with a smile, and started walking again. Zander followed without another word on the subject.

When they reached the Bentley, Zander quickly went around to the passenger side and smiled. "All yours, mate," he said.

"You gotta be kidding. Something tells me I wouldn't be covered, especially after drinking a couple of Boags down on the beach."

"Then you better not mess it up."

Billy had to admit that rose quartz never looked better. "What the hell. No guts, no glory, right?" He shook his head and settled in behind the wheel.

"Wait," Zander said. He stopped a young man who was about to pass them on the sidewalk. "Would you mind taking a picture of my friend and me in this high-dollar Volkswagen?" he said, holding up his camera. The man gladly complied.

"That's one for the archives," Zander said as he strapped himself in. "The only thing I ask now is that you sync up your phone with the Bluetooth, or whatever the hell it is, and give your partner a call. I suddenly feel like we need a woman's voice in the conversation. It's early morning there, right?"

"Right. She's an early riser." Billy quickly went through the prompts. "Calling Claire."

CHAPTER 57

I f Simon's first performance at the Australian Open was a ballet, a graceful display of the youngster's power and athleticism, the second was sure to be a heavy-metal concert. All the seventy-five-hundred seats in Margaret Court Arena would be filled, and the partisans who fueled Neval Laskaris and his theatrical brand of tennis would be in full throat. They always came prepared for a rowdy slugfest.

But Laskaris, who had just turned twenty-four, was more than a brand. He was an ever-present source of conversation in Australia, one of tennis's bad boys, who was quick to weigh in on matters large and small. He believed that any publicity was good publicity.

Most recently, just days before the Open began, Wild Thing suggested on Twitter he'd fight any of his colleagues in a boxing match and was soliciting potential opponents from the public. That drew the usual chorus of responses; most either wondered why his mind wasn't on tennis, or thought he was an idiot. The others simply laughed.

The son of a Greek father and Malaysian mother, who had each immigrated to Australia in their twenties, Laskaris was a must watch. He was dark and dashing, and his talents were unquestioned. He had won six times on tour to steadily move up the world rankings and was now inside the top forty — a threat to win any time he took the court. Few doubted that he had the game to one day become a major champion if he could control his emotions.

In that regard, he was a lot like Simon.

Billy hadn't seen much of his client since the opening-round victory. He knew the tension that was just below the surface, and it was best to leave it there. Rehashing the looming situation at home would only make matters worse for everyone.

This was one of those times when Billy had no firm plan of action. He decided to let things be.

Darren Carter always had a plan, and one of his major assets as a coach was keeping players calm and focused. It's what drew Team Shay to him in the first place. The one thing that worried him about Laskaris was that he thrived on chaos. Few players in the sport — perhaps none — were willing to go as far in their behavior to intimidate an opponent, chair umpire, or any other officials in the way. The unpredictability made it hard to devise a strategy to combat him. The more unruly the scene, the better for him.

Simon could create a bit of chaos himself, but he didn't thrive on it. In fact, when he got way out of line, it was his undoing more often than not. Today he needed to pull back, embrace the villain's role against the home-town hero, and stay cool. Simple as that.

"How do you feel?" Zander was taking Carter's temperature again, and there was no nod this time. The coach looked back over his shoulder with a puzzled expression.

"Not sure," he said. "This one worries me. I couldn't get a good read on Simon this morning, and I can't right now either. It'll be tough."

When the player was distracted on the court, Carter could usually tell early. The mindset wasn't right. Frustration tended to set in before long.

A few minutes into the match against Laskaris, the coach didn't like what he was seeing. Simon had hit a weak shot into the net, sailed another one well past the baseline, and then double faulted to lose his serve in the first game.

The fans were already excited, and with the noise building, Laskaris took the first set 6-2. He had the early momentum. Carter had dreaded that development the most but fought not to show it. He wanted Simon to see confidence on his face when he looked up at the player's box.

Instead of wilting under pressure, Simon suddenly found his mojo and took the fight to the favorite. His aggressive style paid off in three straight games and gave him the second set 6-3.

The chirping from Laskaris had already begun. He swatted away balls after mistakes and banged his racquet head on the Greenset surface. He chided ball boys who were slow with a towel between points.

Laskaris knew he was in for a fight, and that he'd be on the court for a while. If he won today, he'd have to earn it. He'd also have to come from behind.

Simon won the thrilling third set with a forehand tracer down the line — his trademark shot — in the tie-break. The 7-6 win left Laskaris flogging the net with his racquet in frustration and pulled Simon to the brink of a signature victory. Take one more set from the Aussie and he'd move into the third round. More significantly, perhaps, Simon would be in the tournament conversation the world over.

But Laskaris was more than a showman. With fans roaring at every opportunity, he summoned all his skills in the fourth set and surged to a 6-1 win that recharged the crowd. The match was even, and he again had the momentum.

Everyone in Simon's box was standing, except for Carter. He was locked on his man like a laser, blocking out the noise, trying to connect with *that look*. He had gone out on a limb and said it was possible to get two wins in Melbourne. Whether he believed it or not, that goal was now in reach. But did Simon have the mental toughness? The tide was against him. *How much did he want it?*

CHAPTER 58

"**I** haven't been this jacked up in a while," Zander said, rubbing his hands together like a kid at the gates of the Magic Kingdom. "This is amazing."

"You're officially a sports fan now?" Billy asked.

"Absolutely."

Billy laughed. He had sweated through more emotionally charged sporting events than he could count, but the feeling never got old, especially when clients were front and center. Each contest, from a genteel round of golf to a mixed martial arts fight, had its own special rhythm and flavor. This one was no different. Everyone in Margaret Court Arena expected a thrilling finish.

The agent leaned in close to his friend. "Think he's going to pull it out?" Zander was still rubbing his hands nervously. "Hell yes," he said. "I'm a positive thinker."

"I've always liked that about you."

The next few games were a dazzling display of skill and intensity. Both players were completely dialed in, and the crowd was riveted by the action. There was no more gamesmanship on the part of Laskaris, whose countrymen were desperately urging him to the finish line. It was all about digging deep and finding a way to win.

By the time he took a 4-3 lead in the set, Simon had obviously won over a decent-sized chunk of the crowd. Many had probably never heard of the kid from Colorado before, but after more than three hours on the court, they appreciated his tenacity, the way he was battling for every point. They respected him.

The players were forced to go deep into their offensive arsenals, and each held serve through the set, until the score was tied at six games apiece. Most in the crowd stood and cheered as the players changed ends of the court for the tiebreaker. First one to ten points won the match.

As Simon stood at the baseline and inspected the new balls he was about to serve, he shot a confident nod and a smile at his coach. Carter turned around and passed it on to Billy and Zander. He had shown little outward emotion to that point, but he seemed to know something now.

"He's gonna do it, mates," he said.

Sure enough, Simon ripped an ace on his first serve and pumped his fist. He never looked back.

A couple of unforced errors by Laskaris left the underdog with a commanding five-point lead, and the Wild Thing began to come unglued. He argued with the umpire over a line call — the electronic challenge showed it was correct — barked again at the poor ball boy and stomped around like a player who knew he was in serious trouble.

The end came when Simon raced to the net on a weak return and knocked off the volley, just the way his coach had drilled into his head for the last several months.

The men in his box sprang to their feet in jubilation. Everyone looked exhausted after five sets of drama over the course of four hours. "I told you," Carter yelled. "I *told* you."

"I told *you*," Zander said, pointing back at him.

Simon walked to the net for the customary hand-shake, but Laskaris had already headed off toward his chair. Completely spent, he took a seat with a towel draped over his head.

The match was undoubtedly one of the best in the tournament so far, and it kept alive the dreams of an American teenager. He was moving on to the third round.

"Survive and advance, baby," Billy said as he remained on his feet. "That's what it's all about."

Simon flashed a thumbs-up at Team Shay, shook hands with the umpire, and pivoted back to the middle of the court, a radiant smile on his face as he saluted the crowd. There was little doubt now: *Simon wanted it bad.*

Regardless of what happened next, the young American had accomplished what he came to Australia to do. He had made a mark.

The men hurried down the aisle from the player's box to the railing, and Simon came over to shake their hands. "We did it," he said, still trying to understand what he'd done. "We did it."

Billy loved to savor the fleeting moments of cama-raderie. He understood what went into reaching a point where everything comes together at just the right time. That's when all the hours of work, the prodding, and the consternation were in clear focus. All the off-the-court distractions didn't matter.

The experience could be transformational for an up-and-comer like Simon, even if there was still plenty of work in Melbourne left to do.

The dazed winner went back to his chair and began to collect his gear. Carter made his way to the lower level while Billy and Zander stood and watched the crowd disperse. They were in no hurry to go anywhere.

"I'm drained," Zander said. "I feel like I was the one out there for four hours."

On the other side of the arena, Billy noticed a man as he stopped briefly to soak up the last of the atmosphere. Wearing a white baseball cap and sunglasses, with a credential of some sort dangling from a lanyard around his neck, he resumed the slow walk past the players' entrance. He finally split off from the small group and turned the corner.

Michael Shay.

"Let's go celebrate with a beverage and think about dinner," Zander said, easing into the aisle. "May have to try that barramundi tonight."

Billy didn't respond. He was still looking across the way at the rush of patrons.

"Ready to go?" Zander asked.

Billy nodded and followed his friend out.

CHAPTER 59

The lead had started with a serial number on the wing assembly. It matched one that had been listed on another manifest.

The same part that was shipped on the AAF truck from Aurora to Detroit — the truck on which J.T. McClanahan was murdered — was making the return trip to Colorado. *Why?*

That's what Franklin Beckett had wondered when he last communicated with authorities. *Why would a specialty airplane part — and a large one at that — come back to the plant where it was manufactured, just a few days later? And why would it have been shipped under a different company's name?* Franklin always had a keen eye for small details.

The Denver detectives had plenty of questions when they arrived at the Airflex plant off Interstate 70. They were directed to the plant manager, a man named Rick Weston, who was in the warehouse talking to a line worker as they approached. The lead detective, Mike Rollins, stepped forward and flashed his badge.

"We'd like to ask you some questions if we could," Rollins said.

"Sure," Weston said with no apparent alarm. He patted his employee on the back and motioned the men toward the nearest exit. "In my office."

Rollins and his partner followed him out of the warehouse and across the parking lot. They walked to the rear of the small administrative building and remained standing as Weston closed the door to his office.

"What can I help you with?" he said.

"We're investigating a murder that occurred a few weeks back," Rollins said. "It involved a trucking company with ties here in the area. One of their drivers was killed on his truck in Missouri after leaving Aurora with a shipment."

"I'm sorry, I didn't hear about it. What's the connection to us?"

"The driver's name was J.T. McClanahan. Does that ring a bell?"

The manager narrowed his eyes and thought for a second. "I can't say that it does. Should I know him?"

"He apparently worked here a while back. We're just trying to run down possible leads in the case."

"I've only been here for a year, but I can ask someone in personnel to look into it. Do you know how long ago he supposedly worked here?"

"Not exactly. It just came up when we took a closer look at this gentleman and his work history. There was also another issue regarding Airflex that we need to explore."

"Okay. I'll try to answer any questions you've got."

"The truck that Mr. McClanahan was on that day was hauling a full load out of Aurora, all sorts of cargo.

One item on the manifest was a large airplane part, a wing assembly that was fabricated here. It ended up being delivered later to its destination in Michigan, which I don't guess is unusual. You have customers in that area?"

"Sure. Lots of them."

"We noticed that the same part was shipped back to Airflex on another AAF truck. Would that be unusual?"

"Not unusual that AAF would be transporting. We use that line regularly. You're saying it was the identical part?"

"Same serial number on the manifests."

"Do you have the number?"

The detective's partner handed him a case folder, and Rollins thumbed through it. "Here it is."

"Let me walk into the office and see what I can find out. If you'll just wait here, shouldn't take long. I'll also check about the driver you mentioned. What was his name again?"

"McClanahan. James Thomas McClanahan."

"I'll be right back," Weston said.

The detectives looked around and could count at least two dozen workers involved in a variety of projects. Airflex had built a niche specializing in the restoration, maintenance and rebuilding of vintage World War II aircraft. The restoration of a P-51C Thunderbird was currently in progress on the shop floor.

Rollins' partner, Bobby Shirley, turned to him and raised his eyebrows. "Never knew a place like this existed in the area," he said. "Pretty cool."

"Quite an operation. For their sake, I hope everything is on the up-and-up."

Weston returned with a couple of papers rolled up in his hand. "Looks like Mr. McClanahan did work for us a few years back," he said. "He was a riveter. I pulled his personnel record. Nothing unusual about it, and he wasn't here very long."

"Would he have had an intimate feel for the products here?"

"Certainly. It's very hands-on work."

"What about the serial number?" Rollins said.

"That was a wing assembly, as we discussed, for a customer outside Detroit. Not sure why you'd have a duplicate serial number, or even why that part would be returned. We shipped the assembly two years ago. That's the last we ever heard about it."

"You didn't get it back?"

"There wouldn't have been any reason for that, unless it had some defect I'm unaware of. I'm sure it would have come to the manager's attention at that time."

"Was there anything special about that part?"

"They're all special, of course, if you need them. But this was just the outer wing for an Ilyushin; it's an old Soviet plane that was the most produced combat aircraft in WW2. It was an unusual request but a very simple job for us. There was no joint assembly, plumbing accessories or any of that. The customer would have installed all of that themselves. Or they could have just been creating a model plane."

"It was basically a big, hollow piece of metal? A shell?"

"Yes, and fairly light for its size."

"Would it be easy to access the inside?"

"The way it was constructed, sure. I don't know what the customer had in mind. They wired us money, and we got everything in and out in short order. According to our records, that's the only time we've ever done business with them. Icarus Ventures of Mount Clemens."

"So that's the name on your invoice?"

"That's it. I don't know where you're going with your investigation, but I suppose you've spoken to Icarus. Did they say they shipped it back?"

"There actually is no Icarus Ventures in the Detroit area, or anywhere else we can find. We don't know what happened to this part. We're looking for it now."

"I don't know what to tell you. Something like that obviously wouldn't be of any use to most people. If you don't have an old Soviet airplane, you don't need a wing assembly like that."

"At least *that* makes sense."

The detectives thanked the plant manager for his time and began to walk back to their car. Rollins, the older man of the two, couldn't help but chuckle.

"Wasn't Icarus the guy who flew too close to the sun?" he said. "He got too ballsy and crashed. Maybe there's a lesson there."

CHAPTER 60

D etective Shirley sat back in the passenger seat and loosened his tie. "Does this wing thing make any sense to you?" he said.

"There's only one theory that adds up. Someone was using it to smuggle something on these trucks. You could get quite a few pounds of weed in there. If it's powder or pills, then you've got a real payoff."

"Yeah, but why an airplane wing? It's big and bulky. Why not boxes of fake fruit, or tortillas, or frozen fish, or any of the other crazy things we hear about every day?"

"Maybe our smugglers are aficionados of vintage aircraft," Rollins said. "Who would think to open up an airplane wing that's framed for transport and check for drugs inside? I mean, it wouldn't be crossing international borders."

"You have to say it's an original idea. Most of these drug traffickers aren't exactly geniuses, but some of them are damn clever. They're always thinking up something new."

"All I know is that we've done our duty for the day, and we'll pass along the info. The DEA is involved, so there's somebody up the chain that's very interested in airplane wings. Maybe it's a new trend."

"What about this guy that was killed, the driver? There has to be a connection to Airflex since he did work there once."

"He certainly had a familiarity with old airplanes, and he must have known something else that was valuable," Rollins said. "Sounds like he knew too much. Why else would he be shot in the back of the head like that?"

"And that just raises the question of whether this was an inside job. All I know is that when you start mixing drugs and guns, bad things tend to follow. That's at the root of so much that we have to deal with."

The detectives were quiet for a few minutes as Rollins drove them back into town. They were still trying to connect the dots, and they usually worked well together.

"You remember the last briefing we had about this guy, Khai Le?" Rollins said. "He's the ringleader of this group that's been trying to expand its operation out of state. What was the name of it? *Good Budz?*"

"Yeah, I remember. Catchy. It's getting hard to keep up with all the black-market stuff in Colorado, but it sounded like these good buds are close to busted."

"I'm not sure, because we're only getting bits and pieces from DEA, but I believe this thing we're chasing today may be tied to them."

"What do we know about Khai Le?" Shirley asked.

"I spent some time looking at the file earlier. He came to the States from Vietnam when he was a boy. Grew up in Denver and got into the caregiver program a few years back. There's not really much that stands out."

"*Caregivers.* Sounds funny saying that now. It was always good money if you knew the right people, but we things are changing. It's stupid money now, whether you're inside legal channels or out."

"Khai Le wanted to be a bigger player, and that turned into a double-edged sword. Now he has to watch his back twenty-four, seven."

"According to the briefing, Butch Fleenor is working for him, right? You remember the big man?"

"I remember," Rollins said. "Fired from the department for … what was it?"

"I believe Big Butch was shaking down some of the growhouse operators, back when financing was looser than a goose."

"It's still like the wild West out there. Ironic that he'd be on the other side of the line now."

"All I know is that there comes a time for all these guys. It usually doesn't end pretty."

Rollins exited off I-70 onto West Colfax Avenue toward downtown. "The question," he said, "is whether there's more than meets the eye."

"What do you mean?"

"Somebody has gone to a lot of trouble to get this big airplane part fabricated and ship it around. The payoff must be lucrative. Is it just marijuana that we're talking about? Or something more?"

Rollins turned onto Cherokee Street and drove south. The Denver Police Department facilities took up the entire block between West 13th and 14th avenues. He pulled into the designated parking spot, and the detective exited the car.

"I get a feeling we're about to find out," Shirley said.

CHAPTER 61

Khai Le kept a low profile in an upper-middle-class neighborhood on the outskirts of Denver, a single man who rarely had company. So, he was surprised to peek through the blinds and see Devin Walton.

Khai couldn't remember anyone associated with his organization, other than his sister, ever just dropping by unannounced. He didn't often interact with Walton. The budtender at the growhouse, nicknamed "Wiz" for the depth of his knowledge about cannabis products and state legislation, was just standing there on the porch.

Khai cracked the door slightly and looked around nervously. "What are you doing here, Wiz?"

"I'm sorry to just stop by like this, but I wanted to tell you that I'm leaving town," Walton said. "Some federal agents came by my apartment about dawn this morning. They had a lot of questions."

"About what?"

"About you. About our managers. About Butch. Everything."

Khai opened the door a little wider. "What did you tell them?"

"I don't think I said anything that would be a huge problem, but I know some others have been contacted, too. It's not much of a secret anymore that the business has come under serious scrutiny. Looks like we're going to be shut down soon."

"You're leaving town?"

"I don't want to be in the middle of any of this, so I'm moving home to Wyoming. I'm just a little man in this, anyway. I'll hang out with my folks for a while. I'm already packed up."

Khai glanced around suspiciously. "Why are you telling me this, Wiz?"

"I thought you should know, and just wanted to say thanks for the opportunity here. It was fun for a while. We had a good run — developed some amazing strains. The product is expanding everywhere."

"You say that some others have been talking to authorities. What more can you tell me?"

"Not much. There are just a lot of rumors out there. I was surprised to hear that people I thought I knew and trusted might be willing to blow up the whole thing. I guess it's what you'd call a cautionary tale."

Khai tried to muster a smile. "I appreciate you coming to talk with me. Good luck."

Walton started toward the driveway, but he stopped and turned around.

"One last thing, Khai," he said. "You really need to watch Butch. I'm not sure he has your back anymore."

Khai closed the door and immediately went for his phone. If he wasn't rattled enough, the news from a lower-level employee was another telltale sign. Time was running out.

"Butch, it's me," he said. "I've got something we need to take care of."

CHAPTER 62

The player who stood across the net from Tomas Buzek looked a lot like Simon Shay, except for the body language. The young man was slumping, literally and figuratively. The electric atmosphere of two days earlier had disappeared.

Buzek, a rail-thin Czech coming off two impressive wins himself, already was serving for a two-set lead in their third-round match. If Simon were to prevail again, it would take an epic comeback that would extend the match a couple more hours. There was nothing to suggest that was about to happen.

Buzek reeled off four straight points to easily capture the second set, prompting a smattering of cheers and groans. Team Shay sat quietly in the player's box. They all knew that getting to the second week of the tournament was going to be a stiff challenge — a much different challenge than defeating Neval Laskaris on his home turf. But that match had given them hope. Now their man was flailing like a rookie overwhelmed by the moment.

"I need to take a walk," Billy muttered.

Zander nodded glumly. "Go ahead. I'll be right here with the same blank stare on my face."

They both knew the eyes of countless tennis fans were on them, and they had to act accordingly. That was one of the cardinal rules of sitting in a player's box: Never let your depression show when the chips were down, especially on television.

Darren Carter was fidgeting and trying hard to contain his frustration. He would have walked away for a respite himself but knew the message it would send on a tough day. A coach was supposed to sit and suffer with the player, stroke by stroke, right to the bitter end.

Billy felt no such constraints. He often got up and took a walk when things weren't going well for a client, or a client's team, hoping his absence might somehow swing the momentum the other way. Sometimes it did. There was nothing else he could do to help anyway.

The agent walked into the concourse at Rod Laver Arena and took in the scene. The building's retractable roof had been closed for the afternoon matches when temperatures soared into triple digits. That changed the feel of the place and usually meant more noise inside. But the crowd was subdued.

Billy knew today was a missed opportunity for his client. Every time an unseeded player stepped on the court at a major, there was something to be gained. After earning his place on the biggest stage, Simon was about to go out in straight sets with little fanfare.

"How bad does it look?" Billy asked quietly. The response was coming from almost ten thousand miles away. Claire was eating breakfast in Knoxville as she watched the action on her laptop.

"Not terrible," she said. "Just not the same player today. Seems like Simon's energy level is way down. Is he all right?"

"I don't think he's hurt or sick. The biggest problem is that he's just getting his ass kicked by this guy we didn't know much about. He seemed a little distracted this morning and looks like it carried into the match. Maybe he can rally here and at least win a set."

"Well, it's been a good run for him. He's nineteen, and he'll learn from it."

"Words of wisdom from far away. I knew I could count on you, Claire. What's the score now?"

"Lost the first two games of the set. Doesn't look like the rally is happening."

"Then let's change the subject. Anything new and exciting back there that I need to know about?"

"Not much beyond what we've been discussing every day, except I had an interesting conversation with Holly. We spoke for a little while last night. She had some questions."

That got Billy's attention. He hadn't thought much about his favorite golfer lately. In fact, he hadn't thought about her since he left the States.

"Questions about what?"

"Business stuff mostly. On second thought, I'll just wait until you get back."

"Don't leave me hanging."

"No, it's okay. I'll just report that Holly did say her rehab was going well. She's starting a regimen of golf-specific exercises, so maybe she'll be hitting balls sooner than you thought."

"That's good to hear," Billy said. "The sooner she's standing on the driving range with a club in her hands again, the better. Guess her doctor — *Britt* — is making her feel better. They're probably spending a lot of time together."

"Am I detecting jealousy?"

"Maybe."

"By the way, how is Zander?"

"He was fine, until this match. It's a tough job, being a fan."

"Yeah, tough job watching tennis and riding around Australia in a Bentley. I wish I was there suffering like that with you guys."

"Funny that you want to be *here*, and I suddenly feel like I need to be *there*. This has been a guilt trip, for sure, but I guess it's worth it, for Simon's sake. I appreciate you keeping me posted on everything while I'm gone."

"You're welcome. And you owe me."

"That always seems to be the case. Same with Zander. You know, you two need to get together and talk when we get back."

Whatever brought that on seemed to surprise Claire. "Okay … if you say so."

"What's the score now?"

"I think you can start packing your bags, Billy boy. Listen, I've got another call coming in that I need to take. C'mon home, mate."

"Thanks, Claire. See you soon."

Billy disconnected the call with a grimace. He needed to get back inside for the finish. These were tough times for an agent to stomach — watching clients flame out at the end. But outwardly he would be cool, calm and collected. He'd try to manage the damage like he always did, accentuating the positive and moving forward with a smile.

Inside, his gut was churning. Simon faced challenges in his life that could easily undermine his career. They would have to be confronted soon, and no agent could be certain of the outcome.

Billy walked back into the arena just as Buzek took a 4-0 lead, all but cementing the inevitable outcome. Zander's blank stare was still firmly in place.

They clapped as Simon held his serve to avoid being shut out in the set, for what that was worth. But he soon found himself waiting at the net to shake Buzek's hand. His first Grand Slam appearance was over.

CHAPTER 63

There wasn't much said on the short ride back to Crown Melbourne. Simon was sitting in the back-seat of the courtesy car, with Billy beside him. Carter was behind the wheel.

In his usual fashion, Zander was trying to be upbeat. "First time here, you did a helluva job, Simon," he said over his shoulder. "You made us all proud. I'm already looking forward to coming back and watching you win a championship someday."

"I played like shit," Simon said softly. "No getting around it."

"He didn't play that bad, did he, Darren?"

"You didn't exactly follow the script," Carter said, trying to be tactful. "But you got behind early, and Buzek was tough. Gotta give him credit; he's better than we knew going in. He'll be trouble in the next round, too."

"Well, let's look on the bright side," Zander said. "We could be in worse places, and now you're free to enjoy yourself. Anything you want to do here before heading home?"

Enjoy yourself. Simon scoffed at that notion. "No, I'm ready to go back. The sooner, the better. I think I'm just going to lay down for now."

Billy was unusually quiet as the conversation continued. He had learned to be measured with clients while they digested losses. Some took losing harder than others, especially when they didn't give their best effort.

Simon would be a better player for the experience here, but his immediate path forward was going to be difficult. They both knew it.

As Carter stopped the car near the valet stand at Crown Melbourne, Billy spoke up. "Darren, would you mind giving us a few minutes alone to talk with Simon?"

"Not at all. I have some business to attend to before we clear out of here. I'll be along in a bit."

"Thank you."

The men strolled quietly past the bustling casino and caught an elevator up to the player's suite. Simon still seemed deflated as they went in.

"Don't be too hard on yourself," Zander said, leaning on the bar. "You just lost a tennis match. It's not a funeral. No one died."

The expression on Billy's face suggested otherwise. "Zander isn't aware of some things going on," he said.

"What are you talking about? Someone *did* die?"

Billy held up a hand. "Let me ask you a question, Simon. Am I crazy, or did I see your father standing across the arena from us the other day?"

Simon swallowed hard and then exhaled a deep breath. "It was him."

Zander stood up with a puzzled look. "Michael is *here*? Why didn't you say something, Billy?"

"I told Simon I wouldn't."

"I don't get it. Michael comes all the way over here on his own — after I offered to bring him — and then hides out? He doesn't want us to know he's here. *Why?*"

Zander cocked his head and stared at Simon, who turned away. "Simon?"

"He has some things going on back home," Simon said. "I really don't want to get into it now."

"You know that's not going to fly. Lay it out for me. Right now."

Simon dropped heavily onto the couch. He had thought about what he would say to Zander when the time came, but now he couldn't find the right words.

"Did you talk to him before your match today?" Billy asked.

"I told him not to come. He was gonna try to catch a flight home. He's probably on his way back right now."

"That explains it."

"Explains *what?*"

"Your performance. You looked distracted from the start, and now we know why."

"Okay," Zander said, "let's hear it. If Simon can't tell me, I want to hear it from his agent."

Billy nodded and took a deep breath. "What Simon is struggling to tell you is that his father has apparently been involved with some shady people back in Colorado." He took another deep breath. "Drug traffickers."

"What? *Michael?* I can't believe that."

"They've been threatening him," Simon said. "That's what he told me this morning."

"This is blowing my mind. Why would he lay that on you here, on the biggest day of your career?"

"I pulled it out of him. He's rattled. I haven't seen him like that."

"You've known about this?" Zander asked.

"I first found out about it a little while back. He said he was looking for a way to end it. He wasn't going to help them anymore."

"Help them how?"

Simon hesitated again. "With the shipments."

Suddenly it dawned on Zander. "On *my* trucks? *My damn company's trucks?*"

The room went silent. Zander's anger started to build. "Michael is running drugs on my shipping line, and you kept this from me, Billy? You're my best friend, but you said nothing about it?"

"I wasn't going to say anything as long as Simon was still alive in the tournament. I promised him that, even though I started into a conversation with you about it the other day and then dropped it. I know that sounds like bullshit, but I didn't see any benefit for anybody. It's been grinding on me."

"So, here we are," Zander said. The disgust was apparent as he picked up his phone and tapped the screen. "But not for long. I'm catching the next flight out. You guys are on your own."

CHAPTER 64

The dark-haired woman moved briskly down the hallway, wrapped in a long, stylish white coat over brown leggings and snow boots. She still had her sunglasses on when she reached the open door of the special agent's office.

"Sean McGuire?" she asked.

"That's right."

"I called earlier. I'm Jeri Mathis — Glen Chapman's ex-wife."

McGuire perked up. "Yes. Come in, please."

Jeri perched the glasses on top of her head and offered a pained smile before taking a seat in front of the agent. She placed the large yellow envelope she was carrying on the desk.

McGuire got up to close the door. "Anything to drink?" he asked. She shook her head.

"You said you have something to show me regarding your late husband? Or ex-husband."

"This was sent to me shortly after Glen's death," she said, keeping a hand on top of the envelope.

"I'm sorry for your loss."

"Thank you, but Glen and I had long since run our course. I'm still receiving a lot of documents, insurance papers and things like that. Glen had some policies and never took me off as beneficiary; I guess he felt like he owed me."

"And so …" McGuire said.

"And so, I was tossing these things I was getting in the mail into a box. It was just hard to deal with at that moment in time … everything was too fresh in my mind. Glen and I had some fun years. There were always issues, but he was a good guy at heart, a brave guy. For him to die like he did … it was crazy, like something out of a horror movie."

"Did you know the woman?"

"No. I assume it was just another case of him getting involved with someone he shouldn't have. That happened a lot with Glen."

"Apparently so."

"You know, my parents helped him start his skydiving business. And it ended up killing him. I'll always feel guilty about that, but I don't know what I could have done. He loved everything about it — it set him free from some heavy emotional baggage — and we felt like we were helping him get back on his feet. Those times were the happiest he had ever been. Without that, he probably would have killed himself. I don't know if that would have been any easier to take, but we wouldn't be here now."

McGuire wasn't exactly sure where the conversation was headed. He wanted to get to the point, but Jeri was becoming more scattered by the minute. "What is it you're bringing me, Ms. Mathis?"

She pushed the envelope toward the agent. "He said he had been talking to you and wanted to clear the record. This spells it out, in his own words. I'm sorry I didn't see it sooner."

The letter was handwritten neatly in black ink on ten pages of notebook paper. McGuire donned his reading glasses and waded in.

Dearest Jeri, it began, *I feel like my life is in danger again. Only this time, it's my friends I have to worry about. If you receive this, you'll know I'm right. It may not matter now, but I loved you more than any woman I'd ever met. I could always count on you, and I guess that was part of our problem. You made it easy to take advantage. I'm sorry to burden you one last time.*

The letter went on to lay out in detail the infrastructure of Khai Le's business, the various roles people played, the regional connections with buyers, the growing aspirations of the organization, and the dark financial arrangements, right down to the ill-fated run to Texas that led to Chapman cooperating with authorities.

McGuire read with growing interest, and then went back and scanned it again. Finally, he jogged the papers together and tossed them on top of the envelope.

"What you have here is very interesting," he said. "I think it's going to be a huge help. I've heard bits and pieces of it before, but there's a lot of new ground covered. Places we haven't been. Glen led an eventful life, right to the end."

Chapman didn't spare anyone in the letter, not his oldest friends and acquaintances. Not even Michael Shay. His involvement was intertwined in the greater narrative with a cautionary note: *Forgive me, Michael. I told you this was like quicksand. Once you're sucked in, it's hard to get out. You should have been smarter than me.*

McGuire removed the readers and arched his eyebrows toward Jeri. "He's taking no prisoners from the grave," he said. "Does this sound like the Glen Chapman you knew?"

"I'm sure he wrote it when he was feeling down and just didn't give a damn. One thing about Glen – he was a paranoid guy. Between the drugs and the damage the military did to him … he just struggled to ever feel normal. There were lots of hard days where friendships were tested. I tried to help, but it took a toll, you know?" There was a faraway look in her eyes as she recalled their mercurial relationship. "Lots of good days, too. I loved Glen."

Jeri bit her lip and tried to keep from getting more emotional. The memories had been hard to reconcile since Chapman's death, and they only got more complicated when his letter came to light. But she had done what he asked, once again.

"When I first read this, I thought about just throwing it in the trash," she said. "It would have been easier that way."

"Why didn't you?"

"I'm not sure. This is going to hurt people, and I know a lot of them. Most were just old friends looking for a better life and trying to help each other. At least, that's the way it started."

"And they just got carried away, right? I mean, some of your friends are dead. Your ex-husband was killed just because of his involvement in the drug trade. People are starting to talk. That's the way it happens."

"You know that for a fact?"

"Let's just say that we have several cases laid out with ties to this organization. We're about to move forward. Glen has helped us fill in some blanks, a lot of blanks, thanks to you. *You* did the right thing."

CHAPTER 65

The white Chevy Tahoe eased to the pullover in a restricted area of Rocky Mountain National Park. Recent snowfall had made the climb more precarious, but it was still doable once they cut the lock on the gate. The signage made it clear: no visitors allowed this time of year.

It had been several weeks since Khai Le and Glen Chapman had come to the park to hide the duffel bags. Four had since been retrieved, but three others remained stashed away as the heat was turned up on the Good Budz operation. Khai Le was weighing his options. He had decided now was the time to take the money and run.

Khai was retracing the route, preparing to use a GPS tracking app on his iPhone once they got within range. Beside him, in the passenger seat, Big Butch was stone-faced. He had said little since they left Denver, except for a moment as they passed Steamboat Mountain north of Boulder.

"I thought you said we were going to Button Rock," Butch said. "That was the turn."

Khai shook his head. "No. Just a little farther up."

The old SUV slowed to a stop. There were no fresh tracks, so the rangers had yet to pass through on their rounds. But they likely would cover this ground before the day was out. The clock was ticking.

To get the money, the men would have to hike a short distance along a narrow, perilous trail that opened toward the distinctive profile of Sawtooth Mountain. It was a relatively obscure trail even in the warmer months.

Khai knew the drill; he had hiked there on more than one occasion. But Chapman had always been with him before. It was reassuring to have the ex-military man along in stressful situations. One thing about Chapman, he was fearless.

Now Khai was depending on his oversized bodyguard, who wasn't much of a hiker in the best of conditions. Butch, in fact, was taxed by any physical activity in the thin air of Colorado, and he would have to carry his weight, along with a couple of heavy bags, on this treacherous mission.

"Hold on," he said, bending over barely two minutes into the walk. "Let me catch my breath."

The boss stopped impatiently. He already had a good idea where he was going and was waiting for the tracker to lock on to the exact location. "Catch it fast," he said. "It's dangerous to even be back here this time of year. We're flirting with disaster every minute we're here. There's no time to waste."

"Remember, this was *your* idea. Like most everything else."

Their relationship had always been one of expedience more than friendship, and it had steadily frayed since the murder of Gina Simpson, to the point that Khai wondered how much longer Butch could be trusted. And that was before the warning from Devin Walton. If others had begun to turn on each other, it was only a matter of time before the Trust imploded. Then it would be every man for himself.

As the primary target, Khai had become accustomed to constantly looking over his shoulder. But he wasn't the only one. The authorities had begun searching for Butch soon after his interview at the DEA offices in Centennial. They were unraveling the mystery of Glen Chapman's death, and he had become a person of interest. It wasn't much of a leap from that to suspect.

Butch hadn't taken the bait when Sean McGuire intimated that DNA tests linked him to Gina. But hard evidence materialized, and he had to face tough choices. He could turn himself in, try to bargain for a plea deal that would send him to prison. Or he could go dark and run once he was able to finance his escape.

"Over here," Khai said. "It's easy to miss, but I remember. This way."

The spur split off from the trail, sending the men toward the bottom of a steep canyon strewn with boulders. Khai could hear the wheezing behind him, and he stopped and looked expectantly at his iPhone. The Tile app made the phone ring, signaling they were near their quarry; he smiled as the application honed in.

The black rubber duffels, three of them, had been wedged together in one of many crevices scattered between the large boulders. Smaller rocks were piled around to conceal them.

The men leaned in and started digging, and within a few minutes, they had freed the bags.

"Payday," Khai said.

Butch was breathing heavily again. "How much cash is here?"

"I don't know exactly. We just packed them full one night when business was booming and brought them up here. Glen knew the terrain well. Great to see them again."

"You had so much money laying around, you didn't even take time to count it? Damn."

Khai marveled at the thought. "Been a few years of that. Making money was never the problem but finding something to do with it was. Once we got the growhouse faucet turned on, it just kept running."

"Guess that's why we're here in the middle of nowhere on this treasure hunt. It finally stopped."

"At least we found our treasure, so there's a happy ending. You take two bags and I'll get the other one."

"Why do I have to take two?"

"Because you're being well-paid to do it. Glen carried four of these on the way in here. Two on each shoulder, and he wasn't even breathing hard. You're a big boy. Surely you can carry two."

"Keep this up, and you'll have to deal with all three yourself. And a three-hundred-fifty-pound corpse, too."

The men loaded up and started slowly making their way back toward the road. Khai Le was fairly certain by now that this would be the last time he'd see Butch. He got more certain by the minute.

By the time they reached the SUV, the big man was exhausted and angry. It had been a tough slog, and he was growling the whole way. The snowfall had started picking up; soon the area would be inaccessible.

Khai opened the cargo doors of the Tahoe and tossed in his duffel. Butch did the same with one, and then held the other in his hand as he stared at the boss.

"You never said how much my help was worth," he said. "The tab has grown."

"We'll figure something out when we get back."

"I think we need to figure it out now. I'll just keep this bag."

"There's more than a hundred grand in each of those, easily," Khai said. "That's a steep price for a mule."

"Mule?"

"That's right. Your job was to come up here with me and retrieve this."

The tone didn't sit well with Butch. "Was it my job to kill Gina Simpson?"

"I didn't tell you to do that. That's why we're in really deep shit now — all because Glen decided to spill his guts."

"We're in deep shit because you had her tamper with Glen's chutes. We could have worked things out some other way and moved on."

"Moved on?" Glen was about to turn us in. There's no moving on from prison. That's the biggest red line of all, and he crossed it. He knew there would be consequences."

"Well, you know where the story led. And now the cops know it, too. None of this is going away."

"What is it you're suggesting?"

"I just want my money, so I can disappear." Butch unzipped the duffel and looked inside. He nodded as he thumbed through stacks of assorted bills. "This bag right here will cover it."

"One big bag of cash and we're square? That seems fair enough." Khai Le turned and walked to the driver's door.

CHAPTER 66

Butch allowed himself a rare smile and stepped away from the rear of the vehicle. He gazed out at the tranquil winter scene; the Colorado mountains never ceased to amaze. He had grown up in the desert Southwest, a landscape with a much different sort of charm. Maybe he would go back there, try to start fresh, if he ever had the chance. If he could outrun his troubles here.

Those troubles were evolving quickly. When he turned around, the boss was holding a black nine-millimeter pistol with a long suppressor on the barrel. He leveled it at Butch's chest.

"What are you doing?" Butch asked.

"You crossed that red line, too, didn't you? You're just another snitch."

"You've lost it, man. I didn't turn on you, but I could have."

"I don't believe you. I heard about your little meeting with the DEA. You never mentioned it."

"They called *me*, not the other way around. I didn't tell them anything."

"I don't believe you," Khai said. "They let you walk for a reason. Let's go for another little walk right now."

"I'm not walking anywhere with you." Butch opened wide the swinging door and settled on the bumper with the duffel bag in his lap.

Suddenly it was game on for Khai. "Get up or I'll kill you right here."

"We both know you're not a killer, Khai. You don't have it in you. You're a coward at heart. That's why you need people like me around to protect you."

Khai was wild-eyed now. "Sounds like you want me to shoot you. Is that what you want?"

"I just want my money and to be out of here. It's only fair considering everything I've done for you and your organization. I don't believe you have the guts to shoot an unarmed man."

Khai wasn't sure what to make of Butch's strategy, if that's what it was. The big man frequently intimidated co-workers but had never tried that on the boss. Of course, Khai had never threatened to kill him before.

"Let's see if you're right," Khai said, motioning up a nearby hill with the gun. "If you're able to walk back down — if I don't have the guts to pull the trigger — I'll give you whatever is in that bag, and we'll go our separate ways."

Butch apparently had something in mind. He stood up. "Okay, let's walk."

"You first," Khai said.

The men reached the bend at the top of the hill and stopped. There was a small shoulder between the gravel road and a steel guardrail on the right, erected to keep drivers from making a fatal mistake. A small ledge jutted out from the other side, with a spectacular view of the valley. Visitors were known to stand there for selfies with their backs toward the abyss.

"Beautiful, isn't it?" Khai asked. "Walk out and enjoy the view."

Butch didn't move. "Did it ever occur to you that I might have a backup plan? That I wouldn't be foolish enough to come up here alone with you and put myself in a vulnerable position? Once you had the money, you didn't need me anymore."

"It certainly had occurred to me. Why do you think I told you we were going to the Button Rock trailhead? I'll be honest, I was still thinking we might run into law enforcement on the way up here. But then I thought, Butch wouldn't pass up the opportunity to get a cut of the cash."

"You thought I'd set you up if it wasn't for the money?"

"I don't know. What would it look like at Button Rock right now? Word has it there's a lot of people trying to protect themselves."

"We all need protection," Butch said. "Isn't that what Glen did?"

"And you see how that worked out. Bad for everybody, especially him. And now bad for you."

"You're sure the feds aren't waiting for us just down the road here? Maybe I had time to text. Maybe I even texted a picture of you sitting in that Suburban with Gina. You and your duffels of cash won't get far."

"I guess I'll find out, whether I kill you or not," Khai said. He gripped the pistol tighter and clenched his teeth.

"You don't think I have the guts? Turn around and walk to the edge. Let's see."

Butch smiled and took a few more steps. "We don't have to do this, Khai," he said. "We can ride out of here together."

"It's too late. Keep going."

Butch turned around and shook his head. "You'll have to do it right here. *Can you?*"

The first blast caught him in the chest, and the second one ripped through his shoulder, sending him staggering to the edge of the cliff. He dropped to his knees.

Khai moved quickly toward the precipice. Leaning over Butch, he took a deep breath and swallowed hard before giving the big man a final shove.

Their tracks would soon be covered, and that would at least keep the park authorities guessing, if they were ever alerted. It might be spring before Big Butch came to light again.

***

Khai threw the cash in the back of the Tahoe and placed his gun on the passenger seat. He started down the hill, anxiously scanning the landscape as he neared the gate. If the park rangers were aware that someone had broken the lock and entered, they would surely be waiting there.

No signs of life.

The way out was simple now. Only a short series of turns remained, and then a long straightaway descending to the main entrance.

Khai had yet to figure out what came next, but the pieces had always fallen into place for him. He would come up with a new plan and rise again.

The sweat was starting to build on his forehead when he made the last turn.

Trouble ahead.

Several sheriff's department vehicles were blocking the road with their lights flashing. The officers stood by with long guns drawn.

Khai slowed to a crawl and then stopped in the middle of the road to survey the scene. His mind was racing as his cell phone pinged. *Cops are here,* his sister Sierra texted. *Lots of them.*

Khai tossed his phone into the floorboard. This is how the dream would end. *Did he have the guts to pull the trigger again?*

Khai looked at himself in the mirror one last time. He closed his eyes and placed the barrel of the gun against his temple. There was no turning back now.

CHAPTER 67

Simon and Billy dropped their luggage and took a quick look around the condo. No sign of Michael.

They collapsed on the couch together. Spending a full day trying to get back to Colorado had left them exhausted, physically and emotionally, but there was little time to rest.

"That was literally the longest trip of my life," Billy said, stretching his arms and legs. "Nothing wears me out like sitting on a plane, unless it's sitting in an airport. And that was a lot of sitting. Why am I sitting here now?" He stood back up.

"I know I've already told you, Billy, but I really appreciate you going with me. The way things turned out, I'm sure you wish you hadn't. Sorry about everything."

"I'm your agent, so no need to be sorry. Hell, you won a couple of matches, and that's what we wanted to see. I hate what has happened here, but you've handled yourself well under tough circumstances. You're strong."

"I don't know. This stuff with my father is ripping my guts out."

"We'll get through it together."

There hadn't been much discussion on the way back of what had transpired in Melbourne. The weight of the whole trip, the months of preparation, the exhilaration, and then the way it ended, had left Simon numb. His tennis future seemed secondary. He was worried about his father, and nothing else.

"It's all surreal," he said.

"That's one way to put it. I'm not sure what else to say at this point." Billy leaned on the bar. "Just give me a minute."

Simon mustered some energy and rose again to take a closer look at the condo. There was no indication that Michael had been there recently. For all they knew, he could have flown to another country from Australia.

"What's your best guess?" Billy asked.

Simon sighed and shook his head. "He won't answer his phone. I was hoping he'd be waiting here, and we could all talk this thing through, maybe somehow work it out. Zander, too. Dad has to know that we want to help him."

"I don't know how clearly he's thinking at this point. I don't know how clearly I'm thinking either. As for Zander, I wouldn't count on him helping Michael. These are serious charges, and he feels like a victim, too. I've never seen him that angry."

Billy rubbed his face and stretched again. "Have you looked in the garage?"

Simon opened the side door and walked out. The SUV was gone. He also noticed something else: the ski rack and a pair of Michael's skis were not in their usual storage space.

"I know where he might be," Simon said.

"Where?"

"Up in the mountains."

"At the house in Eagle?"

"Maybe, or close by. Through the years we've both gone to Vail to blow off steam when the stress piled up. Lots of times."

"To *ski*?"

Simon shrugged. "It's just the way we handle things. It looks like Dad has his cross-country skis with him, so I suspect he's up there. He may look at it as his last chance for a while."

Simon tapped out a number on his phone as he walked back into the condo. Billy could hear the question: "Is Michael Shay there by chance?"

Simon waited and then responded, "No, he's the owner of the house, and I'm just looking for him. Sorry to bother you." He nodded. "Okay, thank you."

"Who was that?"

"Airbnb renters. They haven't seen him. Dad keeps some ski equipment locked up in a shed at the house, and I thought he might have dropped by to get it, if he wasn't able to stay there. Renters are almost always there this time of year."

"Next question: what do you suppose is going on with Zander?"

"I'd say he's at AAF, probably turning the place upside down. Why don't you call him?"

"Let me think about that. I'm not sure what to say right this moment. And I'm not sure he'll answer my call anyway."

"We can't just sit here and wait," Simon said. "I think I should go to Vail. I can be there in a couple of hours."

"Even if your father is there, how would you find him?"

"I'll find him. It's best if I go alone to look, if you could drop me off to get another rental car. Then maybe you can see what's up with Zander."

Suddenly there was a heavy-handed knock at the front door. Through the peephole, Simon could see two uniformed officers on the porch.

"Cops," he whispered to Billy.

"See what they want."

The door opened slightly, and one of the officers waved documents in front of Simon's face. "Federal marshals. We have an arrest warrant for Michael Shay. Is he here?"

"No, he isn't. I'm his son and just got back into town. I'm not sure where he is."

Billy opened the door wider and stepped up. "What's the charge, officer?"

"Who are you, sir?"

"Just a friend of the family."

"Do you know where we can find Michael Shay?"

"I don't. Can you tell me what he's charged with?"

The marshal looked down at his documents. "According to the warrant, Mr. Shay is wanted for conspiracy to traffic cocaine and marijuana. He's also wanted for questioning in connection with the murder of J.T. McClanahan."

"*Cocaine* trafficking?"

"Mind if we look around? We have a search warrant, too."

"There's nothing here," Simon said. "Come in and see for yourselves."

The officers spent several minutes combing through the place while Simon and Billy sat on the couch and waited.

"We'll keep looking," the one officer said. "If you happen to hear from him, I'd suggest you tell him to turn himself in. It's just a matter of time."

Simon shut the door and turned around with a dazed look on his face. "*Murder?* He can't be involved with that. And I've never heard anything about cocaine. This is getting a lot worse. I don't know what to say."

"Maybe Michael isn't planning to come back here," Billy said. "I don't know what he's thinking, but he's facing serious jail time. He could be long gone."

"I have to look for him," Simon said, slipping his jacket back on. "Take me to get a car."

"I've got a better idea: We'll take mine. I'm going with you."

"This isn't your problem, Billy."

"If it's your problem, then it's mine, too. That's the way things work. Let's go see if we can find your father."

CHAPTER 68

The narrow, two-story structure was built into a stand of firs at the back of the property in Eagle County. From a distance, it looked like a treehouse on steroids, complete with A-frame tin roof, double-hung windows, and an inviting spiral staircase. For the moment, it was a suitable hideout.

Billy followed the tire tracks through the crusty snow, right to the end of the drive where the charcoal gray Range Rover was parked. "Good guess," he said.

Simon nodded and looked around anxiously. *Where was his father?* The trails were nearby, and the ski rack on the roof of Michael's SUV was empty.

"Let's go up," Simon said.

He couldn't remember the last time he stood at the railing in the canopy and looked out over the valley. What a beautiful slice of seclusion it was. The parents of Jenny Riddick, the friend he had rescued from the avalanche the previous year, had designed this place, Kingfisher's Nest, when Simon and Jenny were still kids. Her father was an architect in Eagle and took the project to heart after buying the land years earlier.

"The Nest," as they usually called it, served as a rustic getaway for family and friends who wanted to be close to the backcountry. That included the Shays; they were always free to come and go. Michael was fond of cross-country skiing and liked to connect to the trails from the property.

"You think he's out there?" Billy asked as they reached the first floor.

"I'm sure of it. The trails are close, and there's really not anywhere else to go on foot. You can see where somebody has gone down the path. We'll just wait."

They didn't have to wait long to hear the rhythm of skis gliding on the snowpack. It was distant at first and grew closer by the minute.

Finally, the sound stopped. Michael was just below them.

"Welcome home, son," he said casually, removing the skis and standing them up in the snow. There was a smile on his face. "We're a long way from Melbourne, aren't we?"

"You haven't been answering my calls."

"I'm sorry about that. I just needed some time to think."

"Michael, there's no more time for that," Billy said. "There were federal marshals at your place before we left. We talked to them. They're looking for you."

Simon grew more agitated. "And you know what they said? Not just that you've been involved in trafficking marijuana. *Cocaine, too*. And there's a murder investigation."

Michael started up the spiral staircase. He seemed not to hear. "This is such a beautiful place, isn't it, Simon? I guess I always liked the flatlands a little more than you. You were a downhiller, a speed freak. I liked grinding it out."

"You didn't answer me," Simon said.

Michael went to the cooler in the corner of the deck and dug through the ice. He flipped a bottle of water to Simon, and then a can of White Rascal to Billy. He set another beer on the railing.

"They made it sound like I'm a big drug dealer?" he asked, pulling three folding chairs from a storage bin. "Conspiracy charges."

"That's what the warrant says. I assume they have some evidence. What's the truth?"

"I've already told you the truth, Simon. I got involved with some people that I shouldn't have. And I'm going to pay a price for that."

Simon began to get choked up. "I want to know the whole story," he said. "Tell me the rest. All of it."

"Is that what you want to hear? Are you sure?"

"Yes."

"It's pretty simple." Michael bowed his head and spoke quietly. "Glen and I had an agreement to move marijuana for his organization," he said. "Not huge amounts but enough to make it worth the risk."

"For how long?"

"A while. Not long ago, I found out that one of the shipments we put on the truck had cocaine mixed in with it. Glen knew that wasn't supposed to happen, but he did it anyway."

"How did you know?" Billy asked.

"There's a guy who used to hang out at the airfield. He worked with Glen and was involved in packing the shipments in this airplane wing assembly. We were talking, and it came out that maybe Glen was getting in over his head. He mentioned this other package."

"On the shipment where the driver was killed?"

"Yes."

"You knew?" Billy asked.

Michael nodded and kept his eyes to the ground. "It really pissed me off at the time, because in my mind it took everything to another level. Glen always wanted to do more, from the time we started, and I kept resisting. I mean, I knew it was wrong."

"Did you confront him?"

"No, the wing was loaded onto the truck like we always did, framed up and tucked in discreetly with everything else. But unlike the others, this shipment didn't make it intact. The cocaine was apparently missing when it arrived in Detroit."

"You took it?" Simon asked. "I can't believe you'd do that."

"I never even saw it."

"But you know what happened to it?" Billy asked.

"Not exactly. I'll admit that I was going to make it disappear. When I found out it was going to be on board, I contacted a man who used to work at the place where the wing assembly was made. He said he could get into that thing quick and easy, and it all went south from there."

"This is the driver who was killed?"

"J.T. McClanahan. He used to be a trucker, and he had the paperwork to be on board, if he needed it. He was going to get the package and put it in a backpack and then disappear."

"And then what?"

"I'd pay him off and find a buyer myself. I already had one lined up. Sounds bizarre, I know, but that's what I was thinking."

Billy and Simon listened with rapt attention. "It doesn't sound bizarre; it sounds *criminal*," Simon said. "I can't believe you were involved in any of this. It's like a drug cartel. What's wrong with you?"

"Someone else ended up on that truck," Billy said. "They knew what was going on, and they killed your driver to get the package."

Michael nodded. "Probably made him open the assembly and give it to them. That's a question no one has been able to answer: Who killed J.T.? We may never know."

"Or where the cocaine ended up."

"That's right. It had to be somebody he knew and was in communication with, so there's at least a chance of finding out."

"You told me in Australia that they were coming for you," Simon said.

"I still believe that. There aren't a lot of good choices right now. That's why I came up here to think about it."

"What did you decide?" Billy asked. "Where do things go from here?"

"Downhill, I would imagine. Very fast." He took a deep breath. "I'm probably looking at five years in federal prison. Or worse."

"Have you heard anything from Zander?"

"No, and I wouldn't expect to. Not after what I've done."

"This is a lot worse than I thought," Simon said. "Now you're admitting to everything?"

Michael got up and went to the small chiminea to light the kindling he had already arranged. "I'll certainly admit to being a fool." The fire caught quickly. He took off his vest, revealing a shoulder holster with a pistol underneath.

"Where did you get that?" Simon asked. "You've never needed a gun for protection."

"I bought it recently; it's a Beretta M9. The way things have been going, it might come in handy. I've got enemies now I don't even know about."

Simon didn't want to hear that. "What are you planning to do?"

"Let's talk first about *you*. I didn't get a chance to tell you how proud I was of you in Australia. To play in a major like that, and then win two matches … that's what we've always dreamed of. You're on your way. Wasn't he great, Billy?"

The agent was almost speechless. "He showed his stuff. I wish you hadn't spoken with him before his last match. That seemed to take the wind out of him."

"I shouldn't have gone at all, but I couldn't stay away. I had to see him out there on that court, in that setting. I knew it would probably be my last chance for a while."

Simon stared at the flames and shook his head in disgust. "You definitely shouldn't have gone. You shouldn't have done so many things. It's never going to be the same for us."

"You'll keep going, son, regardless of what happens to me. You'll be the champion I never was."

"We were supposed to do this together. That's what you always said after we lost Mother. Now, I'm on my own."

CHAPTER 69

Zander was waiting impatiently in the parking lot when the men returned to Aurora. Billy had called him and, surprisingly, he agreed to meet them at Michael's condo.

"Where is he?" Zander asked.

"He's on the way, just a few minutes behind us," Billy said as they began walking to the front of the condo. "Let's go in."

"I've tried to call him several times, and he never answered. I'd like to know what in the hell he was thinking, but, at this point, I don't guess it matters. I'll just let the authorities sort it out."

"Well, it's tragic, to say the least," Billy said. "You guys were close. Michael just lost his way. I don't know what he'll say. What *can* he say?"

"So damn foolish. At some point soon, I need to know the full extent of this scheme. I've been running through it with my employees here, and there are questions that need answers. The management team in Aurora is going to have to be restructured. It's just a freaking nightmare."

Simon unlocked the condo, and they walked inside.

"I want to apologize for not saying something earlier," Billy said. "I started into that conversation when we were down at the beach that evening, and then just kind of left it hanging. I wasn't sure exactly what we were dealing with anyway."

"I've been thinking about that." Zander turned away. "Things can change in a hurry."

"It's my fault," Simon said. "I told Billy not to tell you. He was just doing what I asked."

"You should have told me yourself, Simon. I realize that he's your father, but you had to know the potential damage this was doing to my company. You and I have always been able to talk."

Simon hung his head. "I know."

"Regardless of what the courts decide, Michael and I are finished. He'll carry this around forever. And I'll be honest with you, Simon; right now, I'm not sure how much you and I will see each other moving forward. This ordeal is going to be hard to ever put aside."

"It wasn't Simon's fault," Billy said. "He had no role in this. He's been victimized, too."

"I understand that. It'll just take time."

The front door opened, and Michael stepped into the living room. The gravity of the situation showed plainly on his face. He wasn't sure whether to start with an apology or explanation, so he said nothing at first.

"How could you do this to our company?" Zander asked. "How could you do it to me? Of all the managers up and down the line, I've felt closer to you than any of them. I trusted you."

"I have no excuse. It started out as small talk with Glen Chapman — he wondered how easy it would be to do this or that — and then numbers were thrown around. Things just went so smoothly at first … there was nothing to it."

"Just money in your pocket, huh?"

Michael nodded. "Easy money, and I got swept up. As time went on, everything just got out of hand. And I didn't know how to pull myself out of it. I was in between the smugglers and the DEA. And you."

"I guess that's where we are now," Zander said. "I want you to know that the authorities will be here soon. I spoke with the head of the task force as I was on my way over here. I don't know yet what the repercussions are for my business, but to have this hanging over us … I still can't believe it."

"I'll tell them it was all my idea," Michael said. "I know you can never forgive me, but please don't hold what I've done against my son. He needs you in his life; he needs you and Billy both, more than ever. I won't be there for him, and he's going to have to grow up fast."

All the men wrestled with their emotions. Simon went over and hugged his father. He couldn't find more words to say.

"I'll be there for Simon, no matter what," Billy said. "You can count on that."

"Thank you." Michael managed to smile for a second. "Just don't give him your car keys."

There was a knock at the door. Sean McGuire was standing outside with federal agents. He presented the warrant for Michael's arrest as they came in and hand-cuffed him.

"Busy day," McGuire said. "We've learned a lot about this group. We just raided the growhouse they were operating, and guess what else we found there? There was an airplane wing hidden in a storage building on the property. I'll bet you've seen it before, Mr. Shay. Am I right?"

Michael didn't answer.

"And there's something else that I know you'll be interested in, Mr. Fleming. There's been an arrest in J.T. McClanahan's murder."

Zander stepped forward. "Who?"

"It was a friend of his named Clayton Powell. J.T. had apparently told him about what was on the truck that night, and Powell trailed them to Kansas City. He ended up taking the package for himself and leaving his friend dead on the side of the road."

"How do you know it was him?"

"We got a tip that he might have been involved, and his cell phone records confirmed his whereabouts that morning. Turns out that authorities in Florida had been looking for Powell, too. He was wanted in connection to the murder of two truckers down there."

Zander sank into a chair and rubbed his face in disbelief. "This is hard to imagine."

"Michael here can back up the story; he knew all about it," McGuire said. "Isn't that right?"

Michael stood with his head bowed while the special agent continued.

"He was negotiating with Powell to get the cocaine back. He was playing all the angles."

"I thought you didn't know what happened," Simon said. "You've known all along."

"I hope you can forgive me at some point." The agents began shuffling Michael towards the front door.

Simon slowly walked to the window and watched his father being placed in the back of the unmarked car. Zander was struggling to come to grips with the developments. He sat for a moment on the edge of a chair and rubbed his face.

"I hate this, Simon," he said. "We've had some good times the last few years. I don't know if I've ever enjoyed myself more than I did in Australia, watching you out there on the big stage and knowing everything that went into it. You really made me proud." He got back up and opened the door. "And then to have it all end like this … it's just a shame."

Zander turned and faced his best friend. "Billy, if you want to fly back with me, you're welcome to do so. I'll be leaving in the morning."

EPILOGUE

The waters off Key West were calm and crystal blue as *Country Boy* sliced through the light chop on a sweltering July day. The seventy-eight-foot Princess yacht was on a leisurely path to nowhere in particular.

Billy took a sip of his fruity drink and leaned back in the wraparound couch on the foredeck. "Are you really sure you want to build a house in Knoxville?" he said. "I don't know if I can handle having you that close again. You'll distract me and my partner."

"Sorry, it's a done deal," Zander said with a laugh. "I'll be right down the road. You know I'll be here most of the time, suffering in the Florida heat by myself."

Billy looked over the shimmering water and nodded. "At least there's a nice breeze."

"Speaking of your partner, she could probably use a few distractions. How often do you take her out on your boat to have a glass of wine and relax?"

"Not nearly enough. Claire loves the river, and she definitely loves wine. But that's a whole different thing. My boat isn't like this boat."

Billy turned around and looked up at the sport bridge. "Isn't that right, captain?" he yelled.

Simon didn't hear. His long blond curls were fluttering from under a white baseball cap turned backward. The dark shades reflected another bright and beautiful morning in the Florida Straits. The magnetic smile had been on his face since he took the wheel. He was in a world of his own.

It had been six months since Michael Shay was arrested, and he was reportedly cooperating with authorities in Colorado while awaiting trial. Simon had occasional contact with his father but had managed to clear his head and move on with his life and career.

A return to the ATP Tour in the spring had yielded impressive showings at tournaments in Europe and South America. The fans, especially young women, were taking notice of his progress as the outdoor hardcourt season began to heat up.

The breakthrough came just last weekend. Simon put together a dominating performance at the Atlanta Open to become the youngest champion in the event's history.

Billy was there to watch it happen and quickly seized on the opportunity. Late that night, Zander called Simon to extend the invitation: Come to the Keys for a celebratory break. It would be the first time they had seen each other since the fallout with Michael.

There was no second-guessing now.

"It's nice to have him here," Zander said, casually motioning for Simon to turn the boat around. His hair was pulled back in a ponytail, and after all the anguish, the broad smile was back on his face. "He's a good kid."

Billy nodded approvingly and leaned back with his drink as *Country Boy* headed toward home.

***

Thank you for reading, and I sincerely hope you enjoyed *Break Point*. As an independently published author, I rely on you, the reader, to spread the word. So if you enjoyed the book, please tell your friends and family, and if it isn't too much trouble, I would appreciate a brief review on Amazon. Thanks again. My best to you and yours.

-Kelly

ABOUT THE AUTHOR

Kelly Hodge is a native of Johnson City, Tennessee. He graduated from East Tennessee State University with majors in communications and political science and spent more than three decades in the newspaper industry as a writer and editor. He lives in the beautiful mountains of Northeast Tennessee

www.kellyhodge.squarespace.com